ONE HUNDRED

ONE HUNDRED SHADES OF WHITE

ONE HUNDRED SHADES OF WHITE

PREETHI NAIR

With magic

Preetha.

HarperCollins*Publishers*

HarperCollins*Publishers*
77–85 Fulham Palace Road,
Hammersmith, London W6 8JB

www.fireandwater.com

Published by HarperCollins*Publishers* 2003
1 3 5 7 9 8 6 4 2

A catalogue record for this book
is available from the British Library

ISBN 0 00 714345 1

Set in PostScript Linotype Sabon by
Rowland Phototypesetting Ltd,
Bury St Edmunds, Suffolk

Printed and bound in Great Britain by
Clays Limited, St Ives PLC

My biggest thanks goes to whoever is responsible for allowing me to catch a glimpse of universal magic and for bringing together some amazing people who have made this book happen.

Thank you to my family and friends, to the 'sunflower ladies', especially to Tricia Stewart who continues to inspire me, to all the team at HarperCollins and finally to my friend and agent Diana Holmes, thank you for believing in me.

For Ammamma, who loved
us enough to let us go.

MAYA

Chaos seems to gravitate towards me. It has always been this way. At the time of my birth, the milkman lost the bicycle which had taken him five years to save up for; my much needed grandmother had to drag out my screaming brother who had accidentally wandered into the room; the rain decided to fall even harder and cut off the current (it made no difference to the midwife, she was blind anyway) and the cockroaches which had congregated on a fallen bhaji were crushed by an unexpected, heavy foot.

The battle that ensued between Amma and I continued. She pushed with all her life and I held on. And so it went on for hours and hours, years and years. Amongst secret whispers, a meticulous strategy emerged and reinforcements came in the shape of forceful fingertips that belonged to a wrinkled pair of hands. The midwife pulled me out, determinedly. The first thing I saw were the dusty blades of a khaki fan. I cried.

At that moment, I wanted to turn right back and ask God to tell me again what he had planned for me and why, exactly, He had chosen this family. Born into a cold, bewildered room, the midwife left me screaming as she lay me out to count my fingers and toes. I was then wrapped up and handed to my Amma.

'She's beautiful, just beautiful.'

But I didn't glance up to see my mother's face and instead I turned my head to look at my Achan. I saw an old rhinoceros-skinned man sitting in the corner of the room and howled even louder.

He was, thank God, the astrologer who sat through the whole commotion in stony silence. The astrologer noted the time and then shook his head. 'You shouldn't have held on,' he said to Amma. 'The second child always brings change, but this one has come with Mars in the first house and she will surely be the cause of much, much upheaval.' But before she had a chance to reflect on his words, the rest of my family walked in.

The heavy foot belonged to my Achan who was supposed to be away on a business trip. He must have come back just for me. Not sensing my imminent arrival, he decided to escape the commotion to look for my grandmother and little brother Satchin. He found Ammamma entertaining him in a rickshaw and brought them both back in.

Ammamma took a look at me and then ignited like a fluorescent tube light, laughing at me trembling in the cool morning breeze. She wondered which old woman's soul I had borrowed. She reached out her arms to hold me but Achan looked at Amma and Amma said, 'Raul, let Raul take her, Ma.'

He took me in those big strong arms and I felt very, very comfortable. Satchin watched, then he went over to Amma and asked to see the family that would be taking care of me. This was after he had finished stroking my foot whilst he sucked his thumb, using me as a temporary substitute for his beloved blanky which wasn't looking in good shape at all.

'No, Monu, Mol is coming home with us, she's your new little sister.'

'No, no, Am, don't want.'

'Monu,' she said as Ammamma lifted him up so he could sit next to her, 'things will be just the same but better, you now have a little sister to play with.'

It was then I looked at my Amma's face, seeking reassurance. It was so radiantly happy and anything she told you, you would want to believe, for this is the kind of face she had, calm and peaceful.

But they should have paid attention to his little words.

The upheaval that was supposed to mark my arrival, and the subject of much speculation and gossip by the man plotting our lives, was delayed by some inexplicable Jupiter/Saturn conjunction. The fact was that it was some three years later that the full effects of my birth came into force.

God gave me a good deal with my parents. My Achan was handsome and my Amma was really very beautiful. She had extraordinary green eyes that shone when she laughed and long delicate fingers which she hid her laughter behind. Achan came from a wealthy family. He had sixteen cows more than Amma. In fact, his family had sixteen more cows than all the villagers put together but I never got to see the cows or any of Achan's family as I was told they lived far away. Amma and her mother came from the same village but had more of a middle-class background. They had a buffalo that slept in the kitchen with them and who seemed to enjoy the bedtime stories more than Amma did. This I know because Amma said his snores reverberated through the house and many times were mistaken for the tremors of an impending earthquake. Amma didn't have an Achan because he died when she was little, but I don't know how it happened because whenever I asked about him, she became very sad.

I can't tell you either the exact circumstances surrounding my parents' marriage because whenever I asked, it was always hastily explained in one simple sentence, 'Your Achan came to see me, fell in love and so it was arranged that I marry him.'

That's how they did things in Kerala. The man and his family would go and see the lady, who would have to go to the kitchen and make him some tea and serve it in the best cup, along with some savouries, and then he would look at her as she handed the cup to him. The lady would glance at the man fleetingly; if she liked him she would smile coyly and sometimes he would respond by touching her fingertips whilst she gave him the tea. This meant that he really loved her. The rest of the family would sit observing the interaction to see how well it had gone. They were also observing other things like if she was well mannered but then, I think, of course she's going to be well mannered, it's only five minutes while she's serving him, it's not that difficult. They would also take into account family background and history; there must be no scandal with any of the extended family members like divorces or separation. Other things were also important like how much money the family has and if the lady can cook well and, finally, their astrological charts must match. My Ammamma told me that the latter wasn't a huge problem as there was a woman in the village called Laxmiammayi who could doctor unsuitable charts. Laxmiammayi could tweak Uranus or Pluto so they sat in the right house and matched perfectly with the proposed suitor, but she did that for a hefty fee.

If the lady was dark, rake-thin and had buckteeth, then Laxmiammayi couldn't do much about that and the man's family would ask for an extortionately high dowry to take her away. If, however, the family background checked out all right, the lady was pretty, well mannered, not belligerent in any way and could cook, then sometimes they would wave the dowry altogether. It was very rare, but this is what I think happened to my Amma. She was all of those things and could cook exceptionally well, due to the fact that she and my Ammamma were the village cooks. But even not having to pay the dowry didn't make my Ammamma happy; she became upset at the bit when she told me how Amma left home and then said she really couldn't talk about any of it.

My parents married when she was seventeen and he was twenty-six. The astrologer says that when an event takes place, like a birth, death or marriage, then something else happens in quick succession. 'Nature responds,' he says, 'and moves things around in accordance with the new energy.' So after they married, an enormous combustion of luck moved them to a bigger town and promoted Achan once again. He became chief oil importer for India and Amma had to move out of the village and settle in a town near Mumbai.

My brother Satchin's arrival a year later sent my Achan soaring to the dizzy heights of true success and gave my family four more servants, including a kitchen hand for the irritable cook, and ten more cows. It also brought my Ammamma to come and live with them. My Ammamma wasn't really a town person; she said that people are born city people, town people or village people, and she was definitely a village person. Village people understood how nature worked whereas town and city people couldn't because the pace was just too fast to be able to take all the signs in properly. The pace of village life definitely ran through her whole body, she said, and although people gossiped, they had something very solid about them; they were firmly grounded and had time to stop and notice things. But Ammamma never complained about the move to the north and said that sometimes you have to do things even if you don't like them because it makes other people happy and that in turn made her happy.

They all lived in a big, white colonial-style house with a red roof and matching floor tiles. The house was encircled by many, many gardens and was protected by trees and huge iron gates. Although it was near the town you would never have known as a sea of tall palms kept the noise of traffic, pollution and bustle at bay. It was a very comfortable life: my Achan would go out to work, my brother would chase anything that moved, and the whole household would run after him. Amma spent lazy afternoons talking to neighbours who came to visit or went shopping for groceries and other items with Ammamma and Nila, her servant boy, or she would cook. At five o'clock sharp, Satchin would sit looking out of one of the windows, waiting for Achan's blue scooter to pull into the veranda, and then he would indicate by some blubbering that he was waiting to be taken out for a ride.

My arrival hindered this ritual that he had set up for himself. Now at five o'clock, my Achan would walk into the room and head straight for where I was sleeping. He would pick me up and rock me and his odour of damp linen and the musty scent of burnt wood would waft in the air with the motion. His moustache tickled my ear, a soothing presence like his voice which was deep and rhythmic. Whilst I was in his arms, Satchin would pull at his trouser leg, a technique he had learnt with Nila and the mango trees; Nila would shake the trunk and he would watch the mangoes fall one by one. Satchin secretly hoped I would meet the same fate. Achan would laugh and hoist Satchin up and say 'Give our little Maya Mol a kiss,' and so he would salivate over my face, accidentally biting me in the process. Achan would stay for a while and then he had to leave; he was a very busy man.

I was especially close to the young Aya who was assigned to assist with my care. Her particular role was to make sure I got to sleep okay and, if I awoke, to see if I needed anything. She did her job so beautifully and sang melodically whenever she could, the tunes whistled through the gap in her teeth. Aya was unlike the old toothless woman who didn't understand her own job description and thought she was there to make sure my blood circulated correctly. She did this by vigorously knocking my joints with her bony hand. Then she would massage me like she was stretching out a piece of dough and put me in this cradle-type thing made from starched sheets, and hang me out to dry like some old piece of popadom. But this, along with bath time, was the only hardship I had to endure and attentive people were never really far away, my Achan being at the very front of all of them. If he was on one of his trips then it was Ammamma who I needed.

When she went to bed, she would pick me up and take me with her, cradling me against her warm flesh as she told me stories. There was, she began, a musician who lived in the sky who was responsible for changing the seasons. In the dry season, people planted their dreams and then they waited patiently for the musician to send the heavy rains; if they didn't believe enough, the rains flooded their dreams, but if they held on with faith, trusted and let go, the rain would bring them many things and these things came in the month of Shravan, harvest time. Ammamma knew lots about harvest time and food because, as I said already, she was a cook. She and Amma would spend hours in the kitchen and Aya would take me in to watch them.

They worked like two magicians and with smoke they could turn piles of vegetables and colourful spices into feasts. Amma would point at the vegetables and tell me the names and all I had to do was to gurgle something back at her and that was enough to make her laugh. It took me a year to realise that this pointing game was a distraction because as she was pointing, Ammamma was getting the condiments ready for bath time. Bitter gourd skin mashed into a pulp, chickpeas ground into flour, and coconut oil, all prepared and on standby. Before I knew it, my clothes were removed. Aya would be running round quickly heating pots of water whilst I was placed on Amma's outstretched legs. I wailed as she covered me in green gunk and yellow flour, 'for healthy bones and beautiful skin, Mol,' Amma would say, trying to console me. Then as I was washed and dried, coconut oil was poured on my head and massaged in and, after that, she tried to feed me. As a sign of protest, I spat out everything she placed in my mouth so Ammamma had to take over. When the whole ordeal was over, Aya took me to play in the sun. I learnt to hate the sight of the kitchen and when I was old enough to crawl, I would do my very best to scramble out of the situation but they would always get me.

As I began to walk and talk, Satchin found me interesting. He taught me how to put straw up the cows' noses so we could make them sneeze and measure how far the mucus landed with our footsteps. This seemed to divert us for hours and we only stopped this because one of the cows lost her calf and she cried for days. The cow mucus game was replaced with another distraction: Satchin showed me how to open the catch of the chicken coop so they would all run freely on the compound and Amin, the hand, had to go and catch them all. Amin would panic at seeing the chickens everywhere and we would watch him jump up and down, running around chasing them. The driver only helped if he wasn't too busy combing his hair in the car mirror or sitting in the front seat admiring his newly acquired decorations.

When he did help, we would jump into the front seat of the car, lock the doors and begin playing with the horn.

'Sahib will be very upset with you,' he shouted through the side window.

Sahib was what he called my Achan but Achan was never upset with us. He got upset with other people, sometimes he shouted at them fiercely, like when the guard kept him waiting at the gate and didn't open it quickly enough, but he never said anything to us. If anything, when he was there he let us do things that even Ammamma wouldn't let us do.

This was because Achan was away a lot and so he really missed us. When he came back, he brought us many gifts from faraway places. Dolls for me and normally aeroplanes for Satchin and presents for Amma, too. We weren't allowed to play with all our toys; some of the really special ones Achan kept locked in a glass cabinet in the sitting room so when visitors came they could see what we had. On these days, Amma also wore the clothes and jewellery bought for her. If it was a special occasion, we could take our toys out, one at a time, but we had to promise that we wouldn't lose them, break them or take them outside.

Then Achan stopped buying us things because he went to a place called London. Before he went, he gave me a little golden Labrador. Satchin and I fought over the puppy because I was sure that Achan said it was for me. 'Mol, this is especially for you because I am going to miss you very much. He's called Tikko and he will look after you,' he said, handing me the puppy. Amma explained that it was for sharing but that is not what I heard. I thought Achan would come home soon to sort it out but he was away for ages and we didn't see him for what seemed to be a very, very long time.

When my Achan went away, Amma and Ammamma did strange things and were particularly busy making bundles of food which they sent somewhere with the driver. The house was also always full of people. One day it got particularly busy and there was much activity going on; banana leaves were collected, the veranda was decorated with flower petals, and it felt like the whole town had come to visit us. Ammamma said it was to celebrate Onam, a festival to give thanks for the harvest.

This Onam thing confused me because it kept changing; sometimes it was in August, sometimes in September, but Ammamma said that was because the calendar went according to the phases of the moon and then she began yet another story, this time about a king, but because she told me so many, I couldn't remember it. The servants, their families and the neighbours didn't care much about that king story either because they were busy polishing off the food, but they nodded fervently with their mouths full as she was trying to explain it to them.

Other times, the neighbours came with their elderly parents and their children who also finished off all of the food, every crumb, so even the red ants had nothing to fight over. Occasionally, a vada would unwittingly fall out of someone's pocket as they said their goodbyes and made their way back home. At that moment, every conceivable life form made its way towards the food but normally Tikko got it first. The crows would screech with disappointment and attempt their fourth or fifth assault on the rice that lay in the sun but Aya was too quick for them and she waved them away with her palm switch. The polecat looked disappointed and took her eye from the crows and moved swiftly onto the chickens, just in case one of them escaped from the coop. Often, the polecat had to settle for a lazy lizard that couldn't be bothered to move quickly enough in the hot sun and if this was the case, the polecat gobbled him up. Ammamma said you had to always be observant, even with nature, because predators were always about, waiting for an opportunity to descend on the vulnerable. She reminded me about the predator every time we went out of the enclave and as the only time we did this was when we went to the beach, I took the predator to mean the sea.

It was a long ride to the beach on a bumpy rickshaw. Ammamma shouted at the driver to avoid the potholes but he never took any notice and so we bounced up and down on the seat. On the way there we saw lots of rickshaws and taxis lined up like an army of yellowback beetles who had suddenly escaped from wherever they were trapped. It was like a race for them all to be first to get to where they were going and they left behind trails of smoke. Once we were at the beach, Ammamma would run into the waves and urge me to follow, but I was scared, the sea was a predator after all, so I dipped my toes in whilst she ran in with all her clothes on. We then sat together on the rocks to wait for her clothes to dry. 'The sea has many answers, Mol, just sit and listen to it and it will bring back the pace.' She described 'the pace' as a universal pulse. If you felt the pace, you could see the signs but the difficulty wasn't really in seeing the signs but interpreting them. 'Feel it, Mol, breathe it, listen to the waves and you'll hear all the answers.'

The only answer I wanted to hear was her say yes to the balloon seller who often came up to us as we sat there. I was desperate for her to buy me one of his long balloons that he had twisted into an animal shape, but she never did. Other children rallied around him, fascinated by the shapes he had twisted, but knowing they could never have one, not unless he gave them away and this was highly unlikely. Ammamma said that they didn't have Achans or Ammas who could buy one for them and that is why they looked sad and scruffy. 'But we can do things for them, we can make them feel that someone is listening to their prayers and that magic exists,' she said. So every time we went, we buried rupees and paisas along the beach. 'All anyone needs is a little hope so that they are able to trust, and from trust, amazing things can happen,' she informed me as we dug the money into the sand. What we did on the beach was our secret and I wasn't allowed to tell anyone that, not even Achan when he came back, or, she said, she would be upset.

Ammamma hardly ever got upset and she only shouted at us once when Satchin and I kicked over the mountain of colourful spices that she had left out to dry. It went everywhere, staining the white walls with bright yellows, oranges, reds and browns. Nobody could clean it off, not even the dhobi, but that was hardly surprising as Ammamma said she wasn't very good at removing stains. She said she was sorry she shouted at us but it wasn't because of the mess we had made, but the lack of respect we showed for the spices. 'You have to treat them with respect because they can do magical things,' she explained. We didn't see what magical things they did but we said we were sorry and that we would help Amin whitewash the walls. Ammamma said that we had done enough. The walls would have been white-washed the next day had the postman not arrived with a telegram.

Amma tipped the postman, took the telegram and said that it was from England. Ammamma looked nervously at her.

'He wants us to go and join him there as soon as we can,' she said to Ammamma sadly. 'It will only be for a short while, a year. He says he desperately misses the children and me. I am also to sell the house as soon as I can.'

Ammamma nodded.

'Ma, I don't want to go to England. If we have to go, you'll come with us, won't you?'

Ammamma didn't say anything.

'Come, we need you, the children need you,' she pleaded.

Ammamma looked at her, looked down at me, and then back at her.

'He's left a number to call him. I'll sort it all out and arrange it, Ma, you'll see.'

I ran to find Satchin to tell him that we were going to England to be with our Achan. He was helping Amin collect coconuts and dumped the basket on the floor, running to find Amma. 'Is it true, Amma? Is it true that we are going to England on an aeroplane? Is it?'

'Yes, Monu,' she said, but she looked very dis-appointed.

That is how I remember it. The telegram came and

then time went at an exaggerated pace, like the hour hand decided to become the second hand so that it could make up for the things we had missed with Achan. Amma frantically began to sell the furniture and found the servants other positions in the town. Our dog Tikko sensed the chaos and left home so he didn't have to say goodbye. Sellers were turned away as they came to the gates, all were told that we were moving and all looked devastated. I don't know if this was because we were their best customers or because they knew something that we didn't.

The whole move to England was explained to us as if we were going on a big adventure and we would return from our expedition shortly. The way Ammamma got herself into the habit of packing me with old wives' tales, cramming me with every conceivable detail, told me she knew what the sellers did. There was something else that was happening and I was unaware of it, but she listened, listened to the pace and the signs.

It was the month of June, the time when the wild musician took over the skies and began jamming, hitting his drums with such strength that the rains fell harder than ever, flooding people's dreams. The workers abandoned their fields, shaking their heads; beautiful flower blossoms fell, drenched by the weight of the water, and their petals were washed into murky puddles that splashed everywhere; ugly furry caterpillars, red and black centipedes crawled out of the ground; food became inedible and schoolchildren ran as fast as they could to avoid the night fever, arriving home with soaking books to a beating because there was no money to be so careless.

Ammamma, interpreting the signs, went to consult the astrologer. When the rain did not subside as all had hoped, her visits to the astrologer became even more frequent and she took me with her, as if to verify that the child he spoke about was the right one. They got into this shell-throwing routine. He would mumble a prayer and throw three shells across a board. Ammamma would look up at him, he would talk to the shells and then shake his head or ruffle his beard, at which point she would try not to look upset or cry. We followed this routine twice a week, always with the same outcome.

On one of our trips, we stopped off at the beach, yet Ammamma didn't run into the sea but instead sat on the side.

'Mol, promise me you'll try to remember this, all of this, the place you are from when you are older, not just the place but the pace. You won't forget the language, the smells, colours, the people, will you, Mol? Don't ever forget where you're from.'

What was she talking about? I wouldn't forget in one year; Achan went away for a year and I never forgot him. I would remember her every day for that year because Amma said that a year wasn't really a long time. The balloon seller stopped and instead of waving him away, she asked me to pick two, one for me and one for Satchin. I was elated and chose a blue one that looked like a dog for Satchin and a pink one that looked like a bird for me. As we rode back, she told me that it would be hard to say goodbye, that I should try not to cry because crying would indicate that the person wasn't coming back and that was not the case as she would be

16

with me always. 'Mol, sometimes when you have to say goodbye it will feel like there is a monsoon inside. When it feels like this, breathe.'

'Amma says that a year is not such a long time,' I said to Ammamma.

'It's not so long, Mol,' she replied.

Little by little, the house was emptied of our possessions until all that remained were three suitcases packed with our worldly goods, tied with string. The patter of rain-drops echoed throughout the empty house. Ammamma stood at the gates, waving her young family off. Amma would not let go of her, drenched in a pink sari and with wet hair, rain running down her face. Ammamma kept looking over at us both seated in the car and mumbled, 'The children, the children, you just take care of the children.' And then she pulled out a little bronze figure from the pocket of her mundu and gave it to Amma.

'We'll see you soon, Ammamma,' Satchin shouted.

I was sitting in the car, trying desperately not to cry, thinking how was it possible to have the monsoon drum-mer inside and not let it show. I breathed and tried not to look at her.

'Yes, Monu, look after your Amma and be good for her. Bye, Mol.'

I said nothing. I wish I had taken one last look at her.

We arrived in England on my fourth birthday.

I thought my father would be waiting for us on the other side with a big gift, but he sent a driver to come and get us. We pulled into the Hilton on Park Lane. It was cold for me, despite being the end of August. Amma took a big yellow cardigan out of her bag and wrapped it around me whilst Satchin had his nose stuck out of the window, mesmerised by the different types of cars. I didn't feel that way because that was day one of remembering my Ammamma. Although it was just the first day, I felt sad, so I looked down at the floor and occasionally I looked out of the window. The only way I can describe our arrival was that it was like being taken from bright Technicolor into a silent black and white film. No rickshaw noise or horns or buffaloes or cows crowding the street, blocking traffic, no grass-hoppers or croaking toad lullaby or screeching chickens, just a mute, inoffensive calm.

Half asleep, we waited in the lobby for my father. He arrived a few hours later in an immaculate dark blue suit and a big smile and Amma woke us up, telling us that that he was there. Satchin and I went running over to him and I asked him what he had got us. He laughed, squeezing me tightly, hoisting both of us up, and then he went over to kiss Amma. Her lower lip began to tremble and she looked as if she was going to cry, but she smiled and looked at my father saying, 'You know it's Maya's birthday today. We have to celebrate.' The driver came back later with a Dundee cake and a rag doll that he said my father had left behind in his excite-ment. 'She's called Jemima, Mol,' he said, giving her to me. What kind of a strange name was that? 'Jemina,' I repeated.

'Jemima,' he said, making a face.

I made the same face.

'Oh, my funny little Mol,' he laughed. 'You will like England.'

If he said that I would like England, then I knew I would like England.

We sat and played in the lobby and then I was taken off by a deep, deep sleep.

The next thing I knew I woke up in a strange bed with lilac sheets and I was surrounded by beautiful lilac walls with balloons painted on them. Amma must have told him that I loved balloons and so he did that for me. That's how I would say I woke up to my new life in England; happy, in a new, big five-bedroomed house in South London. I went to investigate all the devices and wandered into the bathroom. We didn't really have a bathroom as such in India; Aya brought the hot water to us on the veranda, so the glistening silver taps intrigued me. I turned them and water came gushing out. It startled me so that I fell back, tumbled onto soft green carpets, and then hastily retreated. Then I saw him, my brother, in his room in a peculiar two-bedded house with a ladder. I climbed the stairs to meet him at the top. He was still asleep and so I shook him to wake him up but in one of his strange moments of fright, he rolled over, falling from a great height and crashing to the floor, making the sound of the dhobi's wet clothes hitting the wall.

Amma came running in and found her son's body under a blanket. She began crying, 'Monu, Monu, are you all right?'

He was still for longer than he needed to be, making sure he had her full attention, and then he began to stir slowly back to life. She was kissing him on his forehead and checking if he was okay. He looked fine from where I was sitting – the body occasionally needs a good shake up. Then he began to moan, just a droning type of a sound, managing the word 'Maya'. Her eyes widened as she plucked me off the top of the bed and she was about to shout at me when my father walked in and rescued me from whatever fate she had planned. 'It's just children playing, Nalini, no need to get upset,' he said reassuringly. I was so happy to have him back and was taken into those arms with that familiar rocking motion. Amma made a big fuss over Satchin, which seemed to greatly ease the pain. Both of us looked at each other, with our respective parent on side, and drew the battle-lines. Within a few hours he had made a miraculous recovery, vowing some kind of pay back.

Later that day, Achan took us shopping. We went to a huge department store and he asked Amma to pick clothes for us for our new school and buy us anything else we needed. She didn't know what to do so Achan called over a shop assistant and asked her to bring garments in our sizes. Then he turned to Amma and asked her to buy some English clothes for herself but she shook her head and wrapped her shawl tightly around her. He asked the shop assistant to get some clothes for Amma too and the shop assistant said something to her that she couldn't understand. 'She wants you to try them for size, Nalini.' But Amma refused. Achan bought her the clothes anyway. He bought lots of things for all of us and then he took us to eat.

Amma looked distressed when we went into a restaurant and Achan ordered hamburgers for us. Up until then we had never eaten red meat but Achan said it was important to try new things. Whilst we waited, the waitress came and brought us a colouring book and crayons. This never happened in India; I couldn't imagine Aya bringing us our slate and chalks before we ate. Then the burgers came and they had flags made from cocktail sticks on top of them and came with something called chips and ketchup. It was an amazing taste and Satchin and I looked at each other chomping into our food and drinking cola. I don't think Amma was that hungry because she left hers.

That week Achan had a holiday and he did lots of things with us. We played in a big park, we went to a place called the cinema, we watched television and he let us do anything we wanted. Then he had to go to work and Amma prepared us to go to school.

'Do we have to go to school?' I moaned. Satchin went to school in India and never once did I envy him. The only part that I thought was fun was when Amin took him and collected him in a rickshaw. Satchin came home with a heavy satchel, his slate and lots and lots of things to memorise. He could recite everything about the Mogul empire by the time he was six.

'Yes, Maya, you'll enjoy it,' Amma said, greasing my hair with coconut oil. I subsequently learnt that greasing is not the best technique in England to keep hair healthy and clean, in fact it was the opposite. There was a thing called shampooing but Amma didn't know that back then. She also packed us off with moist sandalwood, bright red stains on our foreheads because we had just said our prayers, and a tiffin carrier each with our lunch in. Thank God we didn't understand a word the other children said to us that first day.

Achan sent a driver and a lady from his office to take us to school and Amma came with us. My class had a lovely, white, round teacher called Miss Davies. They were making crocodiles and snakes from egg boxes when I walked in. Miss Davies stopped all the other children, said something to them, and then they looked at me strangely. Someone pointed at my forehead. Miss Davies said something else to them and then they clapped. All of them were eager for me to sit next to them and I sat next to a girl called Catherine Hunter. Miss Davies handed me a paintbrush to paint the snake she had strung together with parts of the egg box. I wanted to tell them all that Amin had once caught a real snake that had made its way into the house and then he put it into a bag and Satchin and I weren't really frightened, but I couldn't say any of it. Miss Davies smiled at me and I smiled back.

'How was it?' Amma asked when we got home.

'Miss Davies is warm and cuddly and is nice to me, she sat with me at lunchtime, to make sure that I ate properly. She helped me undo all the tiffin carrier tins and then, Amma, all the other children looked at me when I ate with my hands. Miss Davies then taught me how to use a knife and fork.'

She shook her head at the knife and fork part. 'And the other children, were they good to you?'

I told her that I played with a girl called Catherine and I remembered how to say her name because it sounded like 'Kathi', our surname, but I don't think I said it correctly as she kept repeating her name. Everyone else was nice but then our company school, along with our company house and car, was very accommodating and all the other children were told to go out of their way to make us feel welcome. Then Amma asked what we had done that day and playing with the cows and chickens seemed so far removed from finger painting and crocodile egg boxes that I thought it might be too difficult to explain. So we both said that we learnt some new words in English like 'Hello' and 'Thank you' and Amma looked satisfied.

The only time Amma ventured out was when she had to occasionally take and collect us from school. This was if my Achan needed the chauffeur and, even then, she would grip tightly onto our hands, more out of a fear that we would run and leave her stranded in the middle of the road than to show us the way to school. She didn't even go shopping. Groceries and things like spices and other ingredients, which weren't readily available, were delivered to our house every Thursday by a man named Tom. Achan had arranged this as Amma liked to cook. It was the only thing she really loved to do. She could have done other things, like play tennis with Catherine Hunter's mother, and I suggested it, but she didn't want to. In any case, Amma only spoke a few jumbled phrases in English so she wouldn't have understood the scoring system and she wouldn't have worn the white outfit. Amma didn't want to learn English either, as she secretly willed that we would be going home soon and her taking English classes would somehow indicate to whoever was listening out there that this would not be the case. So she spent her time cooking with the ingredients Tom brought.

That first week he came in September, he brought all sorts of vegetables both Indian and English. 'Do you remember Mol, Onam? It's all for Onam,' Amma said, pointing at the vegetables. The prickly bitter gourd looked almost offensive sitting next to a sedate cucumber, the black-eyed beans looked evil next to the green garden peas, and the hairy yam looked as if it was going to eat up the potato. 'For aviyal, olan, thoran.' She reeled off a list of dishes just like she used to do when she trapped me in the kitchen in India and I nodded and made my way quickly out of there before she decided to paste me up with them and put me in the bath.

Her food would often go to waste as Satchin and I discovered that we liked burgers and fishfingers with ketchup a whole lot better. We would gang up against her and make her place these items on the grill instead or tell her how to make English things. The food that was all dressed up on the table would go into our tiffin carriers the following day but it got embarrassing doing that whole tiffin carrier routine day after day, especially when Catherine Hunter held her nose, so we would get the chauffeur to stop on the way to school, run out and throw the contents over somebody's fence. Amma didn't know better and was happy that we ate it all. We also asked Amma if we could get rid of the red stains and sandalwood tribal look. She got very upset at this and said it was God's blessing for the day to us. Satchin asked her if God could put it somewhere else and she almost cried. So instead of upsetting her further we washed it off before we got into class and would tell her that it was smudged off during the course of the day. We also decided against broaching the shampoo concept, that could wait a while longer.

Even though Satchin and I went to the same school,

had the only two ethnic-looking faces and the greased back look, he refused to acknowledge me as his sister. 'Is that your sister?' his friends would enquire and Satchin would swear no relation to me and walk off. I really did envy his group of large friends and longed to break free from my role as 'Danny'.

This was around the time when 'Grease Lightning' took hold of the playground. All the girls with blonde hair became Sandy and because most of the boys didn't want to join in, I was elected to play John Travolta's role. I passed myself off as a cheap stand-in for Danny, even though I hadn't seen the film and couldn't really sing in English. This didn't seem to matter as the other girls just needed someone to twirl them around and because I was quite tall for my age and had jet-black, greased back hair, I seemed to fit the role. The way I just kept saying 'summer lubbing' over and over again also seemed to swing it for me, so at every playtime for the next two months or so this is what I did. Nobody ever knew that I harboured a desperate yearning to have blonde hair and become Catherine Hunter, they just thought it was a strange foreign custom thing that Indian people did when I shaved off my eyebrows.

I took one of Achan's razors and shaved off my black bushy eyebrows so I could draw new ones in with a yellow crayon. It would have looked good but I didn't know how to use a razor properly and so cut myself and then the yellow didn't show. Amma looked horrified when she saw me and she said Achan would be very upset when he got back from his trip. This didn't scare me as Achan never got upset with me. She also said that the sooner she got me out of England the better, adding

25

that it was making me do things that even she couldn't understand.

More than a year had passed by then and, if I am honest, I stopped counting the days and remembering the things that Ammamma told me, because I grew to really like England. I loved my school, my teacher, the food, television, and I didn't want to go back. If I was asked to make a choice, I would choose England every time. It wasn't that I forgot India or my Ammamma but India became less and less important and I thought maybe Ammamma could come and live with us. If she came, I knew she would like England too. I didn't tell Amma that, or that I secretly willed Achan's contract to go on forever.

Dundee cakes came and went to celebrate all the special occasions. Everyone got a cake for their birthday and I was about to have my third one with six big candles. Somebody should have told my Achan that we absolutely hated them and that these cakes only served in joining my brother and I in a perverse friendship. The only time we teamed up was when we threw those chunks of cake behind the sitting-room cabinet. The fear of our father finding this Dundee cake wall behind a hideous mahogany cabinet united us in a way that had never seemed possible. Achan came back for my sixth birthday but he could only stay for two weeks because he had to go back to America again for business. Secretly, I liked it when he went there and came back because he would buy us things that you couldn't even get in England. Once he bought me an air hostess doll that talked and even the teachers were so impressed that they allowed me to take her into assembly to do a demonstration for the other children. I also loved it when Achan was home because he played with us; piggyback rides; hide and seek. He'd understand the games and play what we wanted.

Satchin and I didn't really play together, not even after school. I tried to be his friend but he never let me because he thought I was too messy and chaotic. So after school we did our own thing. He had this endless obsession for colouring with his felt-tip pens, which he guarded with his life. My scrawny colouring pencils were not of the same standard so I didn't relish the prospect of colouring as much as he did. On several occasions, I offered to swap the whole set of my pencils for just his pink and blue pens. His refusal was categorical. So the day these very same pens went missing, all hell broke loose in our house. The only way I survived the neck lock he held me in was by signalling with my eyes at the Dundee cake wall that we had built together. But I suppose that if we knew what was going to happen, then the Dundee cake wall hardly would have mattered. When the cabinet was eventually removed and all the old bricks of cake lay there, nobody said anything. My Achan never got to see it.

Achan's trips abroad became longer and my Amma really missed him because at night we could hear her cry a lot: not a loud inconsolable cry, more of a whimper, a bit like when the school hamster was trapped in his wheel. Amma started learning English, annoying us by interrupting the television programmes we were watching with questions every five minutes as to who was saying what, but she did make a big effort to learn. Maybe this was a sign that we were going to stay in

England for longer. She would even venture out to get some of the groceries herself and collect us from school. Achan didn't see any of this or he would have been proud of her; he was always telling her to be a bit more independent. When he did return it was always to a hero's welcome and his gifts became more ostentatious. Satchin and I could have whatever we asked for; a new bicycle, games, toys, anything. Our only preoccupation at this time was whether we should stay in and watch *Blue Peter* and learn how to make what they had made earlier. That was until the death of Fluffy.

We hadn't really seen death before. The calf's death was different because we never saw her die but Satchin actually witnessed Fluffy's death. Fluffy was my brother's class hamster. To my astonishment, he asked me to come along and attend Fluffy's burial. All the children held hands and prayed as Miss Turnbull said a few words. She said that Fluffy had gone so peacefully and was happy in heaven, playing with his friends, but the truth, confided in a moment of frenzied grief, was that my brother had accidentally murdered him. Dropped from a great height because he had had a fight with Jessica Thomas and didn't want her to take him home for the holiday, Fluffy's death was instantaneous. Nobody saw. So how he could have played in heaven in that state I really don't know. Not unless God had fixed up his tiny legs along the way.

For weeks, Satchin was terrorised by Fluffy's face coming to him in his dreams. I could hear him from my room, crying, shouting and jumping around like a fish in his bed. A truce descended between us when I offered to move into his room and sleep on the top bunk bed.

I managed to convince him that just in case Fluffy decided to come down and get him, he would find me lying on the top bed instead.

Ammamma would say that we should have read the signs, but we lived in a big city and the pace didn't allow it. Three weeks after that, my Achan died and life would never, ever be the same.

Amma picked us up from school. She had a bandage wrapped around her hand, her hair was unbraided and she was wearing a pair of trousers and a light green pullover. She never dressed like that and was always wrapped like a mummy from head to toe in a sari, even covering her head with the final piece of material that remained. So instantly we knew something was wrong.

'What's happened to your hand, Ma? Are you all right?' we asked.

'My hand will be fine, I had a little accident.' There was a long silent pause and then she told us. 'Makkale, Achan had an accident too.'

Was Achan's hand damaged? I thought, but before I had a chance to ask, she blurted it out.

'He died.'

Satchin started to cry.

No, he couldn't have died, my father would never die, he went away but he always came back. There must have been some mistake; you can't die from a hand injury.

'He's not coming back, Mol,' she said again, crying.

I watched her lips move and the only other thing I heard was that, 'He died a hero and there was no pain.'

He was rerouted on one of his business trips and he

went to heaven instead as he saved a boy from having a horrific accident. He would save a little boy, that was the kind of thing that my Achan would do, but he wouldn't die. There was some mistake.

We gripped her hand firmly, more so that she would not run and leave us, and we walked home in silence, not stopping once to jump and scrunch the leaves on the ground as we normally did.

The house was in a mess. Where were his pictures? They couldn't have gone with him. I ran into the bathroom to see if his toothbrush had come back but it wasn't there either. Did Amma think that she could put his pictures away and that we would forget about him? I went into his closet to look for them and saw his clothes weren't there either. They were packed away in a big cardboard box. How could she pack him up like that? In just one day, like he never existed. I told Satchin but he made no response.

'Why are Achan's clothes packed away, Amma?'

'Mol, he's not coming back. Come, eat something.'

Eat? Is that all she ever thought about? How could we eat? She had cooked an elaborate dinner and placed some chicken drumsticks coated with breadcrumbs on a side plate (more as an afterthought that we might not like the rest). We ate none of it and went to bed. The three of us slept together in my Amma's bed. I wanted to cry but I remembered that Ammamma said that crying would indicate that the person would not come back and this was clearly not the case so I couldn't cry. Amma lay in bed with us and Satchin whimpered as she held us. I contained my sadness and desperately wanted to hold both of them but then I decided not to get too

30

attached to either of them. Everyone I ever really loved seemed to disappear.

Death precipitated events, just like the astrologer said it would. With no income and no way of getting back to India, Amma began packing things. The grocery man, Tom, came most evenings to help her. He had a sister who lived in the East End of London and he thought perhaps we could rent one of her bedsits. Tom helped us sell most of the furniture, Amma sold her jewellery and our toys, and she put down the deposit for two months' rent on a shabby room. Satchin and I didn't want to leave and we were sad but Satchin said that we had to be strong and not make any fuss. We did not say goodbye to our teachers or school friends. We left like thieves with the three suitcases, all tied with string, and as we climbed into Tom's van, our childhood effectively ended.

I can't remember much of that journey, except that it was raining hard and that the rain began to fall inside of me, suffocating me and taking with it any hope that I had of Achan's return. The sea predator could not get me so it sent the rain. My heart beat faster and the rain fell harder: the rest, I cannot remember.

The flat was a semi-furnished bedsit off Green Street in the East End of London. We had to share an outside toilet with the man on the same landing as us. He was Polish and he dressed in an old black pinstriped suit every day of the week and rarely left the house, except on Sunday when he went to Church. Tom's sister, Maggie, was the Irish landlady and she lived above us with her two cats, Arthur and One Eye. She was the one that came over to us as Tom parked the van.

Maggie was a fiery lady with bright red curly hair and a big bust that she emphasised with a light sweater. She wore a black pencil skirt which was obviously too tight. Miss Davies would say that she was having her last fling with youth, that's what I heard her say to another teacher about Catherine Hunter's mother who dressed in those type of short skirts. Maggie also had long nails and her fingertips were stained the colour of dried henna, like her teeth. She showed us into our new home. Amma thanked her. Maggie looked down at our three suitcases and smiled at us, a smile that pretended to look reassuring. She ruffled Satchin's hair, which was the wrong thing to do because he only let Amma do that. He stepped back from her and clung to Amma who held onto him. Maggie smiled at me and I smiled back.

'What's your name, darling?'

'Maya, Maya Kathi, and I'm six and my brother's called Satchin and he's eight.'

'Well, Maya Kathi, if you ever need anything, I live upstairs,' she said as she left.

The room had horrific orange psychedelic wallpaper, a decorative attempt to distract us from what it really was; damp, cold and sparse. It had dripping taps, a hob ring for a cooker, and a greasy, thick green curtain to divide the kitchen from the sleeping/sitting area. Tom showed us how to insert the ten pence pieces in the electric meter under the sink. He looked at my mother and he told her that it would not be forever, it was just a start. When he said that, I could tell Amma wanted to cry, but she didn't. He left and we unpacked our things.

Maggie and Tom came back a few hours later with an old iron bed for the three of us to sleep in and a few other bits and pieces which Maggie said she didn't need. 'Tom said you'll need a job,' Maggie said to Amma. We translated and Amma nodded. 'There's a factory a bus ride away from here that is always looking for people. Can you sew?' Maggie waited for us to relay what she had said and Amma shook her head. 'It's not difficult, it'll take a day or two to get into it. I've a machine upstairs. I'll teach you.'

That is how we spent the next two days, in Maggie's warm room with an electric bar heater and a Singer sewing machine buzzing away. One Eye and Arthur were jumping about and playing with us, whilst the television was on in the background. Maggie said Amma was a natural and would have no problems in finding work. We, in the meantime, she said, would have to be good for her and go to school. On Monday, she would take us to enrol at the local primary school and she would then accompany my mother to the factory. I thought that Maggie was another sign and that my father had sent her to show us that he hadn't forgotten us. I could tell, though, that Amma was very cautious of her. I don't know what exactly it was about Maggie but Amma wasn't herself when she was around her. Maybe she didn't understand her.

That Sunday evening, before we went to bed, I wrote a letter to my Ammamma telling her all that had happened to us. I hadn't written religiously like I had promised because we had been so busy, but that Friday,

I began my first letter, not something that I told Amma
to write for me. I really missed her and I tried to remember the things she taught me but I couldn't, so I told
her things that we did and how it was now. I asked
Satchin if he wanted to write anything to her on my
letter. He took it from me and began laughing. He read
from the beginning: 'Dear Ammamma, Who are you?'
    'You mean how, Maya, not who.'
    That was the first time he had laughed since that day.
It was worth saying 'who' if it made him laugh. How/
who, it didn't really matter, because Ammamma didn't
read English anyway. It was just so that she would get
something from me to let her know that I hadn't forgotten her and I wanted to send it because I needed her
now. Amma lit a candle and burnt an incense stick and
placed it near her bronze figurine of a little Goddess
with many arms and thanked Her for whatever she had
sent. Momentarily, the scent masked the dampness and
put us to sleep. It took me back to the veranda, waiting
for my Achan, who would scoop me up and tickle me,
or back to the big house when he came in late at night,
kissing me and saying, 'Who is my best little Mol?' As
morning approached, I had fragments of dreams of my
Ammamma, the smell of the sea vividly invading my
senses as we were running along the beach, or as I sat
on the side, watching her swimming with all her clothes
on. Occasionally, it didn't make any sense, like when
she appeared in a red telephone box. I promised whoever
was listening out there that I would never complain if
I could have those days back with the two people that
I loved most. I awoke to the smell of that urine-stained
mattress.

Amma got up early that morning and insisted on washing and oiling our hair. 'You want to look good for your new school don't you, makkale?'

I thought it was best not to make a fuss because she seemed sad at the prospect that it was the last time she would be able to do that for us. 'If I get work at the factory, I will have to be up very early and go before you wake up, so I won't have time to do this for you every day, not for a little while anyway.'

She helped us get dressed and Maggie came down to get us. Maggie said she would be back for Amma in half an hour to take her to the factory. We kissed her goodbye and left her to get ready. 'Be good,' she shouted through the window.

Maggie held our hands but Satchin released hers as we began walking to school. We passed derelict buildings, shops that were boarded up and covered with graffiti. Some said simply 'Pakis out'. These Pakis were everywhere, according to the graffiti. 'Who are they?' I asked Maggie.

'You've not to take any notice of that sort of thing. Do you hear me children? Just silly people giving other people nasty names.'

There were empty beer cans sprawled along the way, which had been dented by heavy fists or feet, and a group of punks crossed the road. Their hair colour reminded me for an instant of the exotic birds we had back in India. I looked at my brother to see if he had thought so too but he was somewhere else, looking down at his feet. This was the ten-minute walk to school that we would grow so familiar with, and then we went into a very old, grey building.

Maggie accompanied us along the corridor to see Mr Mauldy, the headmaster. He asked us lots of questions and gave us a stack of forms which needed Amma's signature. We said we could sign right there as Satchin was the one who normally signed for her when Achan wasn't around. Maggie smiled at the headmaster, saying that we were always joking around like that, and she took the forms and put them in her handbag, adding she would make sure that my mother got them. He smiled at us uncomfortably and then he took us down the corridor to show us to our respective classrooms.

My new teacher was a lady called Miss Brown; she didn't have the warmth of Miss Davies and when she smiled she revealed a set of piano teeth, with a protruding e flat. 'This is Maya, everyone say hello,' she said, introducing me to my new class. 'This is Maya,' she repeated. Everybody talked over her. She shouted at the top of her voice and they stopped for a few seconds and looked at her apathetically. Nobody volunteered for me to sit next to them and I could feel the hostile eyes of a boy in the front row. Miss Brown pointed to the back of the class to a seat next to a small girl. I went over to her and as I took my seat I smiled nervously at her. She smiled back, saying that her name was Fatima and she gave me a yellow fruit gum. This act of generosity meant so much at the time but, weeks later, I realised that she had packets and packets of them as her mother worked at the sweet factory and the yellow ones were the ones she didn't like and so discarded without a second thought.

Miss Brown was teaching the colours of the rainbow and was asking if anyone knew what followed red. I knew all the colours because in the old school we had learnt a song. I kept putting my hand up and answering questions and the boy in the front row kept looking back at me. I smiled and then he squinted his eyes at me so I ignored him. This aggravated the situation because he mouthed something back, to which I shrugged my shoulders, indicating that I couldn't hear what he was saying.

'He's Mark Fitzgerald, you can't mess with Mark Fitzgerald like that, say you're sorry,' said Fatima.

'But I haven't done anything.'

'Just say sorry or there will be trouble,' Fatima urged.

I never say sorry, especially if I haven't done anything wrong, so I continued to ignore him.

At playtime, Mark Fitzgerald and his big friend came up to me.

'You don't ever mess with me, Paki.'

I did not quite understand what Paki was so I told him I wasn't a Paki and I hadn't messed with him.

A crowd had gathered.

'Not a Paki,' he laughed, pushing me.

'Well, why have you got dirty hair and that Paki smell? Bet you eat with your fingers an' all. Look, Marty, we've got another new Paki,' he shouted to the other boy.

At that moment, I envisaged Catherine Hunter's golden locks and wished that I was still at my old school, twirling around aimlessly in the playground with a Hula-Hoop.

'Bet you've brought some smelly sandwiches with you as well,' he said, grabbing my bag.

Oh God, my lunch box. I hoped Amma hadn't put

in any masala potatoes between the bread or packed vadas. Mark Fitzgerald's sidekick went to open it. I closed my eyes, fearing the worst, and then I heard the word 'cheese'.

Thank you, Amma, thank you for not doing that to me.

'It's cheese,' Mark Fitzgerald shouted, flinging the sandwich, and then he threw my bag at me.

That was the Kermit the Frog bag Achan had brought for me from America.

And then I don't know what happened but something triggered in me and I went for him. I jumped on his back, pushing him to the floor, and pounded him with my fists. All the other children began screaming with excitement and shouted my name. Anger, hurt, sadness all came through my fists as I beat him, I couldn't stop, and then Mr Mauldy prised me away, marching me into his office.

I ached all over.

'This is no way to behave, Maya Kathi, especially not on your first day.'

I tried to explain that it wasn't my fault, that Mark Fitzgerald had started it, but he wasn't listening.

'I'll be watching you very closely. One more episode like that and you're out. Do you hear me? OUT!'

I said nothing, I didn't care. I was very, very tired and sad and wanted to sleep and forget everything.

When I walked into my class, all the other children began cheering. Miss Brown said there was no need for any of that and asked them to stop, but they continued. She added that poor Mark had had to be taken to the nurse's office and then they began clapping. I didn't really care and sat back down next to Fatima who asked if she could be my best friend.

I thought Amma would come to collect us after school but Maggie came instead, saying that Amma had got work at the factory and would be home later.

'Did you have a good day, children?'

I said nothing. Satchin shrugged his shoulders.

'You'll get used to it. It's always difficult at first, especially when you're new.'

Used to it, used to it, we weren't going to get used to anything. I would speak to Amma, she would make sure that we went somewhere better or find a way of sending us back to our old school.

'We're not staying,' I said.

'Not staying where?' Maggie asked.

'Here, here in this horrible place, in your horrible house,' I said, as she opened the front door.

Satchin put his hands on his face.

'Is that right?' she asked.

'Yes.'

'Listen, young lady, let's get a few things clear and then you and me will get on fine. Be grateful, because this is the best there is at the moment and if there wasn't this you'd be out on the streets.'

There were no beaches in London, that's why she said streets.

'Think of your mother. She'll be working hard all day so she can put some dinner on the table for you, so the least you can do is be grateful; at least she's there for you.'

I thought again about the children with no Achans and Ammas who couldn't ever have a balloon, how sad they looked, and then about the fight. It started because

39

he threw my Achan's bag. What would happen if Amma went too? We would be like those children, out on the streets.

I must have looked frightened as Maggie bent down and looked at me. 'I'm sorry to be hard with you, darling, but it's going to be a little difficult at first. That's always the way it is, but it will get better, I promise you, it will get better, but you have to try and be strong and be good for your mother.'

I looked at her and told her about the fight and what Mark Fitzgerald said to me and how I beat him and I couldn't stop. Tears rolled down my face.

Maggie picked me up and cuddled me. 'I'm sorry, darling, not everyone is like him and by the sounds of it you won't have any problems with him no more.'

She kissed my cheeks and made me feel safe, like I could believe what she told me.

'Now, would you like something to eat?' she asked.

Satchin and I nodded and Maggie took us upstairs and made us fishfingers and spaghetti hoops whilst we watched her black and white television and waited for Amma.

Amma came home later looking exhausted. 'Did you have a good day, makkale?'

'Good,' Satchin replied.

'It was really good and we made lots of new friends,' I added.

Ammamma said sometimes you had to do things just to make other people happy and then it would make you feel happy, but I didn't feel anything when I said that. Maybe it was because I felt bad about what I had done to Mark Fitzgerald.

Amma thanked Maggie.

Maggie said it had been no trouble and that we were really good kids.

We went downstairs and went to bed.

The next day Amma got up and went to work early and left us all the breakfast things prepared. Satchin served it all and then washed up and took me to school because Maggie was busy. It was a straight road, left at the crossing and then straight again. It wasn't difficult, but we followed the other mothers and children just to make sure we got there. I don't know why I expected it to be different. The children were much nicer to me but there was still sadness, a sadness which was built into the school walls. There were no pictures or singing in the corridors and assemblies were endless prayers and hymns that none of us could identify with, nobody brought in their toys to show the other children; maybe they didn't have any. You couldn't really sit assemblies out even if you wanted to. Fatima did, insisting her father would get angry as they were Muslims, and she was taunted regularly, but preferred this to what her father would do if she attended. I wanted to sit out with her but just got on with learning the Lord's Prayer.

Assembly was Mr Mauldy's time for imposing his authority with threats of caning for misbehaviour. He held the cane firmly in his hand as he spoke from the stage and lashed it against the podium, but nobody took any notice. What was another beating in the scheme of things? Then came the occasional morale-boosting song, introduced more as an afterthought that maybe this was the way to go:

'*I love the sun, it shines on me, God made the sun*

and God made me. I love the rain, it splashes on me, God made the rain and God made me.'

The bullies laughed at the absurdity that there could even be a God, let alone one sitting and making the sun and the rain, and glared at those who were heartily singing away. They had antennae to identify the weak: nobody could really blame them, for this is what they learnt at home. You had to pretend to be strong, even if you weren't, or you had to find some way of keeping them at bay.

They never touched me, not since that episode with Mark Fitzgerald, and many of them even listened to me. One day Miss Brown had to go in for a blood test which she made such a big deal out of that I thought she might never come back and teach again. 'She's going for a transfusion that might not be a success,' I said, preparing the class for the worst. She arrived back in class the next day, larger than life, to a pile of bereavement cards. 'It were Maya, Miss, she said you were gonna die,' informed Nicola Jory.

Miss Brown muttered something about wild imagination but you only had to look at the size of her plaster to know it wasn't that.

I had to utilise the fact that I wasn't touched by the bullies and find ways of keeping my status, so some playtimes I set up stories narrating colourful scenes and turned even the most hardened bully into a goblin or a prince. As I narrated, standing on the bench, they would turn their overcoats into fantastic capes and would vent their anger by slaying some dragon, or would make wishes to wizards that we knew would never be fulfilled. Never did I finish with a happy ending, always with a bizarre twist of fate, otherwise they wouldn't have played. Fatima became my assistant and made some really good sound effects like the wind and torrential rain. Most times, she was made redundant by the real thing and on those days, I found her something else to do.

Satchin kept his bullies away by mimicking. He imitated his teacher really well, curling up his lip and speaking like she did. He was always full of bright ideas and if any of the kids had problems, he would find a way around it. One day when he saw Amma was struggling to pay for the electric meter, he suggested pawning the Silver Jubilee spoons that our old posh school had given us after prancing around a pole, country dancing. We had kept them safe for an emergency and so, one day after school, we took them to the pawnshop. The broker looked at us and then the spoons and repeated our demands for five pounds a piece. He laughed so hard that his belly shook. 'How much then?' Satchin asked authoritatively.

'Five pence a piece and even then, I'm being generous.'

With his highly developed bartering skills, Satchin said, 'Ten and you have a deal.'

The man paid him and we ran off, triumphant.

We had meant to put the twenty pence in the meter, but on our way home we loitered for several minutes outside Mr Patel's sweetshop. We stood there grappling with the thought of a couple of packets of crisps each, a few boxes of sweet cigarettes, four sticks of liquorice and two packets of Bazooka Joe's bubble gum, and succumbed to temptation and went in. Coming out clutching several brown paper bags, we made a pact to

43

make them last and to share. Neither of us was sure of the terms of this agreement and I began secretly eating the contents of the bags and a few hours later, everything was gone. Satchin didn't fight with me when he found out, he just looked at me, disappointed.

Our relationship changed when our father died and subsequently when Amma had to work. We knew we were fighting on the same side, so it was pointless wounding each other on purpose. Satchin became very protective towards me and although he would not overtly acknowledge me as his sister, he would wait for me near the school gates so we could go home together. He was the one who had possession of the door key and took responsibility for most things. I was in complete awe of my brother, the way he could do things and make things feel so exciting when they blatantly weren't. We would run home chasing each other, or take turns to kick empty cans, but always in a world of our own, averting the glances of strangers, not giving them an opportunity to say anything or make gestures at us.

We were acutely aware that all around us, on the streets, a battle was raging. Poverty is a hideous thing, it fills people with a sense of injustice, frustration, inadequacy, even unworthiness, and from then on, a secret war begins inside them. The battle is to become someone, to prove something, and it never ends. Surrounded by derelict buildings crumbling like dreams, burnt-out cars and pavements stained with venomous spit, people fought themselves and each other. More often it was each other. Maggie's simple home was a sanctuary from everything that lurked outside her battered blue door.

An oasis in the middle of everything concrete and void.

Once inside the bedsit, Satchin heated up whatever Amma had made for us and we ate together, washed up the dishes, tried to do our homework and waited for our mother to come home. Sometimes the wait was just so boring that it was better to fall asleep. What Amma did at the factory, we didn't really know, but she always came home very tired. On Fridays, she brought something back for us: a colouring book, a reading book or matchbox cars, so we always stayed up. We never asked her for things and, believe me, I wanted to; I would have loved some transfers or stickers but Satchin told me not to ask. He said that some nights he heard her crying, saying that she couldn't give us the things she wanted to, and he said that asking for stuff would make things worse.

On Sunday, Amma's day off, we went to the park and she sat on the roundabout and watched us play or, on very special occasions, Tom would take us in his van to the seaside. They thought we would enjoy this but I hated the sea, it was a predator like the heavy rains, and predators took things away when you least expected, just like the rain. Satchin and I ran along the beach or played in the arcades and for those moments we could be children. Then on Sunday evening, we would crawl into bed, knowing that soon it would be Monday and the week began again. It could have gone on and on like that and we wouldn't have known the difference had the seasons not changed.

Despite the cold, winter was like a dream for us. Beautiful snowflakes covered everything that was grey, and temporarily we didn't have to see the reality of where we lived because everything was painted a soft, fluffy white and we could distract ourselves by building snowmen and throwing snowballs at each other. Summer, in contrast, was difficult. Whilst other kids counted the days until the school holidays, Satchin and I dreaded them. In summer it got very hot and sticky inside so we had to be outside but were told not to wander far. We had six long weeks of being together, which meant endless hours entertaining each other. We didn't have a television so we tried to re-create scenes and stupid dialogue from the Laurel and Hardy films that we had watched when we were rich.

Hardy is entertaining some ladies and doesn't have enough money for sodas for all of them, so he tells Laurel (me) to say, 'No thank you, Oli, I'm not thirsty.' And when Hardy checks the order with the girls, he says, 'Soda, soda, soda and what will you have, Stanley?'

Stanley says, 'Soda.'

He pulls him to one side. 'Didn't I tell you we only have enough money for three sodas?'

Stanley smiles and Hardy begins again.

'Soda, soda, soda and what will you have, Stanley?'

'Soda,' I reply. Then Hardy chases me around the room and we fall about laughing. Why we laughed so much, I don't know, boredom and repetition do strange things. Sometimes we got Jatinder and Simon, two boys who lived on our street, to be the extras but they thought this was boring so Satchin told them about this idea he had to make a bomb.

All four of us went out into the yard and began making a bomb from petrol cans we had found in the street and Satchin added some turps we found out in the yard. He doused a rag with the mixture and Jatinder lit the cloth; it went up in flames immediately and set alight the cardboard box that was next to it. Jatinder panicked and threw the box against the fence. Before we knew it, flames were everywhere and we couldn't put them out. The Polish man saw us and fanned the flames with the buckets of water he was using to clean the windows. Maggie spotted the Polish man jumping up and down, shouting, and his suit nearly on fire, and came running with her extinguisher. Jatinder and Simon ran off.

Maggie reprimanded us, telling us how dangerous and stupid it was and how we could have killed everyone.

'Do you understand me, Satchin and Maya, do you understand what you could have done?' she shouted.

She said she would tell our mother unless we wrote a story about the consequences of fire. Mine was entitled 'The Effects of Smoke Inhalation'. I don't know what exactly I wrote as I copied it off the piece of paper attached to the fire extinguisher, but she was very impressed and said there were no two ways about it, I definitely had talent, but it was wasted on doing silly things like trying to burn the house down.

Maggie could have shouted at us a lot more because we gave her much cause to. I think the last straw for her was when we almost became the centre of a hostage situation. One evening, there were helicopters patrolling above our house and policemen surrounding our street. We were playing in the yard and these two men shouted at us to open the gate. We were about to do so when the Polish man ran over, picked us both up, and dragged us inside. I kicked, bit him and screamed because that was what Miss Brown had told us to do if men unexpectedly picked us up. Maggie came running down to see what the commotion was all about and the Polish man told her that we were about to let some escaped convicts who had been on the news into the house.

'You kids can't go on like this. I know it gets boring but I thought you'd have more common sense than to let strangers in, especially armed ones,' she yelled. 'You know it's not safe.'

It wasn't safety that we wanted, it was excitement, adventure, something out of the ordinary to happen, but it didn't.

After that day, she decided that we were definitely a hazard and thought it was probably better if we went up to her flat after school and the days she was there on our school holidays. We could only stay at Maggie's until seven in the evening and then she would have to go to work. Sometimes, when we came home and Maggie wasn't in, she would leave One Eye in our bedsit as a substitute, but when she was around she cooked us stew and played with us. Maggie became all things to me, I could talk to her about almost anything.

Upstairs in her home, Maggie taught me how to sew and to knit. That birthday, she made me a rag doll named Kirstin. 'Here you are, Maya, darling, to replace the one you used to have, Jemima, wasn't it?'

'Jemina,' I corrected her.

Maggie handed me a parcel. I unwrapped the package eagerly, waiting to find a rag doll with long blonde hair but found a creepy-looking thing with black button eyes sewn too closely together. Her black hair was everywhere and she looked like a mad woman who wanted to go out on the rampage. I made a comment about the hair but Maggie said that was fashionable and the current style. I didn't take her to bed but left her on the sideboard where she stared evilly at me. Maggie insisted that we spend weeks just making different outfits for her. The first thing I made was a large pink hat that covered her eyes. 'It's too low, Maya, darling, you can't see her eyes,' Maggie said. Then I was resolute that she have a home of her own so she wouldn't have to glare at us. We got her a cardboard box and made her a house that looked better than ours. I shut her up in there and allowed Satchin to use it as a garage and store all the cars he was collecting, turning Creepy into a parking attendant. He was ecstatic.

Satchin and I also bonded further that summer through the raids we carried out on Mr Patel's shop. We didn't do it because we were poor; Amma often bought us the kind of things we stole. For me, it was the excitement of being Satchin's young accomplice. I would distract Mr Patel by asking him to weigh a quarter of cola cubes, and then Satchin would stuff some Wotsits up his jumper and cough, which meant that I had to then change my mind about the sweets. We would then run out of the shop as fast as we could and laugh uncontrollably. If we were lucky, there would be a packet of Smarties up there too. My brother and I would never have got caught, but one day Maggie overheard us arguing over the stash. The brown Smarties were the source of much contention and, as I threw the whole packet at Satchin, she came in, made us put on our coats, and marched us both into Mr Patel's shop to confess.

We stood there defiantly, following the procedure that we had rehearsed many times, that was, to say nothing or claim complete innocence. After five minutes, the word police was thrown about a few times and Satchin, forgetting our pact, just broke down and cried. So then some slave labour arrangements were made and we had to help Mr Patel and his wife brush the floors and clean out their storerooms. Maggie made out like we had stolen the Crown Jewels or something, saying that she was extremely disappointed in us and didn't think we'd sink to such depths. After going on and on she finished by saying that she would not tell our mother as it would break her heart to know that we had been thieving, but I wished she had, then at least Amma might have had some reaction towards us.

I missed Amma desperately, or maybe I missed the idea of having a stay at home mum who baked cakes and read stories, who shopped and gossiped. I felt sad in the mornings when I followed the other mothers taking their children to school and I wished mine was there too. Looking back, I never felt like I really had her and that she was mine, but then I don't think I ever gave her a chance. It wasn't because I didn't love her, for it was hard not to want to love her, it was because I was terrified that she too might be taken away. So I used Maggie as my security and clung to her so she couldn't throw us on the streets if anything happened. On the days Amma was around, I found it hard, as I also didn't want to be reminded of India, the good times or our culture, because things were bad enough without all of that to deal with as well. I felt we were forced to make a choice and I chose the easiest route, which was to forget the place and the culture that I was from.

At prayer time, when Amma woke us to pray to the Goddess, she would just manage to say the first few words, 'Aum, namo Guru Dev . . .' when I would suddenly cut in with the Lord's Prayer which Maggie was helping me with. It probably upset Amma but there was enough confusion without praying to some foreign God. When she prepared for Onam and told us some king story, I interrupted her with the story about the king who asked his three daughters how much he loved them. And as she decorated the bedsit for Onam, I made no comment at the intricate petal design she put on the doorstep and trod all over it with my dirty shoes. When she cooked Indian food, I insisted on something else. I wish I had never done these things but I was desperate for her to shout at me, to react, to tell me that she didn't love me, that she couldn't cope with it all and that she was going too, but she never did.

On the days that things got really tough, I locked myself outside in the toilet and talked to Achan, begging him to make things a little better from wherever he was. I knew he was always consistent and listened, as things always improved after I spoke to him. That is how I knew that, despite him not being physically present, he was around us. Sometimes, I would ask Satchin if he spoke to him to make things better for him, but Satchin would get really sad. One day he became very distressed and said maybe he was to blame for what had happened to our father because of what he had done to Fluffy. There was nothing I could say to that as I remembered what the astrologer said about the rules of karma so I decided not to bring up the subject again and thought that maybe he did die because of the bad things we did. Maybe that's what happened if we did *really* bad things.

I would talk to Achan alone and I asked him many times if it was this but he never said anything. Other times when I talked to him, I would tell him what we had done in the day, because somewhere I was sure he could hear, even if he couldn't answer. But my greatest wish was that I would wake up and he would come and find us in that house and take us away, saying that there had been a terrible mistake and that he hadn't died.

NALINI

I cannot easily put into words why I told my children that their father had died. To save them from the lies that inextricably led to the fact that the only person he could have possibly loved was himself, I suppose. Not only this, but what do you say to two small children who are about to lose almost everything? Self-worth is fragile enough as it is, isn't it? What was I supposed to tell them? The truth? 'Monu, Mol, your father has had enough of responsibility and if that is not enough, he has another family, he's gone, left us.' Maybe there are one hundred shades for explaining truth, a spectrum of light to dark, depending on the vulnerability of those who have to hear it. Things are not always so clear-cut, they are not either black or white, life just isn't like that. I know my mother would disagree, arguing that there is one immutable truth and it is just a question of facing it. My husband left, just as my own father did, without saying a word. Not even goodbye.

My mother had a series of miscarriages before giving birth to me. She did not really care if I was a girl and she would have to find a dowry for me to marry. I think my mother was happy to prove to her in-laws and everyone else that she could bear children. She was elated when she found out she was carrying me and did not hide her bump like all the other women in the village did.

I was born in a part of India where God had a riot with the colour green; everywhere you looked He had created hues of luscious greens and made the air so healthy and calm. There was, however, not one moment of peace that I can draw from those childhood years. My father was always trying to kill my mother or she was threatening to kill herself by jumping into one of the many wells. The sound of screaming voices invaded the first eight years of my life but the screaming stopped suddenly with the death of my baby brother. My father had already left the day before the baby was born: one day he was there and the next, he was gone. The shame of what she would tell the other villagers meant that we had to leave the village. We walked twenty-seven kilometres barefoot, carrying our scant possessions on our heads, and settled in the village of Collenauta on the border of Kerala and Tamil Nadu.

The only thing my mother could do exceptionally well was cook, so she offered her services to the patrons of the village who owned all the sugar cane plantations and who were immensely wealthy. The story I was asked to relay, whenever probed about my father, was that he had been killed whilst trying to save someone drowning. On hearing me say this with the intonation and facial movements that accompanied the phrase, the patrons, Thampurati and Mothalali, took pity on our plight and offered us a place to stay. That is how we came to be hired by the Kathi family, my mother as cook and I as her assistant, and we lived in the small quarters at the bottom of their land, surrounded by rich banana plantations, mango trees and paddy fields. It was a small room but beautifully decorated with simple woodcarvings and all the utensils we required to do our job along with a buffalo, which gave us fresh milk.

The art of putting together food is a magical thing and if it is done right it has the power to soften the most hardened heart. My mother always said that when you work with what you love, you work with magic. However, if the ingredients are incorrectly administered, or if you work with bad intention, it can also bring the most disastrous results. Subtly, we laboured, convinced that it was the love and gratitude we put into the preparation of the Kathi's food that made them prosper. Just the right amount of cumin to stimulate appetite for life, a cinnamon quill to bring spice or action into stagnant phases of life, lemon juice to diffuse an argument, chilli to relieve pain and turmeric to heal the heart. Freshly picked coriander leaves tempered bad humour and gave a sense of clarity, fiery peppered rasam warmed the soul, and grated coconut added to many dishes soothed and comforted. Pounded lentils left to soak for days made the batter for soft pancakes filled with shallow fried masala potatoes for a sense of pride and stability. Golden beans added to vegetable thoran were for longevity and prosperity.

My mother would watch situations and then prescribe

accordingly under the watchful eye of Annapurna, beautiful pale blue Goddess of food and abundance, lit by the fire and the passion of the sun and the moon. She was placed on a box in the kitchen area and was adorned every day with fresh flowers. We said a prayer to her when we woke up and just before we went to bed, thanking her and asking that she give us the courage to do our job. So I don't know if we could really take the credit for delivering small doses of happiness wherever possible, but we believed it was Annapurna, and my mother said it really didn't matter, for whatever you believed became true.

There was also a little bronze Annapurna, no bigger than my thumb which my mother kept in a makeshift pocket of her kasava mundu. She came everywhere with us and was placed in whichever kitchen we were cooking in and was always given the first offering of food. There were many kitchens the little Goddess visited as word spread rapidly through the village that we had the most amazing ability to cook. As we were hired out for village festivals, births and marriages, things in the village began to change: a new temple, renewed rainfall, and laughter. It was almost as if my mother turned the inability to mend her own life outwards and seeing the pleasure this produced fixed her in some way. She took pride in her work and it showed.

The astrologer first thought that these changes were negligible and had been induced by the new phase of the moon. When one of the village women, who had been trying for ten years to conceive, suddenly fell pregnant, he consulted his chart and once again found two new specks pointing in a northward direction. He paid us a visit.

My mother welcomed him in. He looked around at the walls that had been brightly painted and the kitchen area decorated with freshly cut flowers and then he saw the box with my mother's Goddess covered with garlands and whatever pieces of jewellery she had. The room was infused with cooking smells and the fragrance of jasmine and incense and then he looked down at the floor which had been neatly swept. He felt a little reassured and he removed his chappels. My mother pulled out the best stool for him and he sat.

He was probably in his mid-thirties and had taken over from his father who had died suddenly. He found it difficult at first to speak and coughed everywhere, looking a little embarrassed, as he dabbed his cheeks with his loincloth. His bare chest had red saffron stains and a black piece of string hung diagonally along it. At the other end was a small bag where he kept a notebook, some seashells and a pendulum. My mother smiled at him and brought him some masala tea. He swiftly drank and coughed again. She pulled out some honey-coated jilebies and as she offered him one, his face softened. When that had disappeared, he took another and another, until his whole body surrendered and then he spoke.

'Why did you come here?' enquired the astrologer.

'We were sent,' my mother replied.

'Dates of birth?'

She gave him the name of the rainy season and the time at which I was born and she said that he could plot my life for she knew for sure the path hers was going to take.

'Just do Nali's,' she said.

He took out his notebook and began drawing and calculating. Smiling enthusiastically, he murmured the word 'good' half a dozen times and then he paused, long silent pauses where he shook his head, and then he began to discuss the plans that had been made for me.

'Many men will come from afar to marry you and you will be a beautiful woman but you must not readily accept the first proposal and you must not marry in pursuit of love, for this, too, is an illusion, just a state of mind. You will be a very, very prosperous woman, unimaginably so, but never lose sight of your gift. If you do, you lose your centre and all else falls away. You are already very blessed, for many people must go in search of their gifts. Lifetimes are spent on this. You know where it resides, hold onto it.' He looked up from what he was doing and asked, 'Father dead?'

'Yes, yes,' interjected my mother hastily, 'lost his life in a tragic accident.'

He was about to probe further when I looked at him sadly and said 'drowning' and then I asked him if I would be happy.

He responded by saying that happiness was a state of mind and nature dictates that states are forever changing. He opened his tin of moist sandalwood and placed two dots on our foreheads. Every Thursday after that he would pay a visit, have tea, share his counsel, bless us and leave.

I did go to school when I could but it wasn't something that interested me. What I loved was the preparation of a wedding or a village festival; the anticipation, the chopping of food, the blending, the frying, the colours, the aromas, the tasting then adding, and then the final results offered alongside decorations. My mother understood this completely and the only stipulation she gave was that I learn to read and write.

We gained much respect for the work we produced in the village and although my mother had made enough money to buy her own plot of land, she decided not to, saving the money instead for my dowry. She hoped that the money would attract a good suitor for me.

When I was about sixteen, many young men and their families began to come and enquire if I was eligible for marriage. First, the tree climber and his family came. His job was to collect all the different fruit from the trees but my mother looked at the state of his feet and his fingernails and turned him away. Then the doctors' family arrived, they weren't doctors as such but were twins. In the village, twins were supposed to have curative powers and if someone had an ailment, one of the twins was brought in to touch the patient. If this failed, the other twin was brought in and the patient was supposedly healed. My mother didn't believe a word of it, thinking that most complaints in the village were cured by her fiery pepper rasams. She said that ailments were very simple to cure; cold diseases treated by warm spices and warm diseases treated by cold spices. In any case this was all irrelevant; the family couldn't decide on which twin to marry me to and they began arguing amongst themselves.

Many even waived the dowry like Luxmiammayi; she made her money by casting off the evil eye. Luxmiammayi did this by blowing ashes of holy vibuthi at those touched by the evil eye and purported to fix any number of problems by doing so. One of the farmers was preoccupied that his hens weren't laying eggs; he was convinced that a neighbouring farmer had put a curse on him, so she looked into it and blew. A few days later the hens started laying again. There was, however, some tension between her and my mother because every time we cooked for a major occasion Luxmiammayi would sit and gossip about how salty the plantain upperie tasted or how badly cut the spinach thoran was. My mother could have said many things about her, like the fact that she didn't use proper vibuthi and it was really leftover wood ash, but she said nothing and Luxmiammayi too was sent packing. The only good thing about the son, my mother proclaimed, was that he had shiny white teeth and this was because he had nothing better to do all day except suck twigs from the neem tree. My mother warded them all off with strong garlic which she mixed in their tea. None of them, she said, were good enough. She didn't know that I had fallen in love with one of the Kathis' sons.

The Kathis had two boys, Raul and Gobi. Both were much older than me and I barely saw them when I was growing up due to the fact they both boarded at the school in the main town. Their father made sure they went to college and got respectable jobs. Gobi, the younger of the two, visited town often on leave and I had seen him a few times but never spoken with him. One day, I was delivering trays and pots to his home, balancing one on my head and carrying the others. He startled me, coming from nowhere, and asked if I was going to his house and if I needed help. 'No,' I replied, meaning I didn't want any help.

It took me half an hour to cross the fields, the sun that day was painfully hot, and I arrived at their kitchen door, sweating. The maid started shouting at me, saying that Thampurati was getting impatient with her and it was my fault. She went on and on and all I could think of was how hot and thirsty I was and I needed a glass of water. She was furious and continued banging pots and pans so that the noise brought down several members of the household.

Gobi walked past the kitchen and stopped when he saw me. 'You said you weren't coming here.'

'I was, but,' I hesitated, desperate for some water.

'But,' he continued.

'I need some . . .' I fainted.

I remember waking up in the most luxurious room. Cool, tiled floors, beautiful alcove ceilings, and the noise of a water fountain. 'Who is she?' I heard a voice say.

'She's Nalini, the daughter of one of the cooks,' Gobi replied.

I opened my eyes and there he was. Deep almond eyes looking down at me, full, defined lips, jet-black hair, very tall and sturdy. 'Get her some water,' the man said to Gobi.

He touched my forehead which pulsated and took hold of my hand. It fell into his voluntarily.

'Will she be okay, Raul?' Gobi asked, as he handed him the glass.

'Heat,' he replied, as he put the glass to my lips and poured the water gently into my mouth.

All of a sudden there was a shout. 'Monu, Monu, what's happening? What are you doing? Why are you giving the servant girl something to drink and in one of

61

our best glasses, we won't be able to use that again.'
Raul stared at his mother who had just walked in. He
ignored her, turned to me and said, 'Nalini, drink.'

'They are silly girls, no sense, walk in the full sun,
what do you expect and then, then they land up here
and give us problems,' Thampurati continued.

'I feel better,' I whispered, getting up uneasily. 'I have
to go home.' There was a pause and he, Raul said, 'I
will take you.'

Another loud shrill broke the silence. 'But, Monu,
you can't be seen out walking with a servant girl. Tell
him, Gobi.'

At first Gobi said nothing and then his mother glared
at him. Gobi suggested that perhaps the maid take me
home.

Raul got up, took my arm, and walked with me past
his mother. As we walked together across the fields,
he held up an umbrella to protect me from the sun.
The workers in the fields stared at us, women turned
their heads, shyly pretending not to notice him when
he passed. We said nothing to each other, the silence
between us said more than was necessary. Some of the
older women, like Kochuammayi, stood with their
mouths open. She had a mouth like a buffalo and I was
sure that after her work was done she would run to tell
her husband in the toddi shop. 'Come home, I have
something important to tell you,' she would shout,
attempting to entice him away from his drink, but he
would ignore her. She would then run over to the temple
and sit outside on the bench and add a little more to
the story, sharing it to those who were ready to listen.

I didn't want Raul to see where we lived, because just

for those moments, I wasn't the cook's daughter, I was somebody important, somebody who he wanted to be with. Almost sensing this, he stopped at the tree on the path that led to our dwelling and said with certainty, 'I have to go but will come back to visit for Onam.' I wanted to say, 'Wait, there are so many things I haven't told you.' But I could not say or do anything.

My head was full of so many ideas as I opened the front door. 'Ma, I have found him. It's him,' I wanted to scream.

'What took you so long?' asked my mother.

'Nothing,' I replied.

Nine weeks. Nine weeks until Onam and then I could see him again. Every detail of that afternoon was etched on my mind and played over and over again; the way he smelt, the strength of his hands, the confidence in his stride, the tenderness in his eyes. My mother rushed back in, interrupting my thoughts. 'Nali, you didn't tell me you fainted and Raul Kathi brought you home.'

'It wasn't important, Ma.'

The month of Shravan seemed to take forever to arrive. Onam was the biggest festival of the year where every household celebrated the harvest just after the end of the rainy season. The main celebration was held on the tenth day at the patron's house and they would invite all their employees and give food and gifts to them as a way of saying thank you. This was the busiest time for my mother and I and preparations began many months in advance.

Before the rains began, we collected banana leaves to serve the food upon, we prepared dried palm leaves and saved empty coconut shells to burn as fuel, and jackfruit was preserved to be used for payasam. We pickled tender mango, 'to let dreams ferment for an abundant harvest,' my mother said, as she packed the finished bottles away in anticipation. In this period, we also cooked and served food to all our neighbours who were helping each other build new roofs with sugar cane leaves in time for the monsoon. Then the rains fell hard and people prayed for an abundant harvest and the whole village waited to celebrate Onam.

As we collected and washed the food for the feast, my mother would tell me again and again its significance. 'It's to welcome the spirit of King Mahabali.'

'I won't forget, Ma,' I reassured her as she began again. 'The Asura King was worried that the kind, wise king Mahabali was becoming too powerful, so he enlisted the help of Vishnu to curb Mahabali's power. Vishnu disguised himself and took the form of a dwarf called Vamana and went begging to the king. The kind king asked him what he wanted and Vamana asked for three steps of land where he could sit and pray and the king agreed. Soon the dwarf expanded and became a giant. His first step covered the sky, the second step covered the heavens, and the third was about to engulf the earth when Mahabali offered his head as the last step so the earth wouldn't be crushed. The Gods were pacified by his sacrifice and his spirit was allowed to return once a year to visit his kingdom and celebrate with his people.'

'Sacrifice is important, Mol,' she concluded. 'Spirit will live forever.'

The evening before Onam, every veranda was decorated with intricate patterns of flower petals and in the centre was a four-sided pyramid of Mahabali. I went to collect the final petals to finish off and as I looked beneath my tree, I saw a package: somebody had left a parcel with my name on it. I tore off the wrapping and inside was a bright blue hand-embroidered sari which would have taken us three years to buy. I looked inside again but there was no note. Raul, I thought, he has bought this for me, he is back.

I went back home and begged my mother if I could serve instead of staying behind in the kitchen. 'You don't know the order of food,' she said. 'Not this year, Mol, next year, then I will have plenty of time to teach you.'

'Please, Ma,' I begged, 'this year, tell me now.'

She relented and the two of us sat up late as she took out a banana leaf and explained how to serve on it. 'The narrow part of the leaf must always be on the left, serving begins at the bottom left corner, and first you place a small banana, next to this come the banana chips coated with jaggery, then popadom. From the top left hand of the leaf, mango pickle, injipuli, thoran, olan, khichidi, aviyal. Only after this is placed can the guest begin eating. Wait for them to begin and then at the bottom centre you serve the rice, then pour the sambar on top of the rice. When they have finished, serve the payasam and after dessert, pour the rasam into their cupped hands and then wait, wait to see if they would like more.'

She went over it three or four times until I felt completely sure. Then we fell asleep.

*   *   *

The next morning I woke up very early and headed for the lake to bathe. Frogs were dancing on the lotus leaves, croaking loudly as I washed my hair, scrubbing it with chickpea flour so it shone. Running coconut oil through it, I tied it up with a fresh garland and unwrapped the sari. I would tell Ma it was a gift from the Kathis for all our help, that I had taken it back to Thampurati, insisting I was not worthy of such a gift, but she would not accept it back and asked not to mention it again for that would embarrass her further. I began to get dressed and let all the confidence and power I had seep into every tuck and fold of my new outfit and then I headed towards the Kathi's house so I could serve.

Stepping into their courtyard, my glass bangles jangled and people turned around to stare. They stopped and looked again. The temple drums were beating softly in the background, calling everyone from the village. When they were all assembled, I began serving. Gobi was first. 'A beautiful colour that suits you,' he said. I smiled and continued serving. The drums began beating faster and faster and then I reached him. I could feel Raul's presence without even looking. I nervously poured the aviyal onto the leaf and as I finished, I looked up and held his gaze. Something exchanged between the two of us. It said a thousand things between us and yet it said nothing to those around us.

My mother was annoyed at me, saying that I should not have accepted such gifts and that I should have tried harder to give the sari back to Thampurati. She said that I looked too good and asked if I had protected myself against the evil eye. I laughed at her and she got very angry and mumbled that she would not look after me if I caught a fever in the night. Then, just before we went to bed, she burnt some red chillies and muttered that it was just as she had thought: 'too many eyes.' We went to sleep, protected from watchful green envy who was responsible for so much misfortune.

The next day, my mother came running into the area where I was sleeping and told me that we would be very busy over the coming months. Raul was getting married. Married! No, he wouldn't, he couldn't, I loved him. I felt a loathing, a sense of unworthiness. Was it all in my head? Had I misinterpreted the signs? All I could do was cook. I spent the day cooking and when my mother went out to run her errands, I hit the pots and pans so hard that they left marks on the floor. I garnished the dishes with an excess of hot chillies so that at lunchtime, for the first time ever, those who ate became sick. I went for a long walk.

Contradictory thoughts battled in my head. How stupid to think that I, a cook, could marry into such a family? But then the astrologer always said that a call that goes out never returns unanswered. 'No matter how strange the request may seem, someone is always listening,' he maintained. I waded through paddy fields, my feet drenched in water as they splashed angrily. Undoing my hair, I ran through the clearing and then sat under a palm tree and cried. I cried until I fell asleep and awoke to darkness. Then I sensed him and laughed at the fact that the mind still played such cruel tricks. I turned my head and he was there. I ran my fingers through my hair and adjusted my pavada.

'It is a bit late to be out,' Raul said.

'I was sent to get some provisions,' I replied, looking at my empty hands.

'Come, I'll walk you home,' he gestured, helping me to my feet.

Why? I wanted to scream. Why are you getting married? Why did you make me fall in love with you when all along you knew I couldn't have you? All I could say, though, was, 'Congratulations, I hear you are getting married.'

'It's not how it appears, Nalini. I had to see you once again,' he continued.

I looked up. His smile came beaming back at me, melting any doubts or resentment that I held. As we walked back, he told me he had been able to think of little else but me. The marriage, he said, was arranged by his mother to someone he barely knew. He took my hand.

Raul Kathi, I thought, Why are you doing this to me?

The hour passed quickly as he walked me to the tree, our tree, and squeezing my hand, he told me he would come back for me.

He returned the next day and the day after that and somewhere I chose to forget that he would be getting married and I allowed myself to completely love him.

Our house became suffused with uncertainty and my mother and I began to argue as we never had. Food rotted after just a day. She sensed that Raul had something to do with it and warned me to stay away. She pleaded, saying that love was fleeting and that the constants in life came from the sense of self and not from another. Nearly every cell in my body begged me to stay away. I knew that this person would take me away from who I was and I did try to keep away from him but the more I attempted to avoid Raul, the more intense the longing became and the more persistent he became. I just wanted him, to touch him, to hold him, to be with him.

Two weeks before his wedding, Raul came to me and asked me to go away with him. I agonised over the scandal and the anguish that this would cause my mother. I did not want to leave her and she would not want to leave her home, but I desperately wanted to be with Raul and if I had told her, she would not have let me go. So the next evening, with an overwhelming sense of grief, I packed a few things and left with him. We married and then we went to the station.

The train arrived at Mumbai. The platform was crowded with people: coolies with red turbans, competing for custom; sellers with fruit on their head bombarding descending commuters; tea boys shouting '*chia*'; contortionists making their way over to families and blowing up balloons which they bent like their bodies. Some of the children cried, afraid, others cried because they wanted to buy the balloons and their parents hastily dragged them away. I stood in amazement. Raul held my hand as we walked through the chaos to find the driver.

As we drove through busy streets, I gazed in wonderment at all the women wearing brightly-coloured clothes, some of whom wore make-up and had handbags. Fast-moving cars sped randomly in front of us and rickshaws, bullock carts and bicycles followed far behind. People urinated on street corners or squatted by food stalls. Colourful buses passed them, covering the food with a thick, black smoke. A policeman stood on a box and was trying to manage the traffic with his whistle but nobody took any notice. Even dust seemed to have a life of its own and participated, flying with the noise of engines and following people who were shouting and running or waiting, wearing their best clothes, in long cinema queues. I felt a strange sense of excitement, I wanted to participate, to learn Hindi properly so I could understand it all. The noise, traffic, people and animals eventually subsided and were replaced by lime and mango trees, fields of them. We arrived at Anajaba, sixty kilometres from Mumbai.

The car pulled up to two wrought-iron gates and as the driver pressed the horn, a guard dressed in khaki opened the gates. He saluted us. Raul nodded. There were acres of lawn and then we approached the veranda. A woman with gapped teeth ran out to meet us and she bowed before me, touching my feet. Another man ran out of the house to take the luggage.

'Mem Sahib,' he said to me as he bowed. We approached the house, a large colonial-style, white building with tall ceilings, and the cook came out with a tray bearing water and food.

'Welcome home,' said Raul.

This was home? Everywhere was covered in an opulent red, there was even an imported red leather sofa to match, upon which yellow silk hand-embroidered cushions rested. I couldn't have dreamt of such splendour. Everything looked untouched, from the white freshness of the walls and the polished wood furniture, to the shine of the floor.

Even if we just had each other, it would have been enough, because in those first few months of marriage Raul was all that I could have hoped for. Attentive and caring, he made me feel like the centre of everything. I never believed I was worthy of such a man. He would rush back from work at five o'clock just to spend time with me and would take me out of the enclave so I could experience new things.

We went to restaurants in the town and he showed me how to use cutlery, or took me to sari shops and talked me through the latest fashions. He would then instruct the seller to dress me in one of the most expensive fabrics and then would get the driver to take us around town so I could experience the evening bustle. Sometimes we walked through the crowds, Raul holding my hand firmly. I enjoyed the noise and the activity with the safety of him beside me. Then I fell pregnant and it changed.

'Raul, I'm pregnant,' I said, throwing my arms around him.

He looked at me, horrified.

'Is there something wrong? Aren't you happy? What is it?'

'Of course I'm happy, just a little shocked. Maybe it could have come later, I wanted you to myself for a little while longer, but yes, yes, I am happy,' he said, stroking my hair.

'Are you sure?'

'Of course,' he replied.

As I grew bigger, so did my insecurities. I felt that somehow, by marrying him, I had exchanged much more than a ring and a garland. Moving into a big house, having servants, leading a life of shopping and gossip, made me feel completely useless. The sickness and nausea took away the pleasure I usually felt when cooking and I detested seeing the kitchen, so I stayed away and the cook did whatever she wanted.

Raul came home later and later, something urgent always came up at the last minute. There were days he promised he would come home early and I would sit waiting for him, waiting to go out, and then I would fall asleep. Now I was always second best to a card game or a drunken evening with his friends.

I wanted to ask him, Raul, why? Why have you changed? Is it because the passion that comes from wanting someone so desperately has to wane into a nothingness once you have them? And is this what happens when you finally possess them and take what you need? Have you always been this way and is it I who have refused to see? But his answer to everything was that pregnancy had changed me and I had become far too emotional.

Maybe he was right. Maybe I had time to question things, but I felt so alone and despite being seven months pregnant, I was desperately empty inside. I longed for my mother, for our life together, for peace. I knew she could make everything better but I couldn't send for her. I had caused her enough grief by leaving her like that, I couldn't now ask for her help. So I carried on and did not complain.

Our little son arrived earlier than expected. Raul was away, setting up an office in the Gulf, and he sent a telegram saying that he would be home soon. Although I had servants to help look after Satchin, I couldn't cope. He screamed all night and I couldn't make things better for him, nothing I did was good enough. I kept seeing pictures of my mother's baby boy, blood all over the kitchen floor, no screaming child, but a silent, lifeless one. It played on my mind over and over again. Defeated and exhausted, I stayed in bed for weeks. Sometimes I looked at my little bundle and the enormity of my responsibility and reflected on how life had changed from being so carefree in the village with my mother to this. Satchin continued to cry, it seemed like it was endless and, almost at breaking point, I wrote a letter to my mother, begging her to come and visit. Enclosed was the train ticket. She came two days later armed with her condiments.

My mother arrived in her best mundu and had put in a set of false teeth for the journey. They were too big for her mouth so she pursed her lips together to stop them from falling out. The driver had collected her from the station and as he opened the boot, endless hand-tied bundles of food jumped out. He complained that she had stained his car with coriander; it had come open as they hit one of the many potholes along the journey.

'Coriander is harmless,' she mumbled from the gap in the corner of her mouth, 'especially on the back seat of a car.'

'Raul Sahib will not be happy,' he retorted.

Ma could not hold her lips together as she came to greet me, so she took out her teeth and handed them to the driver who looked disgusted. She held me tight. There was so much I wanted to tell her. How could I say that she was right, that I now understood what she meant when she talked about love, about the importance of the sense of self? But a mistake is only a mistake when you admit it to yourself deep inside. With tears streaming down my face, I told her how happy I was, that Raul was a good man, that he took care of me and gave me the stability that I had longed for and that he was kind, very kind.

My mother said nothing, never once did she reproach me or make a comment on how I had left the village, the scandal that it had caused and the effect that it had had on her. She got on with practical things and helped me take charge of the household. The first thing that needed to be done was to fire the cook. The cook had a bad feeling emanating from her; everything she did was peppered with anger and frustration. She also stole from us and I let her. I didn't have the energy to deal with it and all the other servants said nothing as they were terrified of her. My mother was firm but kind and said that though she had done an excellent job looking after me perhaps she'd like to move on to do other things.

The cook came storming through the house to find me. I was feeding my son. 'Is this right, Mem Sahib, you don't want me here any more?'

'It's not that, Barathi, it's just that my mother is here and she is a—'

'She is an interfering woman! We'll see what Sahib has to say about this when he gets back.'

'I'm sorry, Barathi, you will get three months' salary.'

'Money, money,' she raged. 'You think everything is about money? One day you will learn and you will find out. I could have helped you, but now, now, Mem Sahib, you deserve everything you get.'

She took her wages and slammed the door shut.

My mother's second task was to cover the red leather sofa, for it made her stomach turn knowing that there was a sacred cow or two lying there in the front room for us all to sit on. She sat up all night making a cover with cotton fabric and then she set to work in the heart of our home. Unpacking Annapurna, everything became infused with a goodness that only she could bring. The sound of dancing oil popping in the heated cheenchatti whilst chillies were frying was like music to me, and the smell of warm cinnamon and clove made its way to all the rooms in the house. Piles of ginger and turmeric were laid out to dry on the veranda; beside them, a mountain of golden cumin seeds roasted in the hot sun and full grains of rice were placed on white sheets so they could feel the heat. People that didn't know us began visiting, drawn by the activity and the enticing smells coming from the household. My mother stopped work to make time for all of them, offering them tea and savouries made carefully from fried green bananas. They returned, bringing their children and elderly relatives. My baby slept peacefully and I felt in control again.

Amin was singing away that morning as he was collecting firewood. They were words of half a chorus from a Hindi movie he hadn't seen but had picked up from the gardener who hadn't seen it either. Aya's anklets were jangling as she swayed to his tune whilst collecting water from the well, and a constant beat was provided by the washerwoman who hit the wet cloths against the wall. A car horn and then the roar of an engine pulling into the drive suddenly drowned out their sounds. The car knocked the mountain of cumin seeds over. Everyone began scurrying around, making their way to the back of the house, as the footsteps approached the veranda. He called out my name.

'Nalini, Nalini,' it echoed through the house. He had come home, finally. Satchin was three months old. Raul made his way up the stairs into our bedroom. My mother was bathing the baby, I was getting his clothes ready. He stopped and looked over at the two of them and came to kiss me. 'I tried to come sooner, Nalini, but I couldn't, it was impossible.' He paused as he looked again at our son. 'I'm so proud of you and look, our little son,' he said, as he went to pick him up. Satchin shivered and screamed as he was held in strange arms. I wrapped him up in a blanket and handed him back to his father.

'Achan will look after you now, Monu,' he said, glancing at my mother.

Perhaps I was fooling myself, but things between Raul and I did improve. For a while he was completely engrossed with our son, showing him off to all the visitors that came and, once again, he showed me the tender side of him, the one I fell completely in love with. There was also much more of a balance in my life and I was kept occupied with Satchin, my mother, my home and cooking.

Whilst Raul was at work or away, my mother and I ventured further out of the enclave. We dressed in our worst clothes and would get the driver and Amin to take us into town where the street sellers bustled about for business. Wednesday was market day. Beggars, flies, cats, dogs, anything that moved, crowded around the food. All hoped that a lemon, a mango, a banana, anything, would fall from the sellers' baskets. If by chance it did, they would scramble, fighting over it, even before he had an opportunity to pick it up. Some people sat squatting, waiting for the seller to get rid of the shrivelled vegetables that he had not managed to sell. Often, they waited in vain.

My mother and I learnt to barter and choose the best produce by discarding the miserable-looking vegetables, which were placed on top, and by not falling for the many tragic stories that were told to us. For if they were all to be believed, many of the sellers had ten children each, no wives, and disabled parents to look after. Young children would then run after us, begging to help us carry the goods. As we made our way to the car, we passed gamblers sitting playing cards on street corners, gypsies who were dancing and singing, men who sat on crates watching them with beadies hanging from their mouths. The driver brought us back to the safety of our home.

We cooked the whole day on Thursday and packed up the food in cotton bundles or newspapers tied with string and got Amin, Nila and the driver to deliver them to the homeless children sleeping on the beach. At first, the driver protested, saying that it was not his job and that Raul Sahib would not like his vehicle to be used in this way for such transportation, but my mother had a few words with him and he soon changed his mind.

*   *   *

Two years later, my daughter Maya was born. I never thought it was possible to feel such love for my baby. You think that your heart won't expand to love another so, that there is no more room, but it does and it does so effortlessly.

With her pink feet and tiny hands, Maya brought innocence and a strong temperament, knowing her own mind even at an early age. She was never really in my arms, always being picked up by one of the members of the household who were inevitably drawn to her. If Maya was not with my mother, she searched for her father. She understood from being tiny that not seeing someone makes you long for them even more. When her father approached, her face would beam. I am trying to think what it was about Maya that drew him to her and made him play with her. I didn't know how long this would last, probably as long as she didn't make any demands on him. But she gave him complete adoration and asked for nothing in return; Raul needed this.

Whatever he had to give, he gave to Maya. 'Mol, Achan will give you a ride, come, jump on Achan's back.' 'Mol, Achan has a surprise for you. Look, Mol, a puppy.' Satchin longed for his father's affection, to be touched or kissed, but this sense of neediness drove Raul away. My mother and I tried to make up for this but Satchin didn't like to show that he wanted us and so he surrounded himself with people, holding their attention by laughing and joking. At such a young age, he became very independent, and if he wasn't playing in the house with his sister, he would be off riding with the postman on his bicycle or out with Amin on one of his errands.

Raul's business trips became more frequent and much

longer in their duration but I did not miss him. I grew accustomed to it and built a life with my family and my husband's returns would give us all something more to look forward to, exciting stories and exotic gifts for the children from strange countries. My mother was never happy to see him and would fall silent whenever his name was mentioned or avoid him when he was home. When news came that Raul was chosen to run the Indian Oil Export Company in Great Britain, she was very happy. We all thought he would be in London for a year, two years maximum, but a year into his contract, he called to say we were to join him.

My heart sank when I heard this. We had a routine, the children were settled. I did not want to leave our home, my mother, our kitchen. I should have said no, this is what my heart was telling me, shouting at me but I thought about new opportunities for the children and they needed their father. I said we would join him for the remaining year and I made him promise that we would come back. 'To a bigger and better life,' he reassured. When I said that that was not what we needed, he replied by saying that he desperately missed us and all he wanted was to spend more time with us. He asked me to sell the house because it was pointless keeping it open for thieves. In my naivety, I consented.

My mother said nothing. Not one word. I pleaded with her to come with us but she refused. I should have fought harder with her. Why did she let us go like that? Why? She could have said something but instead she helped me sell the house and its contents and then she found each and every one of my servants new work. My mother said it was time that she went back to her home and so, after helping us pack, she left, saying that she would see us all again very soon. I never saw her again, though, and the letters I subsequently sent to her went unanswered.

England was damp, despite it being the middle of summer, and there were hardly any people on the streets. I didn't understand a word the driver Raul had sent to collect us was saying to me and felt frightened. I held my children tightly as we went to meet my husband. Raul looked like a stranger when I saw him again. Arrogance had filled his head and tilted his jaw so that he no longer looked at you but above you. He took us to a large, impressive house complete with wall-to-wall thick carpet and chandeliers. It was a cold house, with no space around it, filed in a row with others like it. But my children were happy; they were with their father and about to begin a new adventure. Children adapt, it is adults who find change hard. I longed to go home and be with my mother and when the children went to school and when my husband was away or at work, this solitude ate into me and made me ache, a nagging pain in my chest that would not go away.

I tried to go out, but hated the constant reminders that I was in a foreign place. Being in the house was difficult as it was without being introduced to further strangeness. The constant drone of traffic also annoyed me, it was so monotonous compared to the chaos of street-life back home: there was not the jumbled-up sound of people trying to make their way across the road, attempting to dodge the rickshaws and the cows, no pungent smells coming from street corners nor the busy noise of bartering, no street sellers vainly shielding their wares from being polluted by the big, heavy buses passing through town, no vibrant dancing colours. There were washing lines – imagine washing hanging in an orderly manner on lines with no dhobi scurrying about finding patches of grass to put the clothes on! Even the rain fell without conviction. It was so organised; from the traffic, the food in the stores to the houses. Gas, electricity, water, all of it flowed in an organised manner whenever you needed it.

People even contained their emotions; they didn't talk to each other but looked warily, neighbours' curtains would twitch but windows and doors were kept firmly shut. No sellers came to the door offering bangles, fresh fish, material or vegetables and gossip; maybe the catalogue man came and left a catalogue at the door or rang the bell and left. One day, the postman had delivered a neighbour's letter to our door by mistake, so I knocked on the door to give it to her. A middle-aged woman came to answer it. She kept her foot firmly against the door and peered through the gap; she did not invite me in or offer tea or savouries but said a polite thank you and closed the door again. England was a lonely, lonely place.

Raul went to work early and came home late. Occasionally he spent time with the children. Sometimes he went out with his friends but seldom was I invited. Even if I was, I did not fit into the social circle and the blunders I made were all too evident.

'Nalini, don't do it like that, use a napkin,' Raul would complain or he would laugh at me in front of everyone at my lack of knowledge. I sat around tables feeling ignorant as people conversed in a foreign language and all I could do was smile, although I couldn't even do this right because inside I didn't feel happy.

Happiness; happiness was a state of mind, happiness was a state of mind; if I said it enough times perhaps it would seep into my consciousness. I had to do something, anything, so I got Raul to have groceries and spices delivered to the house. At least I could cook to keep my sanity.

I cooked huge meals and placed them on the dining-room table. From morning to night, I would concoct dishes, remembering recipes and stories from my mother, cook and forget the place I was in. I would polish the cutlery and decorate the table. Nobody ate what I made. Raul had either eaten at the office or with clients or friends, and the children preferred their new-found meals of burgers and fishfingers. I would secretly garnish these with spices so that they would never forget where they were from. Every day I got instructions from them to make new English foods. 'Ma, can you make us omelette and toast?'

'What is omelette and toast, makkale?'

'Like mutta dosa with no chillies and hot bread,' Satchin replied.

I beat the eggs with coriander leaves, added half a chilli, crushed peppercorns and onions, and toasted the bread on the cheenchatti with ghee. They complained about the 'green bits'; it felt like I was losing the battle. The children were consumed by the adventure and the only thing that consoled me was the thought that it was temporary and that we would be going home soon.

Tom, the young man who delivered spices, came

religiously every week and I filled containers of food for him to take back. It would have been wasted otherwise. This made me look forward to his visits, even though he had fingernails like the tree climber. Every time he came, he taught me a new English word or sentence: 'This, Mrs K, is called a pumpkin and this is a marrow . . .' Containers were exchanged in this way and a year later, I could understand him and give him whole sentences back as well. He would always encourage me and as he left he would say, 'You're a fast learner, Mrs K, it's coming along really well.'

Raul had gone on a trip that autumn to America and normally when he went away, he would call every week. Two weeks went by and there had been no news. He telephoned the following Wednesday and instead of asking how we were, or telling us when he would be back, he gave me strict instructions to give Tom one of his suits to dry-clean. It seemed such an odd request, so I asked him was it because he would be returning within the next day or so. 'Yes,' he said, 'soon'. I waited for him to ask about Satchin and Maya but he didn't, so I ended the conversation by saying that the children were fine and that we all missed him. He made no response other than to say that he was really very busy and had to go.

Later that afternoon when I was cleaning, I remembered the suit. I went into the walk-in closet and began looking for it, the pinstriped blue one. Finding it amongst the hundreds he had, I took the suit out and placed it on the bed. I went to fetch a bag to put it in and as I folded it, I thought I had better check the pockets to make sure there were no tissues or loose change. From the breast pocket of the blue suit, I pulled out a picture. It was of Raul with his arms around a blonde woman and, placed between them, a young child. Confused, I stared at the photograph. On the back were some words that I could not read. I felt numb. Thoughts went around in circles. Who was this woman? Who was the child? Was there some mistake?

I rooted through his closet and found pictures and letters in a shoebox. None of it made sense; who was she? I needed Raul home. I had to speak to him. He would sort it all out and tell me there was some big mistake. It was four o'clock and the children would be home soon. I put the things back in their place and when they arrived, I made them something to eat, sat and played with them and tried to go to sleep.

Days passed waiting for a phone call, a letter, anything; a week went by and my anguish mounted as the children asked for their father. I made up stories that he would be back within the week and then another week went by. No news. And then I got a call from the office but I didn't want to understand and asked them to call back on Thursday lunchtime. Tom came then. They rang and I watched him as his face turned white and he hung up. 'Mrs K, there is no easy way to say this, but he's gone. They can't find him. Embezzled money from the company and left.' I shook my head, not comprehending. 'He's disappeared. They want to know when you will be leaving the house. They have someone coming next week.'

'No, no, no, no.' I shook my head. Tom came to touch me. 'Go,' I screamed. 'Go.'

'Mrs K, can I do something? Can I call someone? What shall I do?'

'No, no, no,' I cried in disbelief. 'Go away.'

'I can't leave you, not like this.'

'Go,' I screamed again.

He left, saying he would call on the way back home. As the door closed behind him, my hands began to tremble, tears streamed down my face and then I screamed and screamed until there was no breath left in me. 'Ma . . . where are you? Help me.' I lay on the ground like some animal, pulling at my hair, choking on the tears. I looked up and saw his pictures on his table. I crawled onto my knees and threw them to the floor, smashing them with my fists and cutting my hand on the pieces. Why? Why did he bring us to this place only to leave us? Why? Didn't he know what it would do? If he were planning to leave, why didn't he prepare us? Did he? Had I missed the signs? Did he mean to leave us money and air tickets to get back home? Maybe he did? I got myself off the floor and searched the house desperately, overturning every piece of furniture. I went into every room. Nothing. He left us nothing.

'Ma, help me, talk to me, what shall I do?' I screamed. 'Tell me.'

There was silence.

My children, what would I tell the children? In two hours they would be home. I made my way to the kitchen and began to cook frantically.

The blood from my hand covered the marrow as I picked it up and began to chop. Blood and tears dripped into the pan and made the oil splatter. Blood seeped into the wooden spoon as I held the spoon tighter and tighter. I began to stir. Who was this man who called himself a husband and a father? What kind of a person could be that cruel? Why? Security, stability, certainty, kindness; he pretended to have all those things, to give all those things but he took them away so ruthlessly. I didn't know where he was, even who he was, or if he was ever coming back. As the spoon went round and round in circles, I made myself a promise. I swore that this would be the last time he would ever disrupt our lives. No matter what reasons he had, he could never come back, and I would do whatever it took to keep him away from my children. Nobody could come back from this with the pitiful excuse of being a father, he didn't deserve them. And so that was the day he died.

Having everything taken away, brick by brick, puts you in a position where you don't care what else leaves you, there is nothing more to lose. My only concern was for my children, to protect, provide for them and to make sure they evolved into good people. I went to collect them and to tell them that their father had lost his life by jumping in the middle of the road to save a little boy who was about to be killed by a bus.

Maya did not cry or scream. She looked at me. Tears rolled down Satchin's face as his sister watched. 'He's not coming back,' I whispered, unable to get the words out, but there was incomprehension. 'Do you understand, Mol?' I said as I held her. She nodded, Satchin began to cry. My heart felt heavy at the enormity of what I was doing to them but it was the right thing to do, I knew it was. I kissed them both, promising them that it would be all right, that I would always be there for them, no matter what. When we got home, we said a prayer together and lit a candle so that they were able to say goodbye to him.

My children slept close to me as I lay there thinking what would happen to us. Was it better to scrape together the fare to go back to India? Where could we go? How would we manage there? Two children and a woman on her own, it wasn't possible. I didn't know where my mother was, maybe she was still at the village, but I couldn't take them back there, that would be the first place he would look for us, if he ever decided to return. The doorbell interrupted my thoughts. It was Tom. He tried to smile, but all he could say was that he was so sorry and offered to help us in any way he could. He sat down with me and I asked him to read out the letters that were in the shoebox. I needed to know. Tom shook his head. 'Do you really want to do this to yourself, Mrs K?'

'Yes, I need to know all of it,' I replied.

Every one of them was from a lady called Marisa, who asked when he would return and if the minor problems he was having that required him to stay in England had been solved. They were all signed, 'Come back soon because we love you and miss you.'

'I'm sorry, Mrs K, I'll try and help you in any way I can, you just say,' Tom said again as he folded the letters away.

'Do you have a match?' I asked, as I took back the box.

He looked at me and then rooted through his pockets and found a matchbox. I lit a match and set fire to the letters, watching them burn into ashes. 'He's dead now, buried. We need somewhere to live.'

I asked him if he could find people to buy our furniture and anything else of value and help us find somewhere to go. He said he would take it all to a second-hand dealer he knew on the Bow Road and ask his sister if we could stay with her.

By the following Friday, the house was almost empty. All that was left in the dining room were the suitcases we came with, cardboard boxes packed with necessities and a few of the children's toys. Tom came at five o' clock as promised and loaded up the van with our possessions. The children sat between us in the front of the van and Tom was talking to them about his sister, her cats, whilst I sat thinking, worrying. Suddenly, Maya shouted, 'Jemina, where's my Jemina?' Jemina was the doll she carried with her, the doll he'd bought her. 'She's probably in the back, Mol, with the boxes,' I said.

'No, no, I need to see her, I need to see her now,' Maya insisted.

'It's no problem, Nalini, I can stop here so we can check Jemina is all right,' said Tom, pulling over. Maya went with him to check the boxes in the back of the van and then she began crying. 'She's not here, she's gone. Jemina's gone. Gone. She won't come back, will she?'

'Maya, don't cry, sweetheart, I'll go back to the house when the new owners come, when it's daytime, and check for you. She might be there,' Tom reassured her.

'No,' she wailed even louder, 'I know she's not coming back, she's gone.'

I got out of the van to get her. My little girl was lying

on the roadside, Tom unable to console her. I picked her up. 'Amma is here, Mol.'

'No,' she sobbed, burying her head in my hair, her face soaked with tears. 'Achan, I want my Achan.'

We had to move to a place in the East End of London, an area heavily populated by immigrants. It looked poor: filthy children were playing on the streets, fighting over whatever little toys they had. As we drove into the place, people looked weary, shabbily-dressed, carrying black bin liners or plastic bags or pushing them in rusty prams. There were many ethnic faces but, believe me, when I say that there was no sanctuary or familiarity in this. It was a feeling of complete mistrust. That was the climate, a heavy insecure feeling, with looting, rioting and petrol bombs through letterboxes all going on in the background. We parked in front of a Victorian terraced house. Tom's sister Maggie came out to meet us and welcomed us to our new home.

Maggie became one of my closest friends but when I first saw her, I just wanted to take my children and run but there was nowhere else to go. Tom had told her about our predicament and I wary of her kindness, thinking that it was a way of slowly luring me into her profession. So even in those first days, when she spoke and I understood most words, I looked at her blankly because ignorance was the only thing that felt safe. I looked at the shabby home she was offering us and I despaired. Smelly carpets, damp, peeling ceilings with a constant drip, drip, drip from the leaking roof. What kind of place was it to bring up children?

Having abundance brings many choices and when I

am faced with decisions today, I relish them, revelling and indulging in possibilities and consequences. Back then, there was none of this. Even contemplating momentarily how the children were feeling was an extravagance. It was a fight for survival and this eliminates the luxury of emotion: if you stop and contemplate you lose the battle and so I was grateful for the fact that there was no time. We arrived on Friday evening, I spent two sleepless nights learning how to sew and on Monday, I was taken to the factory.

The factory was situated on a run-down industrial estate a twenty-minute bus ride away. These twenty minutes were filled preparing myself mentally for the day ahead and then observing the actions of the workers who clambered on at the various stops. Some of them were Irish or Polish, most were Pakistani women dressed in salvar kamise and shawls. A scattering were Indian women in saris, socks and sandals who glared at me in my western clothes. All managed to find their respective countrywomen and huddled together chatting. The Irish made the most noise and livened up the dead journey with their laughter.

Maggie had taken me to see the boss, Mr Humphries, a fat, bald man who seemed happy to see her. He was about forty-five, chewed on a pencil which he kept behind his ear, and cleared his throat every five minutes. Maggie and this Humphries man had a conversation. I don't know exactly what they said but he showed me to a table with a machine.

Maggie took a piece of red material from the basket and placed it on the sewing machine. Manoeuvring it carefully, she produced the template of a skirt that I was

to copy. After I had done a few, she smiled. The Humphries man came to inspect. He nodded and Maggie left.

It was 1978 and I was alone in a strange country at
the age of twenty-six. This first place of employment,
Humphries & Co, Bow, was a badly-lit factory, where
I sat making shabby dreams for two small children. I
would catch the bus, punch my card in at eight o'clock
in the morning and sit at my machine, just sewing. The
monotony of the noise would take me far away, with
my children and mother, back to India, to a beautiful
home with a veranda surrounded by mango trees. Then
the supervisor, a rake-shaped woman called Veronica,
would stab me in the shoulder with her pen. Spitting some
words at me that I did not understand, her face said it all
and so I would speed up. The noise would bore through
the memories, but I would stitch them together with a
fabric of sunshine and laughter. At ten o'clock the noise
would stop for five minutes as the women drank from
their flasks, and then it continued, the women fuelled
by the tea or coffee inside them until lunchtime. There
was half an hour for lunch and the women congregated
in their respective groups, squeezing every second out
of the minute with gossip and cackling. The machines
then continued their cacophony until six in the evening.
I would be the first person on the bus and the first
person off it, running home in the dark to see my children,
but by the time I arrived, they would be almost asleep and
then whilst they slept, I cooked. Cooked whatever they
needed for the next day, cooked just to forget. Forget that
somewhere I was losing them, that Satchin was becoming
very responsible. At eight, he had responsibilities beyond

his years, and Maya; Maya was very distant, almost in a world of her own. I had to continue. There was no choice. At night, their warm bodies would cling to me as I stroked their hair and touched their sleeping faces, tears rolling down my cheeks, whispering over and over again, 'I know I am not enough for you, not at all enough.'

When I was at the factory I could not allow myself to think of my children's safety. I prayed that God would be taking care of them until I got home and that they would not fall sick. My frame of reference for everything was Friday. The brown envelope arrived every Friday at the end of our shift. I managed to save a little amount from it every week and would work any available over-time on Saturday. The money from Saturday would be used to buy Co-op stamps so no matter what else, we could always eat well.

I didn't affiliate myself to any of the groups at the factory, pretending not to understand the broken English, avoiding the politics this way. Every group had its leader and issues. Instead of uniting against the same cause, they all fought non-stop. The other Indian ladies pretended to be proud and snubbed me or made comments when I passed, perhaps this was because I was from the South or because I was new or wore western clothes. I feigned ignorance at every opportunity, doing my piecework, stepping out for air at lunchtime, slowly accumulating the groceries for the week from the local Co-op and picking up some small toys or whatever I could for Satchin and Maya.

Sundays offered the only opportunity to spend time with my children. They were growing so fast and it was only on these days that I stopped to notice. At times, I didn't want to see because guilt crept into my soul. Guilt that I had nothing to offer them and the only way I could compensate was to cook. Sometimes you see things and there is absolutely nothing you can do so you pretend you don't see them because it hurts a lot less.

We had no money to go anywhere, no money for luxuries, I couldn't even take them to window shop because I thought it was cruel to show them goods that we could not possibly afford. Sunday morning was a visit to the launderette and the children helped me carry the wet bags of washing home which we hung around whatever space we could find. We then sat with the dampness of the clothes. If the weather was nice, we went to the park, but if it was cold we just sat huddled together in bed and I would try to tell them stories. I was desperate to recount stories of their grandmother; I even wrote letters from her pretending that she had sent them, but when I tried to think of other ways to remind them of home, my imagination usually failed me and Maya would continue the stories. Then I would cook, and she would ask if she could go up and invite Maggie.

At first I didn't like this; what kind of an influence was a woman like Maggie on my children? And I barely had enough time with them as it was. But I saw how much Maya loved her and how Maggie was around them and so I eventually gave in. Maggie ate with us on Sundays and occasionally Tom would join us. Some-times, she insisted that she cook a roast for us all, saying that Satchin and Maya really liked it. Before I had a chance to say no, they would be leaping up and down with excitement. So I would go upstairs on a pretext and just before she put the chicken or the meat that she was cooking into the oven, I stabbed cloves and cinnamon through it so that they would not forget the taste of home.

When I did the cooking it was normally on my hot-plate and I went upstairs to Maggie's to serve because it was much bigger and she also had a dining-table. A year had passed and I trusted her a little more, seeing how she took care of Satchin and Maya in my absence, so everything I cooked was from a deep sense of grati-tude. Tom, as always, devoured the food. Maggie found it a little too hot, which was understandable as the spices conflicted with her temperament, leaving her feeling vanquished. I hoped that one day the spices would do their job by diffusing the anger that was raging inside and that she could give up her profession.

Tom continued to deliver groceries to the wealthy and his clients now extended out of London, so he was away during the week, driving and delivering. One particular week, a client had asked for a certain bottle of pickle, not too spicy like the Asian stores in the area made them, but something that had a combination of zest and sweetness. Tom was telling us that he had looked but was unable to find a supplier. 'Maybe Nalini could make some up,' Maggie eagerly volunteered. 'Go down to the market, get what you need, I'll take care of the kids.'

There was a ripple of excitement as I chose the fruit and spices from the market stalls: soft Alfonso mangoes imported from India; deep red chillies; root of ginger; mustard seeds and coarse cinnamon sticks. I got back to the house and washed and peeled the fruit, cooking

94

them, experimenting with the proportions of lemons, mangoes and spices, until I came up with the combination that I felt was right. I gave the pickles to Tom and forgot all about it.

A few weeks later, Tom came back saying that the family had absolutely loved the pickles and asked if they could order a dozen bottles. I spent that Sunday making and bottling them in decorated jam jars, giving them exotic names. Tom offered the surplus to his other customers and more orders came in. It got so busy that I stopped working Saturday overtime at the factory and concentrated on making and bottling hand-made pickles. Satchin and Maya helped. The mixture needed to be stirred continuously so Satchin stood on a chair and did that. Maya wanted to spoon the contents into the jars but made a huge mess, so I said putting the fabric on lids and placing an elastic band to secure them was much more interesting, adding that I really wished I could do that job. So she swiftly moved departments. In just two days, we made a week's wages. Soon, the bedsit was full of brightly-coloured mangoes and lemons, spices and bottles. We had a whole system going and Maggie would squeeze into the room and help with the labelling and packaging.

Tom began visiting restaurants and shops, offering samples and, within weeks, we had more orders than we could have possibly envisaged. I knew I could not fulfil them, not unless I left work. I thought about it, but the idea scared me. It scared me because although I hated working at the factory, it gave me a sense of stability and I knew exactly where I stood; there was no room for hopes and dreams, no room for expectations or disappointment. Tom kept doing figures to convince me that I could make much more money from home, making pickles, and Maggie added that, more importantly, I could be there for my children when they came home from school. I thought about it all as I went into work.

The women piled onto the bus as usual. Some of them were in their forties and fifties, looking defeated, old and dishevelled. That could be me in twenty years' time so used to my life that I dare not dream, expect anything from it but mere survival. The biggest highlight of my life would be theirs: talking enthusiastically about buying a watermelon in summertime; or saving up for the luxury of a shower head to attach to the bath. I would have done nothing except that which was familiar – stitch skirts and take abuse from people who believed that they were better than me. It would show on me like it did on those women; rugged lines of sadness so deeply etched on their faces that they forgot how to smile. At least I had been given an opportunity, a way out; it was up to me to take a leap of faith.

I went into see Mr Humphries, who shouted at me for coming into his office without knocking. I told him I was leaving. 'You're doing what? Don't come running to me when you're desperate. You'll not have a job here,' he added, furious.

I said nothing. This irritated him further so he said he would have to dock my wages for giving him no notice and leaving him short of a worker. 'Fine,' I replied confidently, rolling up my tatty blue overall and handing it to him. I took my last brown envelope and left.

I remember feeling so elated and free, like I could do anything, be anyone if I chose to be.

'It's Amma, Satchin, it's Amma, she's at the gate waiting for us.' I think the whole playground heard Maya. The other mothers stared at me.

'What is it? What's wrong?' Satchin asked.

'Nothing, Monu, this is how it is going to be from now on. Today is a really special day and we are going to celebrate.

'It's not that Onam thing again?' Maya asked.

'No, Mol, it's not Onam. What would you two like to do?'

'Wimpy!' they both shouted.

I shook my head, processed food with processed thoughts, and then I laughed. 'Come on, then. Let's go.'

The three of us sat and dreamt in Wimpy. Hamburgers hanging out of their mouths, Maya made a list on her napkin of all the things she wanted and quickly ran out of space because her writing was too big. Satchin and I talked of a big house with a garden and room to bring friends home. Then I told them about my plans for the business, how it would be awkward for a while, living with fruit and spices everywhere but it would only be for a short time. We walked back home, holding each other's hands, and we stopped off at a photo booth to capture the moment so it would last forever.

It was four o'clock in the morning; I couldn't sleep. Tom would be picking me up in less than an hour to take me to his wholesaler. I lay thinking about life's many ironies: I had once placed all my trust in a man who was completely untrustworthy and I had promised myself not to trust that way again. I was then put in a situation where I had no option but to trust, and the very two people sent to me were the ones that appeared completely untrustworthy: Maggie and Tom. What would I have done without them?

My mother would say that the right people are sent to us just when we need them and they come in many guises. The beggar asking for food may well be a pauper, but it is only our judgement of him that makes him a pauper. 'When we hold our judgements and see beyond, magic happens,' she would say. 'When we believe in someone even if they don't believe in themselves, magic happens.' Where was she now? What would she be doing? What would she say to all of this? I know she would say trust, because according to her, trust prepares the ground for forgiveness. Only when you put your faith and trust back into life, are you able to forgive, and with forgiveness all insurmountable obstacles just dissolve. Strengthened, I got up to get ready.

Tom arrived to take me to Spitalfields Market.

'He's a nice enough man but bargain hard with him, Nalini,' advised Tom, as he was driving.

'Tom, maybe I shouldn't ask, but I need to know – why?'

'Because he can be a bit steep with some of his prices and . . .'

'No, Tom, I meant, I mean, why? Why do you go out of your way so much to help me and the children?'

He glanced over at me and looked hurt by my question.

'Because I don't want you or the kids to suffer like we did. Is that good enough for you?' he replied defensively.

'What happened?' I asked gently.

'What didn't might be a better question.' There was a pause. 'I don't really want to talk about it, Nalini. Some things are best left where they are.'

'Tom,' I said after a short while, 'we do appreciate everything that you and Maggie do for us, I mean, I don't ever want you to think that . . .'

'I know,' he interrupted. 'Anyway, like I was saying, you've got to be very decisive with Mr Prakash. Tell him exactly what you want and the price you're willing to pay. He'll try and say no to everything but you just stay firm.'

It was dark and the wholesaler's was bustling, even at that time in the morning. Traders were shouting out the prices of their products and where they originated. The floor was filthy with rain and tomatoes and other fruit which had been squashed by footsteps. There were no animals congregating around the food, hoping to take advantage of the situation. Mr Prakash was exactly as Tom described him. 'All our fruits and spices are of the very best quality, Ma'am, you won't find any-where better, all freshly imported from India. Smell,' he gestured, inhaling the aroma of a crate of mangoes. 'And the price must indeed reflect the quality.'

'I need a twenty percent discount,' I insisted.

'Twenty percent,' he shouted, 'You'll put me out of business, take the shirt from my back now.'

'Fine,' I said, turning away.

'Ten percent,' he said, muttering.

'Fifteen, and I'll give you good custom.'

'You are indeed a hard woman, but may God bless you,' he replied.

I chose crateloads of the finest fruit and filled jars

with fresh spices, whilst he yelled at one of his assistants to help us load the van.

Maggie managed to source the pickle bottles cheaply from a man she knew who worked at a packaging factory. I went to the sari shop on Green Street to buy yards and yards of fabric for covering the lids and Tom picked up three hotplates from the second-hand shop on the High Street. There was absolutely no space to move in the bedsit and I tried to work when the children were at school or late at night when they were asleep. New worries now replaced old ones: I worried if I could make a go of it, if I was good enough to make a better life for the children, and then I worried about practical things like the intensity of heat in that room, whether they would fall sick from the draft that came from an open window, the constant smell that must have made them nauseous. I worried if I would be able to fulfil orders and if the standard of the pickles were good enough, would the supplier have enough fruit for the following week? And so the worrying went on, but when I cooked, everything paled into insignificance.

Orders increased and it got to a point where we had no room, there was no option but to move out. I decided to rent a one-bedroomed flat across the road so I would not be too far from Tom and Maggie. It was our first real home and it felt like a rajah's palace. There was a separate sitting room and a big kitchen with a black-and white-tiled floor and a small garden. Tom, Maggie, the children and I splashed around that weekend with fresh white paint and we bought some second-hand furniture which we re-painted and re-upholstered. Most of it was done in a rich green and pink sari material which Maya bought with Maggie and the curtains were also made in the same fabric. Maggie managed to get hold of an enormous second-hand fridge and an industrial cooker, from where I don't know and I didn't want to ask. The man at the second-hand shop also saved me a big wooden table where I could chop and lay out all the ingredients which fitted perfectly in the kitchen.

That move was another step for me, another leap of faith, and if I am going by the astrologer's theory, who posited that even the slightest action is responded to by something far greater, then I would say we were rewarded heavily. The children were happy in their new home, we had money, so I could afford to buy them proper shoes to replace their flimsy plimsolls, I didn't have to go traipsing around jumble sales for their clothes and now if they needed money for a school outing, I had it. The three of us could sit huddled together watching television on a Friday night, eating chocolate, or go to the cinema at the weekends if we chose to. I even enrolled at the local college to study English and book-keeping. Customers kept re-ordering and, for the first time, I could afford to pay Tom who delivered the produce and Maggie who continued to help with the bottling and packaging.

My mother used to say that it was forgiveness that worked magic on the soul and made miracles possible. According to her, forgiveness from a broken heart combusted energy that made insurmountable obstacles just dissolve. So if she found Luxmiammayi gossiping about her, she forgave; if a servant boy stole whatever little she had, she let him take it; if I hurt her, and I know I did, she just forgave me. Not the forgiveness that belongs to a coward – he who sees but refuses to believe and so pretends that nothing has happened – but the kind of forgiveness which belongs to a courageous heart, the heart that accepts and says no matter what anyone does, or whatever circumstances are thrust upon it, it will always, always be all right. It does not become embroiled and constrained in anger and bitterness, but moves forward and grows.

If in the village there was a rift that seemed impossible to heal, she would muster forgiveness with bright turmeric, mustard seeds, ginger, garlic, the bitterness of lemon and anger of hot chilli. The latter two ingredients were supposed to counter the bad feelings and diffuse them. She then sealed it all with warm water and made a paste, which she added to whatever dish she felt appropriate, and then offered it to both sides. The results were not instantaneous and many could claim that it was time that solved the problems but somewhere, she was sure, her simple process of forgiveness was working away.

My mother taught me that forgiveness was part of life's learning process. I don't know if my mother simply forgave my father, if she truly accepted, if she let it go and sealed her wounds with the scent of fried ginger and turmeric, but for me it was impossible. Impossible, because how can you forgive a person who takes up most of your heart, who is your everything, your world, who tells you you are the most important thing and then leaves? Suddenly, the food that you help prepare for them is not good enough, the kisses that you give them are not good enough, you are not enough. Despite the fact that my parents were always fighting, my father was always kind to me and I loved him. I thought he loved me too. I would rather not have known the truth about my father. I would rather that my mother had pretended that he loved us and was taken away by some tragic fate. My mother said that to lie is the coward's way and that truth is whole, like black or white. But what if there are a hundred shades for truth?

I think I only really began to forgive my father when I started to let go of Raul. Day by day, I let the feelings of inadequacy and unworthiness burn with peppercorns and chilli. The peppercorns and the chillies would sizzle in the boiling hot oil and expand until they could grow no further and then they exploded, releasing a suffocating smell that choked. Freshly squeezed lemon juice and the ginger would calm and soothe the aroma, evaporating the stench, bringing it back to a neutral place. To this mixture was added a sweet ripe mango, bursting with fertility and promise, limes and honey which held so many dreams, and lightly fried onions that grounded and made things feel safe and possible. All were bottled until the man became a shadow of a memory. It did not concern me who he was, where he was, and the thought of him coming back never crossed my mind. The labels were put on the pickles and the process was complete.

As we sat across the kitchen table, Maggie laughed when I told her what the secret ingredients were that made the pickles so successful. If only life were as simple she would say. She became chief taster, and I got her to put the lids on the jars so she could inhale the contents. Slowly, she began to open up and diffuse her memories with the aroma that emanated from those pickle bottles.

*   *   *

The smells took Maggie back to her childhood in a little town in the south of Ireland called Dara. Everything was green, deep green, but the piercing grey light (that she never got used to despite having been born there) made everything appear duller than it was. She was brought up on a farm where her father worked as a hand. Her mother was busy year after year giving birth and Maggie was kept occupied patching up the hand-me-downs that went from sibling to sibling and doing chores. She was helped by her sister Noreen who was a year younger than she was. Maggie probably had a lot more relations than she knew about as her father, who had a taste for the Guinness, did not quite remember what he had done at night. On his sober mornings, he ploughed the fields and made sure the family kept their home.

Maggie was sent to school sporadically so she could just make out the signs in the village and the notes that were passed to her by the farmer, all written with promises of love, prosperity and a better life. The farmer planted empty dreams in Maggie's head and filled them with illusions so the dull light finally became bearable. She fell pregnant at fifteen. The family covered Maggie's sin with nine months of silence, keeping her indoors, doing whatever tasks needed to be done around the house away from prying neighbours. Maggie's mother took her child, named him Tom, and added him to her collection. The farmer said nothing, gave Maggie's father some extra money and allowed them to stay on the land almost rent-free.

She loved Tom from the day she saw him, all wrinkled and scrunched in a ball with bright orange hair. Hair that didn't listen and always went in the opposite direction to which it was combed. He had inherited that disobedient streak from his mother. When Maggie was asked to help with all the other children she did it without question but she always did the most for Tom. Loving him, singing to him, feeding him. She began working at the local shop, and the money she made went straight to her mother but she did not tell her of the rise she eventually received and with the extra pennies she began saving for things for her son. She got as far as buying him a little toy truck and then she realised he could not play with it because her mother would wonder where it came from. She hid it under her bed.

Shortly after Maggie turned eighteen, her mother died. Maggie's father stayed out all night, she continued working at the local shop and at home but she wanted more, more for herself and for Tom. Maggie felt Noreen was old enough to look after the other children and ideas of going to England began germinating in her head. After a violent argument with her drunken father one night, she decided it was time to leave. Maggie stole money from the shop, took Tom, and fled to England with an idea that she would find her eldest brother, Michael.

The last address they had for Michael was in Bow, East London but when she got there he had gone and had left no forwarding address. She was forced to find work almost immediately. The money she stole only managed to cover the fare to England and a week's accommodation. She rented the bedsit where her brother had stayed, hoping he would come back, and then she took work at the local factory. There was no one to look after Tom, only three years old, so she kept him locked in one room, put food and water out and put up makeshift barricades so that he would not harm himself. Agonising over him, she prayed he would be kept safe.

The money wasn't enough but more than that, she had nothing to offer her son. She went to work on the streets, working at nights, so she could take care of him in the day. At least at night, she thought, he would be safe asleep. Life continued and Tom went to school and then she made enough money for them to move out and live somewhere better. A few years later, one of her regulars died, leaving Maggie a house with the condition that she look after his cats and provide somewhere to stay for his uncle. So she found herself in the boarding house off Green Street. She could have stopped working then, when Tom was eleven, but she continued, thinking she could give him an even better life.

Maggie never told Tom that she was his mother. She did everything for him, worked for him, and then it got to a point where she didn't know why she was working, she didn't know what else she was good for, it had just all managed to creep up on her. When Tom asked about his mother and father, the brothers and sisters that he barely remembered, she said that their mother had died, their father couldn't cope and all the other children had gone to live with aunts and uncles but for her, little Tom, well, he was too special, so she took him and came to London.

When he was old enough, Tom learnt what his sister did but he could handle it precisely because she was his sister and he remembered his mother as the warm Irish woman who died suddenly. His father turned into a loving one who eventually died grief-stricken, of a heart attack. Tom loved Maggie, anyone could see this, and she helped him in any way she could. He had always wanted to start his own business and when he left college, Maggie bought him a van and from there, he made his way. Occasionally, he stayed with her in the boarding house and other times he slept in his van, depending on the journeys he had to make. Then we arrived and threw their lives upside down.

Our innermost conflicts were exchanged across that kitchen table whilst I was chopping ingredients or she was filling bottles. We tiptoed around the very delicate parts of our lives, like Gurkhas avoiding landmines. It's not that we pretended that these parts of our lives never existed but we never probed, and waited for the other to freely surrender the information.

'You see, darling, Tom went through an awful lot, more than I'll ever know. One of the kids at school told him about me working and that. I just kept denying it, but I did it for him. Many times I wanted to sit down and explain it all to him, the whole thing, but I thought he wouldn't be able to handle it. To be ashamed of your sister is one thing, your mother is quite another.'

'Not for one moment did I think of telling my children the truth about their father. He is a man who only knows how to cause pain. I remember how I felt when I was told my father left us. Always hankering after him or any affection shown to me. I was riddled with self-doubt. Was it because I wasn't good enough that he left? I don't want that for them. I want them to feel loved, not feel like they have to work hard to earn it, to prove themselves.'

'They're lovely kids, darling, a credit to you, and their innocence, well, we've got to keep it pure for as long as we can. I wish I'd done better for my Tom. He doesn't believe in himself, he works hard, all hours, and nothing happens and you know why that is, don't you? He doesn't believe he deserves good things. All your dreams come to nothing if you don't really believe they're possible. What do I say to him? Sweetheart, you deserve the best. Well, look where the money has come from to give him the best. That's how he feels, he doesn't have to say it to me but I know that's what he's thinking.

'I hope he meets somebody who understands him. He's a good lad, my Tom, with a decent heart. I know he'd make a great father.'

Sometimes, however, we said nothing to each other and just let the radio that was playing in the background take us to wherever we wanted it to.

The mango and lime pickles were doing very well and I decided it was time to introduce a new range: apple, cinnamon and chilli. Ripe, sober English cooking apples blended with a mixture of temperamental chillies, a hint of toasted fenugreek and asafoetida for vision, all grounded with lightly fried onions and mustard seeds. In those bottles were a perfect combination of stable West and fiery East. It was an acceptance on my part, an assimilation of cultures, fused together with the coarse sweetness of cinnamon.

I needed to find a name for our brand and after much discussion we decided on 'The Abundance of Spice'.

What began as a homespun industry became a profitable business with a turnover that was increasing day by day. I think we appeared a lot bigger to some of our clients. If only they knew how we scraped together our equipment: a rickety mixer from a closing down restaurant; pots and pans from the rag-and-bone man who specifically collected them for us, and a set of cooks' knives bought from a car-boot sale.

One of our main household clients was a man called Ravi Thakker, who ordered forty bottles a month. I don't know what he did with them but we all had a good laugh imagining him eating pickle for breakfast, lunch and dinner. Maggie said that he was probably so full of forgiveness that he surrendered himself to life and was probably some light worker, humming and chanting on top of a mountain. Tom said he was nice enough, a businessman who lived on his own and ordered so many bottles because he missed home.

On one of his visits, Ravi asked Tom if someone from The Abundance of Spice could come and cook at his home for an evening. He was entertaining some clients and wanted to give a dinner party. He was offering twenty pounds, a fortune to us. 'Tell him we'll do it, no problem,' Maggie and I said. Tom drove me to North London to discuss requirements, menu and guests. I also took a sample of my cooking, packed in a tiffin carrier, to see if it was the kind of food he wanted.

A kind-looking man in his mid-thirties opened the door and smiled, introducing himself as Ravi Thakker. I shook his hand. He was pleasant and put me at ease, offering Tom and I some tea. We sat discussing the preparations. He showed me into a very large, tidy kitchen, which smelt new or had retained its newness because it had never been used. Mr Thakker imported and exported rubber and said he had important clients coming to see him from Malaysia and because he would be entertaining them for the week, he wanted them to have one home-cooked meal. There were six guests coming in two weeks' time. If the food that I had brought for him was of a good standard, he would give me a call to let me know which day would be best for him. That very evening he called, saying that my food was 'unbelievable' and so we came to an agreement.

Maggie helped me with the shopping and Tom drove me there on Thursday morning. We let ourselves in with a set of keys Mr Thakker had left. Tom helped unpack the shopping. 'You'll be okay, Nalini?' he kept asking.

'I'll be fine,' I replied.

'If he makes you feel uncomfortable, you call me and I'll come right back,' he said, as he went out of the door. He stopped, was about to say something else when I interrupted him: 'I'll manage, Tom, and I will call if I need you.'

I opened Mr Thakker's fridge and found a few empty milk cartons, leftover takeaways and a stock of my pickles alongside some naan bread. I laughed. It made me feel proud that my pickles had prime position in the fridge. Then I unpacked my utensils, washed them again, took out the fresh produce and began to chop, grind, blend, boil and fry. The kitchen became vibrant with cooking. I didn't want to use the extractor fan because I wanted his whole house to be woken with the smell of freshly ground spices.

To start, I prepared dosa; lentil and rice pancakes with a deep potato masala filling, and dhai vada; fluffy dough balls coated with mustard seeds dipped in seasoned yoghurt. Then, chicken biriyani to keep the guests occupied as Mr Thakker talked, finishing with a selection of coconut barfi and payasam so that they could come to a positive agreement. I found the serving dishes that he had and delicately placed the food upon them, garnishing each dish with fresh coriander, and then I changed into a sari so that I could serve the food. The bathroom upstairs was big enough for a family of four to live in and had gadgets that I had never seen. It was all very clean and the towels were freshly laundered, he must have had a maid or a cleaner that came in and kept order.

I set the table. Mr Thakker arrived with his guests at exactly the agreed time. He introduced me politely as Nalini, the cook, and as I heated the dishes, he settled them with drinks. I served the food and went into the kitchen. All the sounds that come with eating and appreciating good food came through the walls. Half-way through the meal, as I was in the kitchen cleaning up, Mr Thakker came in to thank me and said I had done an exceptional job. After coffee was served, I put on my coat, took the envelope that he had left on the breakfast table and caught the Tube home. I opened it and inside was a note with a simple 'Thank you' and twenty-five pounds. The train ride home was spent thinking of how the children could spend the money. I got home and they were asleep. I slipped out with ten pounds in an envelope and pushed it through Maggie's door.

111

The next morning Satchin and Maya spent the fifteen pounds five times over with a list of requests. They then went off to school and Maggie came around to help bottle pickles. The phone rang and it was Mr Thakker asking why I had left without saying goodbye and thanking me once again. He asked if I could come the following month and do the same. I put the phone down and Maggie smiled. Tom came in later that morning to collect boxes for delivery and Maggie told him but he did not seem too happy. 'I thought it was just a one-off, Nalini,' he said as he left.

On Sunday, we took the children to Brighton. They couldn't decide exactly what they wanted to do with the money so I decided to open a Post Office account for each of them. Satchin liked this idea, he was practical with everything he did and meticulously planned every detail. The money would be in his account five years later and he would draw on the interest. Maya wanted to withdraw it the very next day and buy silk fabrics and tailoring scissors. That was Maya, impetuous dreamer, even at ten. I could guarantee that she would buy the scissors and fabric, make a creation that she would display for a day. To a certain degree, I gave them the freedom to make their own choices whenever they could.

The business was doing well enough for me to hire someone else, Mrs Khan. She was the mother of one of Maya's friends who I had met at the school gates one afternoon. Though her face was covered by a scarf, I could tell she had been crying, so I went up to her and tried talking to her. She spoke very little English but managed to tell me that she had lost her job at the sweet factory and her husband would be annoyed, there was little money as it was. I told her she could start with us the next day.

Farida was quiet, she said very little and worked hard. At first, Maggie was unsettled by the silence but eventually got used to it, understanding that it was just her way. The pickles did not work on her. Maggie and I tried so desperately to get her to inhale the aroma or taste but she didn't trust us and was frightened, too frightened, so that she had completely closed down. Even the slightest noise would make her cower. Maggie tried explaining but she didn't seem to want to understand and then she gave up, saying what was the point of giving someone hope when you knew they were never going to use it. It worked out well in other ways because after school, the two girls would come home and play together, whereas normally Fatima would be at home on her own. After she finished, Farida would take Fatima home.

I was saving for a deposit to put on our own house. I imagined it with every conceivable detail from the size of the bedrooms to the colour of the walls and curtains. The children and I would talk about it before we went to sleep. Maya wanted her room done up with pink polka dots and Satchin wanted racing car wallpaper. It wouldn't take long, I promised them, maybe another year. I could possibly do it in six months but I didn't want to save so they had to go without things.

Mr Thakker continued to employ me. It was over an hour's drive so he always made sure he sent a cab to collect me and take me back home. Making food for him and his guests was a bonus for me. I loved how he understood the detail that went into the preparation of food and how much he appreciated it. Every month, I would go and learn a little more about him, just through the instructions that he left me on the kitchen table. His notes were neatly written; considered words, that were not hastily thrown on paper or which ended abruptly, with a scrawled signature. If he made a mistake, he would simply put a line through it and not seek to mask it or erase it. The notes became more informal as time went on. He ended them with 'Ravi' and not 'Mr Thakker'.

Six months later, Ravi asked me to prepare dinner for two people. I went a little later than normal as there wasn't so much work. He arrived home around six o' clock but there was no one with him. To my astonishment, he held out a bunch of yellow roses. 'For you, Nalini,' he said. 'To thank you for everything,' and then he invited me to sit down and have dinner with him. I wanted to run out of the house and leave, yet a huge part of me also wanted me to stay. I was flattered. We sat down and he served.

He told me how his family had come to England after being thrown out of Uganda. A few years later, his parents left to join his brother in America. Ravi stayed to make a go of his new business which was what he had been doing for the last seven years. It employed ninety people worldwide. I thought he would continue talking about himself but quite suddenly he asked me about myself. His first question was how long I had been with the company and if they were good employers. 'Very good . . . the best,' I replied. He said it was impor-

114

tant to work for good people and I told him that it was my own business and so the boss had to be good or she would be fired. He looked surprised and I explained that it wasn't quite the multi-national he thought it was, more of a cottage industry. Then, as he was eating a brinjal, I said I had set it up because of my children. The brinjal almost fell out of his mouth.

'You're married!' I could have said yes and finished the sentence with, 'my husband left us,' but I didn't. It took just a second to say, 'my husband died'. He said he was sorry and we talked about the children and the business. It was getting late, he called me a cab and paid the driver to take me home. As I said goodbye, he kissed me on the cheek. I felt like I was sixteen again. The journey back went quickly as I replayed the conversations we had, and tried to contain the emotions I felt.

Maggie asked me the next morning how it went and I said nothing about my feelings, maybe because I didn't want to acknowledge them. I wanted to tell her that Ravi was a gentle, kind and generous man. I don't mean in a materialistic kind of way but with his time, his patience and in his sensitivity. If I am honest, I thought he was a good man from the first day I met him. As the months passed, his presence gave me a safe, solid feeling. I knew he would never let me down.

We continued to see each other once or twice every month but there were never any more guests. The two of us would sit, eat together and talk. Not about the past or the future but about each other's lives, the business, Satchin and Maya. When I was around him, I was sure of who I was and I felt I didn't have to pretend to be anyone but myself. A year later he asked if he could meet my children. I agonised over this. I didn't want someone to come into Satchin's and Maya's lives only to get comfortable and leave, so I said no. He accepted this unquestionably.

'Do you love him?' Maggie asked when I finally told her about our relationship.

'Yes,' I replied.

'Do you trust him?'

It was time to introduce him to them.

We never really had guests in the house apart from the children's schoolfriends and Maggie and Tom. There wasn't any space or a proper dining-table with chairs. I had always meant to go and get some but we were so comfortable eating on the floor and we needed the space for the pickles. I told them that the man who bought so many pickles, and who I cooked for, was coming to take us out, that he had become a good friend and he wanted to meet them. Satchin seemed fine about it but Maya looked at me and said, 'We don't need any more friends, especially a man friend, we've got Tom.'

'Give him a chance, Maya Mol, you might like him,' I said.

'No, I'm quite sure. Tom is more than enough,' she replied.

Ravi came before lunch. Satchin ran down the stairs to open the door for him and showed him up. I introduced him to Maya. Ravi brought her a gift; she just looked at him. 'Say thank you, Mol.' She grunted at him while Satchin asked if he had a car, what it was and where he had parked it, insisting that we had better go now to wherever he was taking us as his wheels might

116

not be there if we took too long. Ravi laughed, looked at the flat crammed with bottles, and said, 'real cottage industry'. Satchin offered to show him the rest of the flat, which didn't take very long as there was only the kitchen and bedroom, all packed with boxes full of condiments and fruit.

We drove into the city. I realised I had never taken my children to properly see it and that day, it seemed so beautiful. We drove around Buckingham Palace, Trafalgar Square, the Tower of London and then we went to Madame Tussauds. They loved it. Ravi then took us to Pizza Hut near Oxford Circus. He talked to them and Satchin talked non-stop, not really giving Maya the chance to say very much, but both of them seemed to like him.

He came every two weeks from then on, arriving at the time he said he would, and then it became every Sunday. Maggie really liked him but Tom was never around when Ravi was there, he was always busy delivering orders.

'Stay, Tom, come and get to know him,' I said one Sunday.

'I know what his sort are like and so should you,' he replied.

I was furious, how dare he! He didn't even know Ravi. I said nothing; I wasn't even going to reply to that. The silence would tell him that he had hurt me.

Tom and I grew more distant; even with the children, he did less and less, but he chose to put that distance between us and he didn't want to see how much they missed him, how much we missed him. It's not that Ravi came and took his place; he never gave Ravi a chance or he would have seen what a good person he was. He was nothing like Raul.

One Sunday, we went to Ravi's house and as the children played in the garden, he asked me to marry him.

So many thoughts raced around my mind and I wanted to say 'yes!' but it could never be as easy as that. How would the children feel about it? What about the business? Maggie? Tom? How would Ravi's parents feel about him marrying a woman with two children? How did he feel about Maya and Satchin? Did he love them like they were his own? I stood back on the patio and watched my children play; they looked so carefree. I could offer them most things, but something was missing, they deserved more, they needed a good father. I looked at Ravi and told him that I needed to talk to the children before making a decision.

When we arrived home, the three of us sat on the bed and I asked them how they would feel about Ravi being their new father. Satchin was so happy and asked if we would be moving to Mill Hill. Maya said nothing.

It was so hard to communicate with Maya. Maya never shared her thoughts with any of us, except perhaps with Maggie. Maggie and Maya had some sort of pact so whenever I tried to probe Maggie, she said nothing. I know that the person Maya showed us was not really the person she was, but it was impossible to get through to her, there were no ways to communicate. My cooking did not work on her, she did not really eat the food I prepared, just played with it and spread it around the plate to make it look less and then hid the rice and vegetables under a piece of popadom. Nor did she sit in the kitchen as I did with my mother, only if Maggie was there. Sometimes, I thought I was not the mother she wanted and other times, I felt these were my insecurities and I tried not to linger on them too long.

I held Maya tightly and told her everything would always be all right, that I would love her always, no matter what. She looked at me and there was sadness, plain sadness, in her eyes. 'Talk to me, Maya Mol, tell me what you are thinking. If you don't want me to marry him, I won't.'

'What do you mean you won't marry him, Amma, if Maya says no? Go on, Maya, tell her, tell her,' Satchin shouted.

'No, Monu, both of you have to be happy about it,' I insisted.

She replied by telling me that if marrying Ravi would make me happy, then it was okay. I waited until the children fell asleep and I began to cook.

In cooking, there are always answers. As I squeezed the fresh tomatoes into a pulp, I thought of saying yes to Ravi and then as I chopped and fried the onions, I would agree to move the family to Mill Hill but on the condition that I kept my business and perhaps with the deposit I had saved, I could lease a shop or an outlet where we would work from. As the onions sizzled, I added garlic, ginger, some turmeric and it seemed better to wait until summer when the children's school term would be over and Maya would be finishing junior school and moving to a new secondary school. The green chillies went into the paste with the boiled potatoes. As it fried together with the tomato puree, I decided that Maggie would still be chief taster and Tom could continue with the deliveries. Finally, fresh coriander and a few cinnamon sticks made it smell just right. Things would work out. I called up Ravi and said, yes, yes, I would be his wife.

Maggie was thrilled but Tom said if we moved, Mill Hill would be too far to pick up consignments but he would find us another driver. I pleaded with Tom and when I got no response, I asked Maggie to speak to him. 'He'll get over it,' she replied.

As I was packing up our belongings for the removal men, Tom came to see me.

'You can't get married, Nalini, you know you can't,' he raised his voice.

'He's dead, Tom. It has been five years and he's dead to me,' I replied.

'It's not that . . . Oh forget it, what's the point anyway?' Tom shouted as he slammed the door and left.

I wished I could put things right between us but I couldn't. We had reached a point where we had drifted so far apart that it was impossible to communicate with him. I busied myself packing and finding a shop that I could lease. Ravi helped me look and we found one in Edgware that had a two-bedroomed flat above it. I put down a deposit and then asked Maggie to move in, rent-free. At first she refused, so I asked her to give it six months and if she didn't like it, she could always move back. Maggie said she would think about it. Farida couldn't come with us, so we found her a job with the wholesaler but it didn't last very long and I never knew what happened to her.

* * *

Ravi and I got married in July at the register office in Stanmore. His parents, brother and sister-in-law flew over from America, as did his friends who came from all over the world. His mother was a little eccentric and she kept kissing my face and thanking me for making him so happy. She thought she would never see the day he married. Now, she said, she could die peacefully. Ravi's brother, Anil, was a little distant with him, considering that they had not seen each other in over two years, but Anil was very courteous and polite with me. Ravi's friends that flew in were also good towards me but I detected a sense of uneasiness in the ones who lived near us. In particular, two married couples kept their distance and looked at Maggie with contempt but I let it go; after all, it was difficult to please everyone.

The day before the wedding, Maya fell ill with a stomach ache and said there was no way that she could possibly come. Maggie coaxed her and sat with her most of the night, saying she had better get well so she could wear the creation that she had made for the wedding. In the morning, she felt much better and both Maya and Satchin stood beside me. Maggie was there too. Tom didn't come. 'Just do it for the children's sake,' I pleaded.

'They've someone else now, they don't need me.'

'Of course they do.'

'Let's not kid ourselves, Nalini, you've all moved on.'

Even Maggie couldn't persuade him.

After the wedding, we had a small party in an Indian restaurant and then we went to our new home. As I climbed into bed, there was an envelope with my name on it. I opened it and found a wedding card and the deeds to the shop and the flat, all in my name. I felt a deep sense of gratitude. 'I love you, Nalini Thakker,' Ravi said as I opened it.

'I love you too, I don't think you'll ever know how much.' As I held Ravi tightly, I let go of Raul completely. He had finally, finally gone.

I will not pretend that it did not take the children some time to settle in. It took that whole first year. There were simple things like sleeping in their own rooms. We had all been so used to sleeping in the same bed for so long that it was hard for them to be alone at night and they missed Maggie and Tom. Although Maggie promised to move into the flat as soon as the shop was up and running, it was not the same for them without her. Maya missed her terribly and called four or five times a day to report any new thing that she had done or seen. Then there were the practicalities of getting used to living with another person. Maya tested Ravi, goading him into scolding her, but he never did and Satchin, he adapted quickly, but I knew he missed his friends.

We continued making pickles throughout that summer. Ravi wanted to take us on holiday but we were too busy moving the production line into the conservatory downstairs whilst the shop was being fitted. It wasn't the ideal place because the sun came pouring through the windows and made it uncomfortably hot for the four of us to work in. Maggie came for two days a week, staying overnight, and Ravi's cleaning lady, Ana, found two local Indian women to come in and help on the days Maggie wasn't there.

The upheaval of the move cost us a few clients because we couldn't fulfil orders on time. Some of the consignments also came back with customers saying that the pickles didn't taste the same. This could have been because they were exposed to too much heat in the preparation phase, so we all moved to the kitchen, which was chaotic. My mind was also chaotic; it was more impatience than apprehension or uneasiness. The building work seemed to be taking forever and I was distracted because I had to keep going in to check how the workmen were getting on.

The builders were extending the back room of the shop, putting in a kitchen and fitting in the machinery to make pickling and bottling more effective. There was ample space for a team of ten to work easily. I also had a side room built to make it easier for the driver to collect the finished consignments.

I had the decorators paint the whole kitchen area white which made all the new equipment shine even brighter, then large black and white tiles were laid down to finish off the back rooms. There were no fluorescent tube lights, they reminded me too much of the sewing factory, so I had spotlights, which everybody said were too costly and impractical, but it had to feel just right. The decorators were in the front of the shop painting the walls the deep red colours I had requested and the carpenter came to make the counter, shelves and the sign. Little Annapurna was positioned on a tiny shelf especially made for her in the kitchen so she could watch over us. It was all finished in time for Onam.

The following week the children started their new schools, Maggie and her cats moved into the flat above the shop, and we were all preparing for the opening. The shop felt magical as we displayed all the pickles on the newly made shelves. Maggie made a window display and bought different coloured sari fabrics, some of which she sewed around the woven baskets filled with straw, and on top she strategically placed a few jars of pickle and fruit. An aroma of dried lavender floated in the air to give a feeling of peace and wind chimes hung above the door, so each time it opened the sound cleansed the air. I managed to find a priest through a friend of Ravi's who would bless the shop and he was due early in the morning, the day before we opened.

The chimes rang and a thin old Indian man with a white beard entered. He introduced himself as the priest and took off his shoes as he walked into the shop. He looked around first and then looked straight into my eyes. As I pulled out a stool for him, my eyes filled with tears and a lump grew in my throat. I felt my mother's presence, an odour of sesame oil and ginger, with her saying, 'Just look after Nalini, I am okay.' Was I doing all right, Ma? Are you proud of me? Was I taking care of the children as you had expected me to? I began to cry streams of tears and the priest held my hand and as he held it, the more I cried, inconsolably. He sat there in silence.

Slowly, the waves that inundated me drifted back to wherever they had come from and my self-control returned. I was just very tired, I said to the priest. He said nothing. He then took out his shells and threw them over the counter. 'Now that you have mastered forgiveness, let it flow through all those who come through these doors and then serve, serve gratitude, but only when you are ready.' I looked at him and asked how I would know. 'You will, when the time is right, you will feel it.' The priest broke a coconut which he stained with saffron. The coconut milk ran over the step that led to the kitchen, he said a prayer, blessed the shop and reached in his pocket for a little pot of moist sandalwood. He placed a spot on my head and left.

My mother had always said that trust prepared the ground for forgiveness. It was essential to have faith and trust in something and forgiveness would then have a firm anchor. Essentially forgiveness was the first step and gratitude was never far behind. Gratitude could come in a hundred forms, like all the different-shaped savouries, offered unconditionally. Gratitude, she said, was the only form of showing appreciation, a way of paying the rent for being allowed to do what we loved. The savouries were offered to the Kathis who gave us an opportunity; the astrologer who came every Thursday with his guidance; the children living on the beach; neighbours who came to visit. Gratitude, she said, kept fear away. If we focused on what we had, it grew, but if we thought even momentarily of what we feared, the fear would multiply and take us backwards. So she even gave thanks for the bad things that had happened, thanks that my father had left. She put behind her the fact that he had ended up a drunk, leaving a series of women behind as he went from village to village. She also said that gratitude brings all the ugly things to the surface and an abundant life is one that faces all that is ugly and lets them go.

After the priest left, I spent the day up to my elbows

in the abundance of freshly ground cornflour and sesame oil, which made each grain of thanks come together, pasting into a dough with the comfort of lukewarm water. Adding just a little salt, pepper, paprika and crushed bay leaves, made bundles of gratitude for my life as it was: the children, Ravi, Maggie, our home, my staff and the shop.

If we were back in India, the savouries would be flattened into different shapes and left out in the sun, soaking in the heat and the energy: here, I left them with the light in the kitchen so they expanded with the heat and when they were ready, I fried them in hot groundnut oil so they would set hard, solidifying in time.

I called out to Maggie, who was out in the front polishing the counters. I asked her to try the golden brown crispy ringlets. She crunched into them and after she had finished, she licked the crumbs around her mouth and took another. She asked me what it was. 'Gratitude,' I said. Maggie rolled her eyes and gave me her Maggie laugh, a cackling sound where she tilted her head back so she could send the noise into the air. It didn't seem right at that time to package the savouries and serve it as produce – we hadn't established 'forgiveness' yet – so we placed them on plates to welcome our new customers. We were ready to open.

It was a Saturday morning and our first customers were Ravi and the children. The children bought some pickles, asked for a receipt, and gave Maggie and I a good luck card that Maya had made. They left to go into London with Ravi. Maggie was in charge behind the counter as I moved between counter and kitchen.

There weren't very many customers at first and the

ones who did come ate the savouries and left without buying anything. Maggie got really annoyed when they returned to eat some more. She said gratitude and patience were running out pretty fast. After lunch, a few more people began coming by. At first they said hello, looked at different varieties of pickles and randomly selected whatever they felt they needed. Maggie wanted to advise them but she held back and talked about the weather, to which they would nod, say nothing, purchase their goods and leave. 'Not very friendly around here, are they?' she whispered. 'We'll soon change that.'

Back in the kitchen, my assistants were the same two Indian ladies who worked with me in the conservatory, Anita and Deepa. Anita was married and had a young son. Deepa was her young sister-in-law who lived with them. Govind also worked in the back. He was a kitchen hand at the local Indian restaurant but lost his job because he shouted back at the tyrant cook. We were there when it happened so I said he could come and work for us and we would see how it went.

Deepa's job was to wash, chop and prepare the fruit and other ingredients as requested. I came in and added the condiments in their required proportions; then she and Govind cooked and boiled the ingredients. Anita would make sure that the machines correctly bottled and labelled the pickles. She then packed them either for the shop or for distribution. Maggie, like myself, was in her phase of gratitude and served at the counter or helped customers choose the pickles that were right for them.

Tom visited infrequently, always choosing the days

that I wasn't there. Maggie wanted him to sell the house and come and live with her above the shop but he refused. He didn't even bother to see the children, just cut himself out of our lives. He sent a new driver called David who brought us fresh produce every two days and took away the consignments that needed to be delivered.

The shop was like a magnet that drew many broken hearts. These fragile hearts came in with layers of armour so they appeared very strong. We had an array of customers: matriarchal Indian women who seemed to know how to hold their families together; young Jewish and Polish women who knew what they wanted out of life; middle-aged affluent English women who looked like they had everything under control; single men, married men and old men. All entered with an air of certainty. Unbeknown to them, the sound of the chimes and the various smells disarmed them and made them feel safe, they felt secure in the store and they didn't even know it.

At first, they bought random jars without saying anything, trusting that their instincts were guiding them and then they came back, buying different flavours so they could make a decision on which ones they preferred. Some had regular orders which they would collect every week and these were predictable; raw green mango for decisiveness, apple and fried ginger to soothe disputes, sweet mango and lime mixed with a hint of red chillies to restore forgotten dreams. Others could not quite decipher which their particular favourites were and so changed their order every week. Some said they were buying them as gifts for other people and bought boxes.

Maggie diagnosed this as symptoms of loneliness and talked as much as she could to make up for it.

Maggie was often right. She had incredible perception and often knew what people needed. She didn't thrust her advice upon them, but would recommend and then they would engage in conversation with her, confirming the diagnosis she had in mind. 'You'll do well trying this one,' she would say, running around the counter to hand it to them.

The shop ran smoothly apart from the occasional disputes between the staff. Maggie sorted those out and I rarely got involved. As the store became packed with regular customers, I hired Govind's younger brother, Amit, thinking that this would even out the balance between them all in the kitchen. I also asked Ana, our cleaning lady, to come in three days a week to help Maggie serve behind the counter. Maya came in on Wednesday after school and on Saturdays, and Satchin and his best friend, Suri, helped the kitchen staff box up the consignments and get them ready for David who now delivered every day.

Wednesdays I took off. In the morning, I continued going to college, enrolling at the one in Stanmore, and in the afternoon, I experimented with new recipes and combinations. At least twice a week, I made sure I was home by four o'clock so I could get back before the children did and make dinner, normally two different types, as Maya still didn't like Indian food. Ravi came home around six-thirty, he would shower and we would all eat around seven o'clock. I know the children hated this as they wanted to watch television. 'Oh, Amma, none of the other kids at school have to do this dinner ritual thing,' Satchin protested, but it was the only thing I held firm on. Dinner was the only time in the day when we could all sit, eat and talk together but on Fridays, I allowed them to get a takeaway and eat in front of the television.

The evenings were time for Ravi and I, and sometimes to entertain friends. I could sense a reserve between his friends towards me and when Maggie joined us for dinner, they made polite excuses and left. This was despite the fact that Maggie's outfits had become very respectable. Maggie said she thought that we scared the wives, who no doubt gossiped about what we got up to. She laughed and mimicked in an Indian accent, 'How do you think they met each other?' 'I don't know but I don't like that Maggie woman, Nalini should know better. What is Ravi thinking about?'

Whenever they came into the shop, Maggie prescribed the extra-hot chilli pickle, to add spice into their lives so they could have something of their own to gossip about.

A year went by and the shop exuded prosperity. I sensed the time was right to introduce packaged savouries. I taught Deepa and Govind how to mix the proportions of sesame oil, water and cornflour and how to get the groundnut oil at just the right temperature so that the savouries did not break and float about. They all eventually came together and became such a good team that I didn't have to be around all the time to supervise them.

Gratitude did amazing things to the shop. People came and stocked up with boxes as they served pickles and savouries to friends and family who came to visit.

There was something indefinable in the air and over the months, things began to change, as if multiplying the cause and effect of events. Deepa, who had lived with her brother and sister-in-law because she had been thrown out of the house by her mother, announced that she and Govind were marrying in the spring. Anita was moving to a bigger home with her husband. Amit was promoted, Ana won a sizeable amount when playing bingo, but she said she still wanted to clean for us and work in the shop and Maggie, Maggie had fallen in love.

Jack was a Scottish man in his mid-fifties who first came into the shop a year after it opened. He had stumbled across it because he read out a piece in the local paper to his wife and she asked Jack to visit so he could describe the shop in detail to her. Sandra, his wife, was dying. Jack hesitated at the entrance to the shop for ten minutes before he came in and then he took a good look around. He stood out, only because the layers of sadness did not leave when he entered the door but followed him around as he bought a selection for her to sample. Maggie joked and said that he would be busy and he sternly told her that they weren't for him. Their conversation ended, but he came regularly to the shop after that. He could have bought a box of six, but he enjoyed the walk to the shop and being inside it gradually reassured him.

Maggie sensed that his harshness was because his heart was breaking and she gave him a combination of ground ginger, orange and cumin to diffuse the rage that was inside him. Some time passed before he came into the shop again. His wife had died; he saw no sense in coming in but just wanted to let us know that she had gone. I gave him a bottle of honey and lime and hoped somehow he would find some serenity. He came in every Friday evening from then on and talked to Maggie if she wasn't busy serving. Eight months later, he mustered enough courage to ask her to go to the cinema with him. 'About time,' she said, having asked me on several occasions to specify the proportions of garlic, asafoetida and red chillies. 'Maggie, you have enough courage for an army,' I had said, not realising that it wasn't for her.

We should have known by the fact that she wore her favourite dress every Friday and had her hair done on Thursday evenings but somehow it escaped us. Then, one day, she asked me how much notice she would need to give to move out of the flat.

I was devastated, thinking I had failed miserably as her friend and how would Maya feel to hear that she was going back to the East End. She couldn't go back, not now, not now that we had come this far. Maggie looked at me and laughed her Maggie laugh and said that she was only moving up the road to live with Jack. I hugged her, and then I went downstairs to tell Govind and Deepa that their wedding gift from Ravi and I was the flat upstairs and that they could live in it rent-free for six months.

Ten days later, gratitude came to tell me that I was pregnant. It was almost coming up to the second anniversary of the opening of the shop.

I was shocked and very apprehensive about how Maya and Satchin would take the news. That evening when

Ravi came home, I told him. I have never seen such happiness on a man's face and this in itself made me welcome the baby that I was carrying. We sat down and told the children the next evening. Satchin didn't really seem to care, he was a teenager and had many other things to think of than babies, but he managed to grunt something that indicated he was happy. Maya said nothing but looked surprised. Ravi said to her that she would always be our number one girl but I don't think that this was the right thing to say. She left her dinner and went upstairs. I followed her up there and could see that she had been crying. I asked her to talk to me but she kept saying she was fine, then she kissed me and said she would be happy to be a big sister and she came back downstairs to finish dinner.

Having the baby inside of me seemed to bring a new wonderment into the shop and we were busier than ever before. Things ran well and the staff helped out in any way they could, not allowing me to carry anything more than two pickle jars at a time. In the meantime, I was teaching Maggie how to balance the proportion of fruits and spices so they could manage in my absence. Months passed by, then one day, Maggie and I were behind the counter, I was serving Mrs Zanuski who was telling me about the problems she was having with her daughter-in-law and as I reached to get her prescription, my waters broke. I finished serving her and signalled to Maggie, who was deep in conversation with Mr Matthews. I threw an orange in her direction and told her it was time to go. 'Already?' she said. 'But you've two weeks left.' She could not get hold of Ravi and so she bundled me into Amit's car and we went to the hospital. Twelve hours later, my daughter was born.

I will not say that the birth was effortless, but it was much easier than when I gave birth to Maya. It wasn't done in total obscurity, no strange people were walking in and out like last time and I could scream without the midwife telling me to shut up. Ravi sat holding my hand throughout. He could not believe it when our little girl came out. He kept shaking his head. As they handed her to me, he kissed her little forehead and held her tiny fingers and looked at me, speechless. I knew it was impossible to love this man any more than I did. We named her after my mother, Ammu, and as I slept that night with her beside me, I smelt the scent of sesame oil and ginger lingering above us and I knew she was there.

The children came the next morning to see her. Satchin looked into the cot, touched her head and then went over to the mirror to comb his hair so he could impress the nurses. Maya sat looking at her and then picked her up and held her. I said little Ammu had smiled at her and she said that it was probably gas. Seeing the two of them like that made me so happy and I held Maya's hand. Maya had changed somehow, almost surrendered, and accepted Ravi in a way that I never expected. Maggie had been right, she had said all along to be patient and give it time. Maggie then came in with Deepa and a big teddy bear and said that everything was under control as she was adding the proportions as I had instructed her and none of the customers had complained or fallen sick. Everyone seemed to be managing and the next day, I took our baby home.

* * *

When I had my other two children, I was barely a child myself, and the people around me took charge. I fed the babies and that was all. I let my mother do whatever she wanted to with them as if to compensate for the one she lost. My father had left her the day before she went into labour. I heard him shouting at her and thought he had gone off to work in the fields and had returned that night. Just after I woke up, I heard her screaming but took no notice because it was a regular occurrence and I thought she was yelling at my father, just another fight. After ten minutes, when it still didn't stop, I got up to see where she was. She was bent over double in the kitchen and the baby was hanging out of her. There was no time to go and call anyone, so I panicked and pulled the baby out. I didn't notice that the cord had wrapped itself around his neck and that he was turning blue. Blood covered my hands.

My mother said it wasn't my fault, that at the last minute he had decided not to come and stay with us, but I kept seeing that scene over and over again, blood all over the kitchen floor and the look of utter despair on her face. She had wanted a little boy so much. Was I ever enough for her? Perhaps if my brother had lived, my father would have come home, if not for me, at least for him? I made my mother hot soups of rice gruel so she would heal quickly and I resolved to help her whenever I could. We had to move away because she wanted good things for me and nobody would marry me if we stayed in the village, knowing that we had been left by my father. My mother and I set up our new life and we were happy cooking together. I felt at last she was proud of me and I had turned out to be all that she wanted, then I went away with Raul and broke the promises I made to her and myself. And when I left for England, I took her grandchildren away from her. She probably knew what life was going to be like for us and it must have broken her heart but she let me go, let us go. I should have fought harder, done more to keep her.

With baby Ammu, I had an opportunity to make up for things. Just holding her, watching her sleep, gave me such peace despite Ravi's parents being there. Ravi's parents came over before she was born and they were to stay for at least four months whilst I went back to the shop part-time. When they arrived, I couldn't leave my little one, not even for half a day. His mother got very upset when I followed her around as she changed the baby or bathed her. It wasn't that I didn't trust her, I just wanted to do it all myself. She would probably say that I was too smothering but I found my mother-in-law suffocating, though I know she meant well. It was a race to see who could get to the cooker and she was always there first, allowing me no space, not even in my own kitchen.

Maya seemed to get on with her quite well and showed her around and took her to the shops when she needed to go. Satchin didn't really care if they were there or not and only got annoyed when she told him to keep his music down. She treated Ravi as if he were a child but he was calm about things, saying that she had nothing better to do and was harmless, but she had a hundred and one things to do with her new friends, couldn't she stay with one of them?

'It's just for a short time, Nalu,' Ravi said, but they seemed to stay forever.

They hardly left the house and I escaped all the social gatherings she threw by taking the baby to the park or popping into the shop. I never stayed too long, I didn't want to. Maggie insisted that it was time to get back to work but I kept saying I wasn't ready. It wasn't that I was depressed after having the baby, but sometimes it felt like I was in a void and had nobody to communicate with, nobody could fully understand the way I really felt about things. I would sit in the park and talk to the baby about how life had been and doing this made me feel scared. It was the first time I had stopped the busyness of my life and listened to all that had happened to us.

Four months went by, and my in-laws had still not left. I tried dropping little hints but nothing. Feelings of inadequacy grew with my mother-in-law's presence and I, who had prescribed a million pickles, was unable to solve the problem and the more I thought about it, the more it grew. At the back of my mind, I could hear 'let it go,' but my mother-in-law seemed to know and touch on my very insecurities.

One evening, she told me how she had bumped into Ravi's long-lost girlfriend and was debating whether or not to tell him. She said that the reason Ravi never joined the rest of the family in the States was because he came looking for his fiancée who he thought was in London. They had been separated by Idi Amin's coup. For years he was searching and then he met me, but she wasn't sure if he had ever given up hope of finding her. I asked her why she was telling me all this. She said she just wanted an opinion.

When Ravi came home, he would head straight for

Ammu's nursery. If I was feeding Ammu, she would turn her head to look at him and he would come over to kiss her. This simple act reminded me of Raul and I shuddered at the memory. At around this time Ravi had to go abroad on business trips and I began to feel a familiar insecurity. I was losing control and I knew it.

Maggie came over and begged me to go back to the shop but I couldn't, I felt stuck. She said that we could take the baby with us and get someone to mind her. I thought about this but the shop was always so crowded and people would be forever poking and prodding her. 'No,' I said. 'We're fine.'

When Ammu was old enough to crawl, she went around the house looking for Maya, calling her M'o, M'o. Maya would scoop her up and talk to her, cuddle her. Both my daughters loved each other and this put my heart at ease. Maya had changed so much since Ammu's birth, not just with me but with everyone; I could talk to her, laugh with her, she was open and not guarded. The baby brought the two of us together. Ammu would be all right with her big sister, I thought, despite the mother-in-law being there. I could go back to the shop and work in the evenings.

It was a month before Ammu's first birthday and I hadn't been in the shop for a while. As I walked in, a stale smell hung in the air. Maggie was not there; Maggie was always there and if she was sick, she would call. Seeing the state of the shop, I panicked; something was very wrong, she would never leave it like this. I phoned Jack. He sounded worried and asked me to visit her, he didn't know what the problem with Maggie was, she didn't want to see a doctor and she wouldn't get out of bed. When I walked into the bedroom, I did not recognise her. She had lost all spirit, her hair had not been dyed, no bright red lipstick, and she looked gaunt. 'What's wrong, Maggie, what is it? Are you sick?' She shook her head and handed me a letter. It was from Tom. She seldom saw Tom these days. He said that he had found himself a lovely girl and was busy with her. The last time I saw him was when I was three months pregnant and this was only by complete accident. Maggie needed to be somewhere and I said I would stand in for her at the shop and Tom came in. 'This is silly, Tom, you can't go on avoiding us like this, the children miss you, I miss you.'

'I heard your news. I hope the baby brings you happiness,' he replied coldly.

Tom had gone to Ireland with his girlfriend, Elaine, and thought he would look up family whilst he was there. Maggie was a little anxious when he first asked her but she had given him the names of towns so far away from their own that she thought there was not even the remotest possibility that he would find anyone.

I opened the letter:

Dear Maggie,

So you are my Mam, but I can never call you that.

You had so many opportunities to tell me but I had to hear it from a drunk in a bar who says he's your brother.

Why couldn't I have heard it from you? All those years of lying. I don't know what is real anymore. Our life together has been based on lies and deceit, as are those whom you choose to surround yourself with.

*It's enough now, and I don't want to have any part
of it, none of it.*

*Elaine and I are married and are making our home
here in Ireland.*

Tom.

Enclosed were a set of Maggie's house keys. There was
nothing I could do to console her as fear swept over me.
'Maggie, he'll come around, he's angry, you'll see, just
give it time,' was all I could manage, but I didn't quite
believe what I was saying. 'Come to work, take your
mind off it.' But she refused. 'Shall I send Maya around?'
I asked, desperately. She shook her head and asked me
to leave her alone for a few days.

So Maggie had not been in the shop and nobody had
bothered to call me, not even Anita. She said Deepa
had gone off four days ago; she didn't call because she
thought she would be back. Govind had gone to find
her and there was no sign of Amit, there hadn't been
for the last week. David had gone home because there
was nothing to deliver and the produce he had delivered,
crates of rotten shrivelled mangoes and other fruit, lay
there because no one had cooked it. Anita said she
thought she could retrieve the whole situation without
me knowing. The kitchen was a mess. I looked at my
little bronze Annapurna and she was a dirty black. It
was as if the customers could smell the fear and stayed
away. I decided that the only thing to do was to close
the shop until we got ourselves sorted out.

Putting the closed sign up, I washed the shelves, the
floors, the counters, trying to remove the stench that

filled the air, but the stains that had seeped into the wood on the counters couldn't be removed and the smell lingered. The windows and doors were kept open but it was useless; I tried lighting incense sticks and scented candles but nothing helped. I couldn't understand it; it was only two weeks since I had last come in, how could I have not noticed? It couldn't have got like this in just a week. How could I not have seen? Anita helped mop the floors and tidy all the empty boxes that cluttered the hallway. I trusted those who worked with me, trusting them completely, giving them the freedom that was so lacking when I was at the factory, but they had taken this without realising its value and had thrown it away. I called the priest; he would be able to do something. He said he would come into the shop the following day.

There was no sound of wind chimes when he came in very early that morning. The look upon his face said it all, like he was going to turn back because he thought he had come to the wrong shop. I told him that anxiety had taken over every corner of my mind and managed to permeate into the shop, fear had taken this space that I had created and filled it with its own clutter and chaos. What was I supposed to do? How could I make it all better? He took off his shoes, stood in the centre of the room and looked up, gazing at me: 'When gratitude comes, Nalini, it shines its torch on all that is ugly, so all that is ugly and not you, all that is not real, can make its way out. There is nothing I can do. You have to be bold, sit still and face all that comes with honesty, courage and dignity, then let it all go.' He reached for his little tin of sandalwood and placed a spot on my forehead, said a prayer and left. I didn't feel comforted by his words; they left me with a sense of foreboding.

Did he mean that I had to let the shop go? I couldn't, we had worked so hard for it. Nothing would make me let it go, I was bigger than fear. I left Ammu with my mother-in-law in the mornings and concentrated on getting the shop back together. Placing a sign outside the window saying 'Closed for Renovation', I set to work, scrubbing and cleaning, emptying all the old containers of condiments. The remaining jars of pickles were removed from the shelves and emptied. This was something I had to do for myself so I told Ana and Anita to take some time off. The counters were re-varnished that week and new tiles were put down to replace the chipped and broken ones. Every day, I reached home, exhausted, but going home to that smile and those tiny arms that threw themselves around me recharged me.

Ravi said if I needed any help he would send in some industrial cleaners, but I said that it was something that I needed to do. He then said that his brother was coming over on a business trip from the States with a colleague and maybe his parents would take a decision to leave with him. A huge burden would be lifted from me if he could arrange that and we could get back to being a family again. I could finally take charge of my home again. He said they would be coming over in ten days and would be staying in a hotel in Central London. Ten days, ten days would give me enough time to finish the shop and then I could get back in the kitchen and cook them a meal. 'I'll cook something nice,' I said. Ravi looked surprised; it had been a while since I had cooked anything at home and Ravi said there was really no need. His mother could do it or we could eat out. 'No,' I insisted. 'The shop will be finished and I really feel it is something I want to do.' He put his arms around me.

Every day, I worked in the shop to bring it back to its former state. I called Maggie as I still had no news from her and she said she needed some more time off. Jack was thinking of taking her away for a week. 'Just make sure you come back safely because it's going to be better than ever,' I told her. There was still no news of Govind, Deepa or Amit so I decided to advertise for staff in the local paper. Anita begged me not to and I assured her that I would sort things out with them when they came back, but in the meantime, we needed staff. Upstairs the flat looked like a chaotic jumble sale that everyone had rummaged through. All that remained were the leftovers and a few suitcases. I tidied up, putting the clothes in the cases, and took it all into the spare room, cleaning the flat from top to bottom. Everything was finished by the end of that week. I could now concentrate on cooking for my guests, something I hadn't done in a long time, and I began to retrieve the sense of perspective that I had lost.

My mother-in-law got very excited at the prospect of her eldest son coming to visit her and was thinking about the meals she wanted to cook him. I told her on the first day it was important for me to make them feel welcome in our home so I would cook. She wasn't happy, but then I added that the baby would be pleased that her grandmother could play with her and that appeased her. I thought about the menus the day before and went shopping in the market.

The fishmonger had fresh trout that had come in that

morning which I could marinade and lightly fry. I packed the rest of the bags with fruit and vegetables that were in season. I knew it was going to be a special meal, a new start for us all. On Friday evening, I marinated the fish with yoghurt, tamarind and spices, smelling the calm of a salty sea. It was quiet in the house, very peaceful; Satchin had gone to football camp and I had allowed Maya to stay over at her friend's house for that weekend. Ammu was in the kitchen crawling about, putting whatever she could find into her mouth. She was almost a year and was trying to stand up. She would stand and make a noise for me to watch her and then after I smiled at her, she would tumble back down and give herself a clap. I talked to her, telling her what I was doing whilst preparing the fish, and although she was banging a saucepan lid with a wooden spoon, her presence was soothing. My in-laws had gone to see some other relatives and Ravi wasn't back from work.

On Saturday, I spent the whole day chopping, mixing, frying and the house was alive again. The cooking smells floated to the upstairs bedrooms, bringing my father-in-law down to investigate what was happening. He never really spoke to me; he never spoke to anyone, and looked like an old cinnamon stick, walking two paces behind his wife, agreeing with whatever she said. He said that the smells took him back to his childhood and it was a long time since he had smelt the fragrance of freshly ground spices. So he stood for a while in the kitchen just inhaling and I gave him something to try. 'Check for salt,' I said. The old man was delighted.

The cooking was nearly finished; all that was left was the saffron rice and the cauliflower vegetable dish. The iddlies were steaming and the sambar was bubbling away. Ravi had prepared the table. I went up to change. I was looking for turquoise stones to match my sari when Ravi came in to tell me that the guests had arrived. 'Five more minutes,' I said. A few minutes later, he called out for me. As I ran down the stairs, I thought I heard a familiar laugh but it was drowned out by my mother-in-law's voice. I walked into the sitting room and saw Ravi's brother, Anil. 'It's been a long time, Anil Bhai,' I said. About to continue, I glanced to the side, and came face to face with Raul.

'Let me introduce you to my friend, Raul Karta.'

'Raul, this is my lovely sister-in-law, Nalini.'

I froze. He stared at me, holding out his hand. I wanted to run out of that house and keep on running. A surge of emotion rushed through me and I held back my tears. Clearing my throat, I managed to whisper, 'Hel—' My mother-in-law gazed up at me from where she was sitting. Why? Why now? How had he come here?

'Nalini is a fantastic cook,' Anil said.

Raul smiled that same half-smile that he used to capture my heart.

'Do you have children?' he asked.

Children? I wanted to scratch his eyes out and hit him and say yes, yes, but you walked out and left them and didn't give a damn what happened. You left them with nothing. Tears were pushing their way to my eyes as I fought them back.

'Three,' Ravi said, walking towards a photograph of the three of them. 'Satchin is sixteen, Maya almost fourteen, and the baby is nearly one.'

As Raul was handed the picture, my hands trembled and my body began to shake, the room spun around and I wanted to vomit. 'Nalu, are you all right?' Ravi asked.

'No, no, no . . .'

'What is it, Nalu?' Ravi came rushing over to support me.

'Sick,' I stammered.

'Is there anything I can do to help?' He, Raul, said.

I couldn't breathe and fell forward onto the floor.

Ravi picked me up and took me upstairs. He put me in bed and picked up the phone to call a doctor.

'No,' I said.

'What is it, Nalu? What is it?'

'Need to sleep. Go down, will be fine,' I mumbled.

'I can't leave you, not like this.'

'Please,' I whispered.

He went reluctantly.

I could hear footsteps beneath me, my mother-in-law scurrying around in the kitchen, insisting that they stay and that she serve the food, not to worry, I would get over whatever it was that I had, it was most probably a twenty-four-hour bug. I could hear Ravi saying that it might be better if they left but she was adamant. They sat at the table to eat. He sat at my table to eat. How could he bring himself to eat in my house? Food that he once rejected, children, home and wife, all rejected. I went to see my baby, carried her into bed with me, and cried until there were no more tears.

The whole night I lay awake thinking what I would do and the next day I decided to go to the hotel and see him. They were staying at Lancaster Gate, just around the corner from where he first brought us, nine years ago. Five hard years I fought, fought to make life better; anything could have happened to us. What kind of a man did that to his family? A man with no conscience, bereft of any feeling. I would move if I had to, taking my children with me, before letting him catch a glimpse of them.

I left early in the morning. Ravi was worried about me, but I said there was something that I urgently needed to sort out. Sitting on the tube, I was shaking, tears rolled down my face as I thought about the day I left my mother, the day he made me leave her, the afternoon I told my children he had died, Satchin sobbing, Maya lying crying on the roadside, endless hours at the factory whilst they sat and waited for me. The couple sitting opposite me looked embarrassed and began talking to each other. I thought I was doing my very best for my children and if I had to make that awful decision all over again, I would do what I did back then.

I wiped my tears as I arrived at the hotel and called up his room. He was expecting me, he said, and it would be better if I came up. He opened the door and my fists lunged at him with odious rage. He grabbed them. 'Why?' I screamed. He had no answer. 'Why?' I shouted again.

He said nothing; he did not even attempt to make pathetic excuses. I sat on the bed and began to sob hysterically. He came to touch me and I flung his hand away. 'Don't you ever touch me.'

'You cannot see the children,' I cried. 'They think you are dead and I wish you were. It has taken us years to find security. They think of Ravi as their father and you cannot take that away from them. Promise me. Promise me!' I screamed.

'I cannot simply walk away from them,' he answered.

'You can't do what?' I shouted. 'You left them, left them with nothing.'

'You don't understand, Nalini, it was difficult, you were difficult.'

I spat at him.

I asked him what it would take for him to disappear and promise never to come back.

Fifty thousand pounds. I bought a promise for fifty thousand pounds. Money that I could only raise by selling my shop, the business, everything we had worked for, dreamt about. He left that evening with an assurance that I would wire the money into his account as soon as I had it. If it wasn't done within the month, he would return, this time to see the children.

I am ashamed to say it, but I sold myself twice to him, twice he robbed me of my dreams. We are tested on the things we most fear and I failed miserably. My mother would have said to me that gratitude had brought me to a place where it was finally time to face the truth, no matter how hideously ugly, and the foundations upon which new beginnings are built would be much stronger. But my children had grown to become secure, they loved Ravi and their little sister, and the thought of Raul re-entering their lives repulsed me and made me physically sick. I did not want to lose them, to cause them any more pain or further disruption. I didn't want to lose Ravi or have our lives torn apart by a man that didn't even deserve to be in the same room as them.

I made arrangements to sell the shop, telling Ravi that I had made a decision to spend time at home looking after Ammu. Maggie said it was worth doing when I told her about Raul's reappearance, that she would have given anything to keep Tom from finding out. She would help me by giving me some of the money from the sale of the house off Green Street.

'Get rid of him, just get rid of him,' she said. 'It's in the past, we can start again.'

MAYA

My mother-in-law to be, Señora María Carmen Gonzalez del Hoyo, was a fearsome woman who took charge of the wedding preparations like a general in command of a military operation. She had set the date for Marcos and I, after weeks of orbiting like a satellite around the priest so she could find out which combination of dates were the most auspicious. Five months to the day, he said. I don't know how she coerced the priest into marrying me in church, but she did, dressed to kill in her combat outfit of grey angora skirt and jacket and perfectly set hair. Señora Gonzalez del Hoyo took charge of an army of caterers, decorators, musicians, and florists, manoeuvring them all with timely precision and occasionally gunning down a violinist or a decorator who stepped out of line.

That particular morning, I was in the flat, emptying out my clothes from the cupboards. She rang the bell, more as a warning that she was letting herself in than a request for entry, and launched herself like a missile. Steaming into the apartment with excitement, she pulled out the wedding invitations. I was about to say that she had put an 'o' in the wrong place and that it really didn't matter when at that very moment, the phone rang. It was Ravi, calling me to say that Maggie was seriously ill, that the doctor had given her a few weeks at most.

I put the phone down and ran to the bedroom hastily throwing things in a suitcase. María Carmen was shrieking Spanish in a high pitch tone in my ear. 'I have to go to London, right now,' I said. She seemed startled as if uncomprehending. '*Voy a Londres, ahora mismo, mi tía está muy enferma*. I have tried to call Marcos but there is no reply, he must be in court, tell him I will call him when he gets home,' I said, shutting the suitcase. She buzzed around me like a queen bee that would not go away, saying that I could not just leave her, what about the invitations, the wedding, the preparations? When would I be back? I ran out of the door as she threw me her fur coat. I went back to kiss her goodbye and told her that I would call her soon.

Hailing a cab, I arrived at the train station. It was a two-hour rail trip from Palmadoro, hidden away in amongst the hills, to Madrid. The train was late and when it came, the driver got out for refreshments so we had to wait another twenty minutes whilst he had his coffee and smoked his cigarette. I was exhausted and slumped into a seat next to the window. I loved to see the hills and the countryside as we rode up. A February sun managed to muster enough courage so it could shine, despite the fact that it was cold outside. People were bothered by the way it came pouring in brightly and pulled the shutters down. I took the huge coat that María Carmen had given me and placed it on the chair next to me to make it look occupied so I wouldn't have to worry about whether the sun bothered them or not.

The coat looked like a huge dog. Palmadoro did not really justify such a thing, except for a few misplaced days in winter, but the ladies liked to parade in them with their long pearl necklaces, comparing quality and price along with the other gossip from the town. Most of them had nothing better to do and would sit in the cafés and restaurants with their aperitifs, go to the hair-dresser's to get their hair set yet again and then wander back home to cook and wait for their husbands.

I had been there for years and still had not managed to make it into any of the inner social circles, despite Marcos being the town's foremost barrister. This might have been due to the fact that Celia de la Casa Morales spotted me one morning in what she thought were my pyjamas. I could not be bothered to put on the customary twinset and skirt to go to the supermarket so I went in one of the outfits I had made. It caused angst amongst the other shoppers who began peering through the shelves just to make sure what they were seeing was true. Celia was there and the way the story returned to us was as though I had run through the town naked. '*Un poco de discreción*, Maya,' was the best Marcos could come up with.

The coat fell to the ground as the train moved and as I picked it up, I heard Maggie's laugh. I was eight years old and had put on Bogey. Bogey was Maggie's fur coat

152

which had been given to her by a friend, the same one who left her the house and the cats. Maggie had named it Bogey because, she said, the man always had a spot of mucus dangling from his nose and it was so out of place as he came across so suave, she never had the heart to tell him.

I wore Maggie's red stilettos, which were far too large, and her necklaces, put on Bogey, took her cigarette holder in which I placed a sweet cigarette which kept falling out and then paraded around her living room. 'Rule number one, Maya, darling, always make sure that your nose is clean and you've tucked your knickers in correctly after you've been to the loo and then success can't fail but to see you,' she said. I placed Maggie's handbag on the table and pulled my skirt down correctly from where it had been lodged. 'See, that's much better already. Success, he's seen you now, he'll be on his way shortly.' Success didn't recognise me and hit my mother instead. A few weeks later we moved to our new house across the road from Maggie and Tom.

One of the foremost memories of my childhood included the three battered suitcases stacked on top of a cupboard, my mother hastily pulling them down and stuffing them with whatever she thought was important. When those suitcases came down, I knew the contents of the house would be sold and that we would have to say goodbye to the people we cared about although she would promise that we would see them again. We never knew what happened to most of them, especially the ones we loved.

I always thought if I was ever asked to write a book, I would begin each chapter with waking up in a different bed: the cotton contraption made from a white starched sheet which was doubled up into a triangle and tied to the door where I spent my first few years; the bunk bed I shared with Satchin where I slept on the top because the thought of the legless hamster descending upon him was all too much; the wrought-iron urine-stained bed in which hundreds of people had probably slept, before it was occupied by Amma, Satchin and I, and then there was the 'normal' double bed which we bought in the sale for our new flat. The new flat was number 64a and the bed had a bedroom to go in and that is where my mother and I slept. Satchin slept in the sitting room on the sofa. Well, he was supposed to sleep on the sofa bed but often, in the mornings, I would find him on the other side of Amma. This was our happiest home and I remember splashing around, flicking paint at each other whilst we were decorating it.

We lived above the downstairs man so we couldn't run about and make lots of noise or he would hit his ceiling with the end of a broom and shout lots of abuse. Ordinarily, it wouldn't have mattered, but he was also the landlord so Satchin and I tiptoed about. He still hit his broom hard against his ceiling. On the occasions he got really abusive, Satchin and I let down the tyres of his black Ford Cortina, but I understood how the noise of clattering jars must have irritated him. We lived with a whole family of pickles, there were hundreds of them, everywhere you went there was a pickle jar. I, too, hated the smell and the sight of them.

The pickles followed me to school. When my friend Fatima came to our house to play, she would see the pickles and think she was being original by suggesting setting up a pickle shop. I had to consent because she had a pretend cash register which she brought around especially and if I said no, let's sell clothes or something, she wouldn't let me have a go on it. The pickles permeated her psyche and she would bring that game to school and all the other children queued up to be customers and fought over being the shopkeeper. It is amazing the power a cash register can wield. Then, when her mother came to work with Amma, Fatima, also succumbing to a pickle overdose, swiftly abandoned that game and we moved onto other things.

We became 'Boney M'. We were short of a few singers and explained to our doll audience that Boney had gone off and we had regrouped into a band called 'M'. Sometimes we just became the girl singers from ABBA. I never got to be the blonde one though. I could have been if I really wanted to, but I gave in to Fatima because nobody else did. Fatima desperately wanted to do our concerts in the garden because she didn't have one but to get to it was worse than *The Krypton Factor* assault course. The door that led to it was stacked high with pickle boxes and then, once you finally got past it all, you had to attempt to make your way down the stairs, bypass the colony of snails that had set up home there, and finally kick the door hard to open it.

Maggie was often at our house; she went part-time so she could help my mother out and so we saw a lot more of Amma. She took us to school and I made sure everyone knew she was my Amma. I held her hand all the way and once at school, shouted, 'Bye, Ma' in my loudest voice. Satchin would run off, sensing what was to follow, an even bigger, 'We'll see you after school.'

On the way back home, I told the lollipop man who used to help me across the road when I was going 'solo' that there was no need, my mother was there. She looked at him and smiled, at which point he pulled out an assortment of sweets from his pocket and handed them to me saying, 'Oh, I know, dear, but I still have to make sure you all get across the road safely.' Looking at Amma, I replied, 'I really mustn't take your sweets, sir,' so she could see what a well mannered child she had brought up and I crossed the road hastily, dragging my Amma's hand, hoping that the lollipop man would not mention the times when I used to ask him for sweets and then wolf them down.

Just her being with us made that walk to school so nice. There was a Trebor factory near to where the lollipop man stood and the smell of sweets that emanated from the chimney would follow us home. As we walked past it, she said that the smell reminded her of home when the sugar cane was being harvested and processed. Bang on cue she said that, every time we got to the top of our road. By the time we stepped through the front door, that sweet smell would be beaten off with a chilli/garlic waft which seemed to attach itself to our clothes, and no matter how much they were washed, the odour lingered. The other kids who played on the street with us used that smell against us if they didn't get their own way and it was the cause of many fights. Satchin and I could have retaliated, we had loads of ammunition against the other kids: Jatinder tied up his hair in a bobble and wore blue National Health glasses, we could have called him 'four eyes', but we didn't. 'You take no notice,' Maggie would say, cleaning us up before presenting us back to our mother. 'Your mother will be so proud to know that you've been good.'

We played on Maggie's side of the street and so she could hear an impending fight with all the noise. Just before it got dangerous, she would look through her window and come and extricate us from the point where bricks and stones were brought in. Then it changed when Amma bought Satchin a second-hand Budgie bike and me a Space Hopper, all the other kids wanted to know us then.

I loved the evenings, especially in autumn when it began to get dark quickly. Maggie came in and Satchin and I would help her stick the labels on the jars. She was a really good story teller and told us about the castle her family used to live in and stories of when she was growing up in Ireland. Tom came around on some evenings but we saw him mostly on Sundays. Sometimes, we went for a drive with him, Amma and Maggie, occasionally as far as Brighton, and they would let us play in the arcades. When we got back home, that Sunday evening feeling crept into bed with us as we slept but now it was a safe feeling because whenever I woke up, my mother would be there.

'¿*Perdone, Señorita, está ocupado*?' I looked up and an elderly gentleman pointed to the seat. I didn't have the heart to say yes. Bogey 2 was scrunched up and placed in the rack above me. The old man began to blink furiously and put his hand above his eye. I pulled the shutter down, not all the way, but just enough so I could still see outside.

The countryside was still beautifully breathtaking

even though I must have seen it at least a thousand times. I knew the way most of the valleys dipped and the streams that ran through them, the villages that were scattered between stations and the animals that were interspersed between the hills. The first time I came, I saw none of this. Armed with a phrase book, I was too busy practising my one sentence for the taxi driver so he wouldn't sense that I didn't have a clue where I was going and that I was scared.

I was twenty and had been sent to this little town through unexpectedly winning a competition at university that I had entered as a bet. Competitions were not my forte and still traumatised me, so I knew it couldn't possibly be me who would win. The first one I went in for was when I was nine and it was to make a robot from batteries and tin foil. Nicola Jory had told me that she had inside information, her mother was one of the teachers and also a judge and she said that I had won first prize. The winners were announced at assembly in reverse order and when Mr Mauldy said, 'The first prize goes to . . .' I stood up, but the prize went to John Saunders. Everyone laughed hysterically. I did not have any real inclination to learn Spanish but I went because I was led to believe that the prize was a luxury holiday with a bit of Spanish tuition thrown in.

The cab driver that picked me up from Palmadoro station had shifty eyes and greased back hair. I spoke my one phrase that I had rehearsed over and over again, '*El monasterio Santo Paulo, por favor.*' He began a conversation with me, to which I yawned, indicating that the trip had been very long and I was in no mood to converse. Fifteen minutes later, we arrived at a secluded place in the middle of nowhere. I thought that *El mones-terio* was a five-star hotel so I kept insisting that there was some mistake. He shook his head vehemently, pointing to the monk who was making his way towards us. The monk said nothing but indicated the monastery. So I followed him, wheeling my suitcase through the cloisters; he left me at the reception area.

The monastery was run by Father Antonio, a bearded man who had eyebrows that knitted heavily together in a knit one, purl one sort of style and eyes that were perhaps a little too close together. 'So pleased to meet you. Let me show you to your accommodation, Señorita Thakker.' I was relieved he spoke English.

'There must be some mistake,' I said, 'I'm looking for *El monesterio*.'

'Yes, yes, yes and welcome,' he said, patting my back and then he took me to my room. It was sparsely fur-nished with an old bed, a cupboard, a table and a lamp. Four weeks, I thought. He said his office was just two floors below if I needed anything and the dining room was across the cloisters, a large hall which I couldn't miss. Dinner would be served at eight. It was all so quiet and there was nothing to do but to wait for dinner. I began to wonder what I had got myself into.

I strolled across the grounds to the dining room and as I entered, I was met by a hundred and fifty pairs of eyes, all male, waiting to eat. I walked nervously in and Father Antonio came over. 'The foreigners' table is over there, none have arrived yet, they are expected in the next week, but please make yourself comfortable, join us.' I joined the head table and just smiled, as I didn't understand a word of what they were saying. After finishing the meal, I left and a torpedo of men came after me. I let them all pass by with a '*no entiendo.*'

Nobody told me that monastery rooms also served as halls of residents for the male university students who were studying in the town. Come to think of it, nobody had told me anything. I sat in complete boredom, until the other foreigners came. Most of them were elderly people from Canada who had decided to take up Spanish for their retirement years, but there were also a few French girls, and a Scottish couple whom I latched onto.

The course consisted of Father Antonio droning on at us, teaching us Spanish for four boring hours every day. One day, I needed to speak to him because I had decided that I wanted to go back home, so I knocked on his office door and went in. There was another door at the back of the room so I knocked on that too and even though there was no answer, I entered. In that room was a four-poster bed covered with purple silk sheets, a television, video recorder, hi-fi and photos of women everywhere. I panicked as I heard footsteps, closed the door and ran out. Not looking where I was going, I bumped into someone.

I looked up and was met by a pair of deep blue eyes. 'I'm sorry,' I said, 'Uhmmm, just looking for Father Antonio.' He smiled, nodded and walked away. That was the first Spanish man that didn't attempt to strike up a broken conversation with me which always led to the words 'you' and 'me' and 'coffee'. As he walked away, something came over me, taking away all thoughts of going home. Father Antonio walked up the stairs. 'Can I help you with something, Maya?'

160

'No thank you, Father,' I said, thinking of my finger-prints all over his door. 'I was just passing. Just wanted to let you know how much I am enjoying the course.'

'Good, good to hear it.'

Every evening, to entertain ourselves, we played cards. Sometimes a few of the Spanish students joined us and when they played, I lost the thread of the game, thinking that maybe the man with the deep, blue eyes that I had met outside Father Antonio's room would come in. So I kept looking out onto the terrace, missing my turn, but I never saw him. Miguel the Poker King's favourite words were, 'Maya, I'll let you cheat if you want, but just play.' He thought I was one of those people who couldn't cope with getting myself up and dressed in the morning and he took it upon himself to take care of me. He already had a girlfriend, Lucía, about whom he talked endlessly, so I felt he was safe and allowed him to show me the town.

As I was going back to my room after dinner one night, Miguel called out to me, 'Maya, I want you to meet a good friend of mine, come over here.' I looked back and there he was, the man with the blue eyes. 'Let me introduce you to Marcos, Maya.' As I said hello, I gulped, so my heart wouldn't pound out of my mouth and make me say something silly. He spoke some Eng-lish and I some Spanish. They were words that were really useful at the time like, 'Where is the post office?' but I sat with them both for half an hour and then I left. I went to bed with my head full of this man called Marcos, hoping that I would see him the next day.

Before dinner, Marcos appeared. The French girls were hanging around him so I went onto the terrace and sat on the wall. Soon after, he came to join me. Typical of fate, I thought. I had less than a week left and I was attracted to this man in a way that I couldn't even begin to explain. Maybe it was the way he seemed so in control. A man in control allows no room for instability, chaos or change; you knew where you were with such stability. Women flocked around him but he seemed not to care.

Véronique, a French girl who was really very attractive, came over as we sat talking. He asked her to get a lighter from his room and handed her his keys. When she came down and stood with a lighter and a box of cigarettes in her hand, he turned to me and said, 'Have dinner with me tonight.' He had Véronique in the palm of his hand, but he didn't want her, he wanted me. I met him that evening and the next, and then on the third evening, he kissed me and I felt like everything that had gone before didn't matter so much.

Ravi Thakker was the man who replaced my father and the one who threw our lives into chaos once again. When I first met him, I thought he looked like a duck. We barely had time to have Amma to ourselves and then he waddled into our lives. First with a big box of assorted chocolates and a pink jack-in-the-box, I mean, what did he think I was going to do with that? Then as the months went by, he came loaded with games, toys and other gifts, trying to buy our affection.

The first time he arrived, he took us to see some boring waxworks and we went for a pizza. That was the best bit of it because it was the very first time we'd had pizza, all stringy cheese and tomato. I loved it, Amma liked it too. She normally never ate with us when we went to Wimpy, but at Pizza Hut, she pulled out a Tabasco bottle from her handbag, put it on her pizza and ate it all. Ravi Thakker made some comment, I can't remember now what he said, but Amma laughed. She always laughed when he was there, he probably made her nervous. When he left, Satchin and I called him 'Duck bum'. 'Did you see how Duck bum drove his car?' he would say, imitating him, but as the months passed when I did it, Satchin didn't find it funny any more. He grew to like him. Every time we got settled somewhere, something came along to uproot us, and I knew after a few weeks of seeing Ravi, that he was there to stay and that Amma would marry him.

There were the little signs like the way she got dressed up on Sundays when he was coming, brushing her long hair over and over again. She put a deeper colour of lipstick on so it showed. If she was going to marry anyone, I wanted her to marry Tom. Tom was always there for us and he would do anything for Amma. He was the one that invented the pickle story about customers wanting pickles so she would have something else to focus on. I heard him and Maggie talking about it when I was upstairs with them. I was lying on their sofa pretending to be asleep.

'We've got to do something for her, she's an awful lot going for her and I don't want her to end up here for the rest of her life,' Maggie said.

So they talked about ways they could help Amma. When I heard some of their ideas, I wanted to jump up and shout, 'no way', but then they both decided on the pickle story and that was quite good. It was Tom who came up with that. Only after she had begun making those pickles did he find her customers that wanted to buy them, driving for hours and hours. Tom was kind to her, kind to us.

Even when he was tired he would play with us. When he stayed at Maggie's house we would wake him up by jumping up and down on his bed and instead of shouting, he would grab us by the legs and fight until we said 'surrender', he would get us caps and show us how to let them off without a gun and teach us karate moves. When the ice-cream van came he would give us money to go out and get a Flake 99 each and would sit on the wall with us until we finished eating it. Sometimes, on a Friday night if we were at Maggie's, he'd let us watch *Starsky and Hutch* with him; that's what he'd call us, Starsky and Hutch. He really loved us and we loved him and then we had to leave.

'Don't do it, don't marry him, Ma, can't you see he's just some fat duck that wants to take you away from us,' I wanted to scream when she told us. But I had lost Satchin as my ally and deeply regretted cutting off the sleeves and the hood of his parka coat to make myself a body warmer the week before. He looked at me as if to say that he would not support me and would make my life hell if I said no to Amma. So I said yes and then I left Amma to pack my things. Just heaped all my dolls, material, sewing things, scissors and clothes in a corner and said there, that's it, all done. Maggie said she would come and be near us again and Tom didn't say anything, not one word, so the day I was supposed to go across the road and say goodbye, I went to see Fatima instead.

Seeing as it was probably the last time I would see

her, I thought she would invite me in but she didn't. I handed over my Space Hopper because she loved it and could never get enough goes on it and I couldn't see myself jumping up and down on it in Mill Hill. The kids there probably had roller skates and sophisticated toys. I also gave Fatima a paper and envelope set that I made up for her. In my haste, it wasn't done as professionally as it could have been. She looked disappointed at the jagged edges but she said she would write. I said that I would phone her and then I remembered her family didn't have a phone. Her mother called her back in and she ran off. I took a long route home, walking slowly along the filthy grey pavements now covered with cherry tree blossom. 'Achan,' I whispered. 'She's getting married to a man called Ravi Thakker, but I won't forget you, ever.' They were waiting for me outside and I didn't have enough time to say goodbye to Tom or Maggie and that was the only thing that stopped me from crying.

Amma's wedding was horrific. I was followed around by Ravi's mother who thought she was my newly adopted grandmother. She kept pinching my cheeks with her oily fingers that she had not bothered to wipe after the buffet. 'Such a cute girl,' she said to everyone who passed, 'Looks exactly like her mother.' How would she know anyway? I could have been the spitting image of my father. Another woman called Nita agreed, nodding furiously, and then looking over at her own children added, 'but Beta, such a pretty girl could have chosen a prettier dress.' Ra-ra skirts and puffy blouses or pedal pushers with T-bar shoes were not for

165

the style-conscious, only for sheep who wanted to follow the current fashion trend. 'Maggie and I made this,' I said defiantly, looking in Maggie's direction. 'Yes, yes, that would make sense,' said the chief spokeswoman.

I followed this Nita specimen into the bathroom and, as she went in, I jammed the lock with a few hairpins. Nobody missed her and she came out an hour later, looking shaken and dishevelled. She gathered up her two meringue-attired children, found her husband (who was engrossed with Jack Daniels) and left. The oily-fingered grandma came over, screeching, 'You must come to America, Beta, and visit us. We'll take you to Disneyland,' heaving me into her bosom as if Disneyland were situated there. The grandpops splattered his Bombay mix everywhere as he said, 'You and your brother, come anytime, we're related now.' What kind of a family was this?

Ravi Thakker's house smelt of polished floors and fresh paint. It was obviously redecorated to impress us. He had done up my room with horrible bright pink polka dots which kept me awake at night. I couldn't really sleep, so I wandered into Satchin's room and slept in the spare bed he had. Satchin didn't like this and filled the bed with his trainers and I had to stop doing this. When he reached his teens, he put obstacles between us, obliterating all that had happened before and so I reminded him of the stories of how it used to be and what we used to do together. It was no use, Satchin wasn't interested, he had bonded with the cricket-loving Ravi. Ravi had won and Satchin was on his side. I made it clear to Ravi that no matter how many gifts he brought me or wherever he took me, he would never be my father. That he didn't even come close. 'Okay, Maya,' was always the way he responded, he never shouted. Okay, Ravi Thakker, it was them against me, but Maggie would be moving out of the East End of London and she would be here soon.

The train pulled into Valamoro and lots of passengers got off as it was market day. Valamoro, the neighbouring town, was much bigger than Palmadoro, it had a lot more shops, restaurants and bars. I often came to the market here on Sunday mornings just to feel the bustle of activity and to see the gypsies who would come in and sell their handmade goods. I always bought something from the children, a handwoven bracelet or necklace, but I couldn't wear it back in Palmadoro as it caused such unnecessary arguments between Marcos and I.

'If you need a bracelet, Maya, I will buy one for you, but don't wear things you have bought off the street, it's cheap.'

The first time we argued was three days before Father Antonio's course finished. One of Marcos's friends had informed me that he was thirty-two and not a student, as I had been led to believe.

'You're twelve years older than me and you are not a student. You lied and I cannot cope with deceit, any form of deceit,' I shouted.

'I never lied to you, Maya. I didn't say anything when you asked. It doesn't make a difference, does it?'

'Don't you understand, it's not the age . . .' I stormed out, unable to finish my sentence.

A few hours later he came looking for me. I was

sitting alone in the games room. He came in and locked the door behind him and said that it was different with me, he knew from the first time we had met that there was something special. He took out his wallet and showed me strands of long, black hair. 'Yours,' he said. If anyone else had done that, I would have thought it was sick, but the way Marcos did it made me laugh. 'Maya, I promise you, I will tell you no half-truths. I want you to stay here, it's summer and you don't have to be back yet for another three weeks.' He said the words with such certainty. The day after, he changed my flights and I stayed on.

Father Antonio was delighted that I took such an interest in his course so he continued with private tuition. Marcos and I spent the rest of the summer together and then it was time to go back home. He drove me to the airport and he assured me he would come and see me in Edinburgh in a month's time and, in the meantime, he would call. I wasn't upset that I was leaving, it wasn't like I had an overwhelming urge to stay, and in the back of my mind, I prepared myself for the fact that he might not call, maybe it was just a holiday thing. We parted at the airport.

I spent five days at home and then term began again. Summer seemed so far away as I went back to study. Architecture was boring, it wasn't how I expected it to be, and the people on the course were pretentious. Maybe it was me; everyone else managed to find a group and get into the social life. As soon as I got back, I took up Spanish as an extra module and also developed a keen interest in Spanish architecture. Marcos called every day like he said he would, early in the mornings waking all my flatmates, but it didn't matter. His calls were what I waited for because I grew to really miss him, I made myself miss him.

It was difficult to concentrate at university. I didn't go out, I didn't really want to. Being away from Marcos just seemed to bring us closer. Two months passed and he came to Edinburgh. I met him as he stepped off the airport bus that came into the city centre and it felt like we should never have been separated. Holding each other on that windy afternoon, nobody else existed and for most of those two weeks we were inseparable. I think you can love someone just from a desperate need to feel part of something, to belong to someone, to make the loneliness inside go away.

Marcos didn't understand a word when the Scottish guide was giving him an in-depth explanation of Edinburgh Castle. Marcos stared at him and nodded in agreement and winked at me. We both burst out laughing in the eerie silence of that place. The other visitors tutted and were annoyed as we couldn't stop and had to be escorted out.

That is how it was for those two weeks, we laughed, we understood each other and he made me feel safe. I got to see a very tender side of him, a side that only I knew existed. As if by being away from Palmadoro, he became himself without the constraint of pretending to be someone important, he was free and was almost childlike and vulnerable. Maybe it was ego, but I felt I did this to him, he needed me as much as I needed him. And I think now, that was what it was, he touched a part of me that no one else had managed to, it was a need to take care of someone and make things better for them, a vulnerability I could understand. I didn't want the two weeks to come to an end. As the taxi took us to the airport, an anxiety took hold of me and time stood still when he kissed me goodbye. When I went back to the house, I discovered notes and gifts from him hidden in every conceivable place. I tried to carry on as normal but thought only of Marcos.

At Christmas, I decided not to go back to study; I wasn't enjoying the course and another year couldn't be wasted pretending I did. So when the time came to pack my bags and head back to Edinburgh, I told Ravi and Amma that I wasn't going. I said I didn't think architecture was for me, I wanted to take a year off and go to Spain to study Spanish. Ravi and Amma were shocked and did everything they could to dissuade me. They called Maggie in but even Maggie wasn't enough to stop me.

Maggie liked Ravi Thakker's house and said it was like a palace. To my horror, she even liked Ravi Thakker and said he was decent. Decent, she hadn't met his parents yet, the mother and father duck. Maggie moved into the flat above the pickle shop and of course Ravi helped her, he knew how to play tactically, I would give him that, he was a good opponent. His great weakness was a dislike for animals, it was more a fear. Maggie made him a cup of tea for the trouble he had gone to in helping her move, seeing as Tom was busy. As Ravi sat down, I placed One Eye on his lap, expecting him to shake the cat off, kicking it away with an erratic gesture or that jerk thing he did so we all could see his true nature, but he sat there, looking petrified. Maggie pulled the cat off him. 'Maya, now don't do that again, you know your father is allergic to cats.'

'My father loved cats actually, we had three of them,' I retorted.

They both looked uncomfortable and then he said it was time he was leaving. I stayed to help Maggie unpack.

She tried to convince me to give him a go but I said the best I could manage was not to cause trouble and, given time, everybody would see what he was really like. Time would tell. 'Life doesn't always work out the way we imagine. Sometimes the worst things end up being the best and other times, what we think is the best thing that ever happened is not necessarily so, and people we don't like end up being the kindest, most generous people,' she said. Maggie wouldn't understand, she always had her father there, not some intruder who came with lots of money. Maggie had so many outfits that they couldn't be squeezed into the cupboards, so we left most of them in a suitcase and put it under the bed in the spare room. I asked if I could move in and she said no, it was always better to be a visitor.

Over that summer, before school started, I went as often as I could to see her. When she wasn't working in the shop with Amma, she helped me make clothes, showing me how to cut patterns. Maggie had bought an endless supply of fabrics and colourful pieces of sari material before she left from the Indian lady on Green Street. Soft material that went on and on that I could tear into angry pieces or snip with calm precision. All could be stitched together, making whatever creation we wanted to. I had control over the fabric, the rest of my life was out of my hands.

The summer ended as it had begun, busily and too quickly. I started a new secondary school. It was all girls and I had to wear a pale blue uniform and lose the rough accent. I didn't really lose it, it just got polished over with refined tones so that after eight weeks nobody could distinguish between Sandra Bailey, star pupil, lacrosse champion and netball team captain, and me. I was in a nice class led by Mrs Harrison who took no nonsense. It's funny how things work; for years in my old school, I tried to be popular and now that I really didn't care, they wanted me around. Some of the girls even copied the way I wore my skirt and tie. I don't know if it was being aloof that drew them to me. I made friends with everybody but nobody in particular as I didn't know how long we were going to stay this time and there was no point in getting close to people. After school, I taught Amma how to do fractions and also long division; I explained that it would come in useful when she was in the shop. On Saturday, I was allowed to go in with her.

Maggie loved the shop and it was hard to separate her from it. Most of the customers became her friends. It was a hang-out for lots of blue-rinse oldies who would stand there talking for hours about hip replacements and pacemakers; the only time they would draw breath was when they remembered to collect their pensions to pay for the many jars they consumed. They would coo at me and ruffle my hair as I rang up their purchases at the till and then I had to be polite and offer them a plastic bag, but they always asked me to come across to them and place the goods in their trolleys. Another excuse to prolong conversation by talking about my height or my hair.

Smart women came in with really expensive clothes. They were probably aware that Edgware was not quite the fashion metropolis they had hoped for but they didn't seem to mind. Other customers would sniff at the bottles of pickles, smearing them with their dirty fingerprints and then they would put them back on the shelves. Amma caught me one day asking a man if he was going to pay for it now that his grubby fingers were all over the jar. She pulled me to one side and told me that the people that came into the shop were special and the last thing they needed was to be spoken to like that. Both Maggie and Amma decided that customer services was not my forte and assigned me to help out in the back. Fatima would have been in her element there with a real life-size cash register, but I was glad. It got very boring listening to people go on and on about the effects that an old mango or a crusty lemon could have on them, I mean, really. It was much more fun being out back.

The kitchen was like a Bollywood movie set with Hindi music playing in the background. One song that was played over and over again had a wailing woman being serenaded by a squeaky-voiced man set to a funky disco beat. The action began with dramatic tears from Deepa which were trickling over the mangoes. She had been thrown out by her mother because she was caught dating a Muslim boy across the road from where she lived. Her sister-in-law, Anita, tried to comfort her, but there was work to be done and she took it upon herself to be the kitchen supervisor. After an afternoon of high drama, Anita offered her a place to stay until she made it up with her parents. That was the first week and then it continued like a serial.

Govind, who fancied himself as Amitabh Buchan, was taken on a week later. He looked nothing like the film star, and was weedy enough to have easily been sucked up by the ventilation fan, but he was very funny and had these really weird dance moves. He danced around the kitchen, looking at his face in the pots and pans whilst giving orders and instructions on how best to use the machinery. There were confrontations between Anita and him and many times she nearly hit him with a spatula. He took no notice. Deepa had to appear to side with her sister-in-law, as four weeks had passed and she knew she was outstaying her welcome. The situation with her mother had deteriorated and had not been resolved because Deepa could not get her lips around 'arranged marriage', but she made out to Anita that peace-keeping negotiations had begun and the terms of a formal agreement were being drawn up.

The next week I went in, Deepa was wearing a tight red sari blouse which was covered by a flimsy nylon sari, the end of which accidentally slipped into the big mixing bowl, so Govind had to fish it out and put it back on her shoulder. At this point she giggled quietly so Anita could not hear and then Amma came in to ask if anyone would be interested in overtime. Anita said she couldn't because she had to go and get her little boy from the childminder, Govind said he would stay and then Deepa hurriedly agreed too. I don't know what happened after that because I had to go home and do my homework, but the next time I saw them, I caught them glancing across at each other over the pickle machine and that same evening when they thought nobody was out the back, I heard him whisper to her that he 'lubbed' her.

The drama unfolded when his younger brother came to work at the shop. He was a lot more attractive and did not wear his hair in a centre parting that did him no favours. Not ascertaining the situation, Amit made advances towards Deepa in the form of a cheesy smile and wink. She was flattered and looked down to concentrate on washing her mangoes. David, the driver, also made some comment about how nice she was looking these days and Govind, sensing the competition, stepped up the tempo, took her out to the Chinese takeaway and told her again that he would do anything for her. At around the same time her sister-in-law was fed up of her leaving her clothes and dirty cups everywhere and asked her to move back to her mother's house. She told Govind to prove how much he loved her and he asked her to marry him. I can't remember how long they lasted together, but I remember Deepa leaving and Amit shortly following her.

Satchin and his best friend, Suri, also came to the shop on Saturdays. They would both laugh at the outfits I made and wore. 'Nice trousers', he would begin, then Satchin would burst out laughing and follow suit. Suri's parents were both doctors and he seemed to know everything about anything. He was an only child and it showed because he stuck to Satchin like a leech. He appeared out of nowhere and attached himself to our family. First he came to borrow books after school, then to play on the computer and then he stayed for dinner. He did this by flattering Amma on some snacks she had offered him and before you knew it, he had almost taken up residence in our house. 'Don't be so grumpy, Maya, he is an only child and his parents work very hard, he probably misses them,' Amma would say.

Oh yes, the infamous doctors who were busy saving lives. I couldn't believe why I had been sidelined in favour of a boring know-it-all who did his break-dancing moves behind the shop when he thought no one was looking. He also had absolutely no style and wore purple Farah trousers and chequered green tank tops. But then I suppose it could have been worse, they could have been yellow. Suri did acknowledge me, smiling and nodding when he saw me, which was more than Satchin did now, and sometimes he helped me carry the trays of finished pickles out to the side room. As time went on, I made a point not to go into the shop on Saturdays wearing my creations, but dressed in trainers and tracksuits, hoping that one day they would invite me along to the park where they always went after finishing in the shop. I even took my tennis racket along, but usually I had to go home.

One day, though, they were really desperate and asked me to stand in as wicketkeeper because they were a man down. This was the lucky break I had waited for. I knew it had to be a matter of time. I walked to the back of the stumps and concentrated really hard so I wouldn't let Satchin down. It was going really well and then it all stopped abruptly after half-time when I threw the ball back at the bowler, missing his hands, hitting his head and knocking him out. Suri told me not to worry about it, that these things happened, but Satchin was furious and didn't talk to me for weeks. Amma told me not to worry because there would be more people in the house to talk to. She said we were expecting guests and I would be busy with them.

Ravi Thakker collected me from school as he had taken the day off work to get the oily-fingered grandma and the spluttering grandpops from the airport. They had arrived from Chicago to give my mother a hand with the new baby but there were still another two months to go. The idea was probably to get comfortable so we would have an invasion of the duck family and it would be hard to relocate them afterwards. Fingers was waiting for me with the door open and almost suffocated me with her grip, saying that I had grown to be so tall and that I was looking so pretty, growing to be like my mother every day. The grandpops shook my hand and squeezed my shoulder with a, 'So lovely to see you again, Beta, you have grown into a big girl since the last time I saw you.' He indicated my height back then, pointing to his rickety knee. It had only been two years and I thought he might be suffering from the onset of some debilitating memory loss so I didn't make a comment.

Fingers had only been there for five minutes but she had managed to find the time to lay on a big spread. I didn't really like Indian food and Amma always cooked me something different, but I made an effort not to be rude and I sat and ate with them. Amma was relieved, she was looking a little bit tired and since she was pregnant, I decided not to be so awkward and give her a hard time. Everything was going okay until grandpops told us the story of how the customs officials had stopped them and checked the contents of their numerous tins. Fingers interrupted him, saying, 'But I told them, it was only the food I made for my children.' The idea of the food going off on a long-haul flight, only to be fingered by a customs official, made me want to be sick. I got up and ran, but didn't manage to make it to the bathroom and it landed on her suitcase, which was blocking the door. Amma and Ravi Thakker looked horrified. Fingers was good about it, but followed me around for days saying that it was good she had arrived because I needed looking after.

Maggie liked her, but then Maggie never said anything bad about anyone. 'She means well,' she would say, but Maggie didn't hear what Fingers said about her, especially when she found out she was living with Uncle Jack and wasn't married to him. Fingers had managed to herd up a group of friends, I don't know from where exactly. I think she might have shepherded them in from the local temples, community centres and old family connections that she looked up. It was all under the premise that she could calculate their astrological charts and tell them exactly which direction their lives were heading. She looked very professional making her calculations, adding it all up, hesitating for a moment before drawing square boxes, but as time went on, I realised that she did exactly the same for everyone and had a strategy where she would elicit information by randomly dropping in questions and then make it look like she had worked it all out. Then she divulged the information to the other women, adding a little bit more here and there.

The house was filled with her friends, you'd open rooms to find another Indian lady and another and another, brightly dressed, of all shapes and sizes. All hoping that she might impart some of her wisdom and tell them things were going to get better. She soon whittled all the ladies down to form an inner clique, who she invited around every two days. They all sat in a circle, dressed in bright saris and wrapped in cardigans that looked like they came from the Help the Aged shop. If it was really cold, Fingers got out her woolly hat. Sometimes they sang bhajans together. One of them was an old grandma who nobody could touch because she was keeping herself pure for God. She refused to eat anything from our house, even drink masala tea because she said that the smell would put God off and he wouldn't listen to her prayers. Five minutes later, she pulled out a snuff box and inhaled the contents. So God was against the scent of spices but he wasn't averse to a bit of narcotics then.

Another granny wasn't that old, about fifty-something, but she looked haggard. It was quite unfortunate because she worked in a shoe shop but she couldn't pronounce her 'Sh's'. 'A soe sop', she repeated when I asked her where was it again that she worked. We wouldn't use her for nursery rhymes when the baby came, especially not 'Ba ba black seep' or 'she sells sea shells on the sea shore.' They provided a much-needed source of entertainment for me, despite the fact they made lots of noise with their uncontrollable cackling and gossiping.

One day, I heard Fingers tell her closest ally, Nita, about the time she found Ravi Thakker at her door. I stopped doing my homework and put my ear to the wall. They were living in India at the time and making preparations to go to Uganda when a little boy who was six years old wearing threadbare clothes came knocking at their door. He was an orphan, a beggar boy. When she said that, an image came to my mind of him; he

179

was one of the beach children, hankering after a balloon. Her mother-in-law took him in to train as a servant but soon Fingers grew attached to him because he was kind and thoughtful and made them laugh with a song and dance act he picked up off the street. He was also very smart and could learn words and numbers after seeing them just once. When the time came to leave for Uganda, she didn't want to leave him behind so took him there as her own. It was very difficult, as her older son disliked him intensely and always treated him as an outsider, but Ravi made good friends and studied well and managed to get himself to university. He was going to get married when Idi Amin suddenly took power and his fiancée's family were forced to leave overnight, so there was no way of telling him where they were going.

He thought she might have come to England as she had close family here so he came looking for her. Years passed and he never found her. Fingers thought he would never get married and then he met Amma. Fingers said quite frankly that although my mother was not educated, from a different class altogether and had two children, it was better he marry her than remain alone for the rest of his life.

I began to see Ravi Thakker in a completely new light. He knew what it was to lose someone, to feel that heart-wrenching loss that cannot be made better by anything, and then to have life turn completely upside down: twice he had experienced that. I had lost my Ammamma and Achan, we shared the same thing. He made my mother happy, anyone could see that, and he tried with us, although many times he got things wrong. A week later my new sister was born. I brought them a card and signed it to Amma and Dad and I let him kiss my forehead.

Much to the disappointment of Fingers, they named my little sister after my grandmother Ammu. She was born two days after I turned thirteen. As I held her, she looked so vulnerable and innocent. The new baby's arrival meant a new start for all of us and everything that had gone before seemed not to matter so much. I told Ravi that if he still wanted to change my name to Thakker so it would fit with everyone else in the family, then it was okay by me. He was absolutely shocked.

The ticket inspector called out for tickets. This was the one who thought he was Casanova of the railways and took every opportunity given to extend conversation with any woman on his train. He would caress their hands as he took their tickets to clip. I pretended to have that just-woken-up look as if I didn't know where exactly I was.

'*¿Dónde va morena?*'

'*A casa,*' I replied curtly, as I snatched the ticket back off him.

'Home' sounded really strange as I said it. Spain was now my home, I meant . . .

He tried to continue the conversation but I closed my eyes.

Ravi and Amma brought Maggie around to persuade me to go back to Edinburgh and continue with architecture. 'You can't keep running away, Maya, darling,' she said. 'One day it all catches up with you and you've got to face it.'

'You mean like you did? Faced up to everything, did

you?' I retorted. The words came out before I could stop them and she looked at me, hurt and disappointed, but tried not to let it show. I wanted to say I didn't mean it, that I was sorry, but I couldn't.

'I wouldn't mind if you went because you wanted to travel and see the world but you're going because you think you have found something else, Maya, and you haven't. What you are looking for has always been right here. It is not what you think it is, it is not over there, it's right here. I know it gets a little hard, darling, but ride it through. Talk to me about it, you know you can, you always used to. You always used to come around and tell me things. What's happened to us, Maya?' she continued.

Maggie just didn't know and I didn't want to say anything because whatever I had to say she wouldn't understand, she couldn't. I shook my head. She pressed my hand and kissed me. I looked down as she got up to leave. I wanted to go after her, give her a big hug, and pour out everything and tell her that I needed her, that I wanted it all back, the way it used to be between us, but I left it. Locking my bedroom door, I crawled into bed, pulled the duvet over my head and fell asleep. A few hours later, a little knocking sound would not go away.

My little sister began calling out my name so she could come in and pester me. I let her in and she ran towards the bed and immediately began trying on the shoes and the clothes that I had emptied from the cupboards.

'Where are you going, Mayo?'

'Away, Bobo.'

'Why are you crying?'

'I'm not crying, Bobo, I'm just tired.'

'When will you come back?'

'Soon,' I said.

'When is soon?'

I lifted her up and sat her on the bed. 'By the time you have learnt all your times tables, that is when I will come back.'

She looked upset. 'But you know I don't like them and that will take forever.'

'It won't, you know your two times already. What are eight twos?'

'Fifteen,' she replied.

Maybe not, I thought.

'You won't go away like Satchin, will you, Mayo? You won't leave and not come back?'

'No, Shorty.' I pushed her over the bed so she lay on her back.

'Mayo, Mayo, is it really true that if you swallow an apple pip, the seed will grow into a tree in your stomach?'

'Of course it is, so maybe by the time I come back you'll have turned into a little tree.' I began to tickle her stomach and she laughed hysterically.

Amma didn't come to the airport, taking ownership of a bad headache. It was just Ravi and myself. Ravi talked around Spain; the fact that India had lost the cricket; how traffic was slower than usual because of the icy roads, and the direction that the Conservatives might take since Major had taken over from Thatcher. That was Ravi; he never hit things head on but walked delicately around them so as not to offend or upset. He was like one of those buffers, safe and reliable, preferring not to see what was in front of him but looking around to the sides, hoping that whatever it was that was coming towards him might veer off the road and go away. We got to the airport and I said he didn't have to come in but he wanted to. There was still an hour and a half to wait but I wanted to get to the departure lounge. I said goodbye to Ravi, adding that I would see them all very soon.

'This is for you, Maya,' he said, pulling out an envelope. I kissed him again and went through the gates. As I sat waiting for the plane, I opened it and inside was some money with a simple note: 'We love you. Ammu, Amma and Dad.'

As the baggage was being unloaded at Barajas airport, I went into the ladies' and made up my face, putting on the lipstick colour that Marcos liked best and trying to draw a straight black line across my eyelids. The eyeliner went everywhere, a combination of nerves and because I wasn't used to it, so I covered the mess with some eyeshadow and made my way to find my case.

Marcos stood there waiting for me at the meeting point and I abandoned my trolley in the middle of the walkway as I ran towards him. Kissing him and holding him, he hoisted me up and swung me around. I knew I had made the right decision. 'Maya, I can't believe it, you came. I can't wait, I have something that you will love, Maya, you will adore it.' He held me tightly. My heart leapt as I thought of the possibilities: a ring would be too soon; the painting, I thought, the painting that I had done of the two of us, perhaps he had it framed as promised. We walked out of the terminal, clutching each other, and went into the car park. He pulled out a set of keys and pointed it around so that an alarm went off and lights began flashing. 'Do you see it?' he asked me, pointing, 'It's mine.' We got into a new metallic silver BMW and the seats could not have been any lower than my heart was at that point.

'It's . . . really nice,' I replied.

I got a full explanation of power steering and suspension. Maybe I was feeling this way because it was late. We drove to Palmadoro.

Marcos had moved out of the halls of residence into a flat shared with two friends, Miguel and Roberto. We arrived in the middle of the night so I didn't get to see them immediately, but I bumped into Roberto mid-morning, after I woke up, and he introduced himself. Marcos had gone back to work and left me a note on the kitchen table along with a glass of freshly squeezed orange juice and a set of keys. It will work, I kept saying to myself, he remembers the small details. I got dressed and ventured out.

The sun was beaming down, despite the fact that it was cold outside. The local bar was bustling with people shouting above each other, clattering coffee cups, and waiters who did their best to look in control of the situation knowing that they were fighting a losing battle. Orders were fired at them as they charged around carrying trays stacked with cups, cutlery and wet dishcloths, running between the women, their fur coats and prams; the workmen who were restoring the church; the town hall officials who had popped in for a quick ten-minute respite, and a group of elderly men who were playing cards in the corner.

People stopped to stare momentarily, finding me an exotic curiosity. Then they got back to what they were doing. A few of the workmen whistled and said things that I couldn't understand, the older ladies began laughing and shouted retorts across the table. I sat at the bar, ordered a coffee and let the different tempo wash over me. Another new beginning, I thought, drinking my coffee. I had retreated to a place where once again, I was the outsider. I left my harassed waiter with a tip as he had managed to keep smiling throughout and then went to the supermarket to pick up a few things for lunch and dinner.

Miguel had arrived back at the flat and opened the door as I struggled with the key. 'Maya, how are you?' he shouted enthusiastically. 'Marcos said you were coming.'

I felt relieved to see a warm, familiar face and I hugged him. 'It's so good to see you.'

'You know, Maya, I never thought it would last longer than the summer, but I am really happy that you are back.'

Are you? Do you think I have done the right thing? I wanted to ask but at that moment Marcos rushed in. He said he could not stay for lunch as he was teaching law at the faculty over lunchtime. He kissed me fleetingly and said he would be back for dinner. Miguel tried not to look embarrassed and invited me to sit and eat with him.

After lunch, Miguel and Roberto went for a siesta. I didn't know what to do and after flicking through all the TV channels and finding nothing but huge peroxided ladies displaying their goods on every programme, I decided that the best thing was to go to sleep as well.

After I woke up, I went for a long walk. On the side of a hill overlooking the town a cross had been built. I sat there looking at the miles of stone wall that snugly enveloped the monastery and buildings, keeping them safe from invaders. Suddenly, I felt as unwelcome as they would have been. Around the wall were cypress trees, growing taller so they could get a peek at what was going on inside. Over to my right was some misplaced scaffolding that seemed to represent the mess and confusion of my own head. I went back and waited for Marcos to come home.

Killing time, I started cooking some disastrous concoction of eggs, garlic sauce and pasta. How Amma would laugh at me if she could see me now, struggling with the ingredients. So many times throughout my childhood she tried to get me to cook with her in the warmth of her kitchen, and perhaps in my early teens, I spent a few moments there but that was all, a brief moment. Many things were sent to come between us and the result, my feelings of absolute rejection, was symbolised by what was cooking now: a few basic packet ingredients thrown together chaotically which tasted bitter and smelt burnt. I had a bath, got dressed up, put on some make-up and waited for Marcos. It was eleven o'clock before he arrived home.

A month into my stay, this emerged into a standard routine. I thought of Maggie seeing me turning into a woman occupied by cleaning, lunchtime soap operas, siestas, shoulder pads and lipstick. 'Oh, you'll never make a lady, darling, Maya, all that prettiness is wasted on you. You have to make an effort with yourself every day instead of hiding behind that sweatshirt of yours,' she nagged, on the days I went to the shop in a tracksuit. I called my family to say that I was really happy and life in Spain was great. I ended the conversation by saying that I didn't understand why people lived in England. Ammu picked up the other line to kiss me goodbye and recited her three times table. She ended by saying that at this rate, I would have to come home soon. If only it were that easy Shorty, I would come home on the first flight back.

Sensing my boredom, Marcos enrolled me on a Spanish course in Madrid. I commuted four hours every day and had four hours of language courses which were divided by a huge lunch. Things improved greatly as the days went by and I met other foreigners who had come to Spain. Most had become English language teachers. A particular student who looked as lost and confused as I did was a girl called Jennifer. She had come from the States to forget her boyfriend, Steve. Not really to forget him but he had asked her to marry him and she got scared and wanted to see if she could survive a year without being with him. If, at the end of it, they both felt the same, she would go back and marry. Initially, I began smiling at her when I sensed that she too did not understand the purpose of the subjunctive. Then we went for out for coffees which turned into lunches.

Our friendship grew quite quickly in the way that it does when you are in a strange place. You feel the need to tell a new friend everything about yourself, maybe because this familiarity is the only thing that is solid and stable in all that is foreign, or perhaps it is because we sense that the friendship is transitory and so we try to cram as much as we can in our time together. Spain did this to many of us; we made it into a safe place where nothing mattered so you could share your innermost thoughts with people that didn't know you, or you could escape whatever you wanted to. Jen thought it was crazy to commute to Palmadoro every day and said that I should move in with her until the course finished.

I spoke to Marcos about it that evening and he didn't want me to go, saying that he would leave work a little earlier so we could spend more time together. It wasn't the fact that I needed to spend more time together, it was more a question of finding my own space. I said it would only be for another six weeks and then I would move back and, in the meantime, I would come to Palmadoro on Friday evenings and leave on Monday mornings. He agreed reluctantly and that is what I did.

Madrid was amazing. It came alive at night with so much energy. People squeezed every minute of fun out of the hours. Eating, dancing and drinking until the early hours of the morning, not caring that they had to get up and go to work in the morning. Jen and I would go out most evenings with people we met from the course or friends of friends. I couldn't last until three or four o' clock in the morning so I left around one and the rest of them would continue on. Friday nights, I would catch the train back to Palmadoro, spend the weekend with Marcos in the hills and then catch the first train on Monday, which left at five-thirty in the morning. Things were getting much better between us and we made the most of the weekends by visiting places and doing things. I loved him when he came out of Palmodoro and stopped trying to be important.

The six weeks were almost over and I thought that there was no point in going back to live in Palmadoro. Jen said that the school where she was teaching were always looking for English speakers and she would ask around to see if I could do anything. On Tuesday, I went in for an interview and on Friday afternoon, Loretta, the head of the English School, asked me to come in to see when I could start and to discuss the classes I would take. She gave me twenty-five hours a week of children's classes and said that in the hours I had off, I could attend the Spanish classes that they also ran. I was elated.

I took the first train back to Palmadoro to tell Marcos. Marcos was furious, arguing that there was no need for me to work, especially in Madrid, that he thought the whole point of me coming to Spain was so we could be together. 'We can,' I insisted, 'I will come up every weekend as I already do.' We spent the rest of Friday in silence until I broke it by making some stupid joke.

'I'm sorry, Maya *cariño*, but you know it is only because I miss you.'

'I know and I miss you when you are not around,' I said, reassuring him.

Sometimes on journeys back to Madrid, I questioned why I put up with such outbursts, the long period of silence that followed every argument and the constant reassurance that I so needed myself but gave to another. On each trip, I resolved to do something about it but then when I saw him, I caved in; it was like I had this overwhelming compulsion to make things better, even if it was to my own detriment. At other times, I remembered how it was in Scotland or the times we went on holiday together, thinking that if only he could manage to get out of Palmadoro, he could then be himself, the Marcos that I knew he was and not someone who was desperate to prove how important they were.

I didn't realise at the time that it wasn't him that needed to be rescued.

I taught two age groups; four to eight years and twelve to sixteen. The younger children were like my little sister, jumping out of their seats, coming to sit on my lap, distracting me, telling me things like their dad had forgotten to brush their teeth for them that morning or whatever else occurred to them. The elder children had more concentration and I tried to make it much more of a structured class, not like with the little ones, who I allowed to disrupt me. It was different with the older children, they had to sit exams and had parental aspirations firmly propping them up in their chairs. It was amusing watching the relationships evolve between some of the boys and girls, secret and innocent, that first love that is impossible to experience again. Hormones would be flying around with the notes and glances that were exchanged when I turned to write on the blackboard. I hoped that they would guard their feelings safely and look back on them with tenderness when they were older.

When I was fifteen, my mother sent me on an errand to pick up some spices from Wembley which was about half an hour from where we lived. Wembley has a street which is like being in Mumbai: different shops and stalls selling saris, Indian jewellery, exotic fruits, vegetables and spices, wall-to-wall stalls lined up on both sides of the road, heaving with bright colours, pungent smells and noise from the street, a replica of a little India built to help take away some of the homesickness that the inhabitants felt. Amma often sent me there when she ran out of things, realising at the last minute she needed fundamental ingredients. She seemed increasingly absent-minded at that time, as if she had something playing on her mind.

After a while Amma sold the shop so she could spend more time looking after my little sister. Fingers had finally left. I think my mother had had enough of her and my little sister didn't particularly take to her grand-mother, turning back and crawling in the opposite direc-tion when she caught sight of her. Amma and Maggie worked a couple of days a week from the house, nothing like they did before. Amma seemed to let the business slide, not really having any more passion for it. The air of magic that surrounded her, which made everyone stop and look when she walked into a room, had dis-appeared. Several kilos took up residence around her waist and she made no attempt to hide it with her sari. Ravi loved her anyway and didn't say anything.

I didn't really want to go to Wembley that Saturday, a few of the girls from class were going to catch an afternoon matinee and I knew that I wouldn't make it on time.

'Maya just do it please, no arguing,' Amma shouted. Satchin had been taken hostage by exams and so he couldn't leave the house, so I went. On the way back from picking up the saffron and bay leaves, I stopped at a newsagent's.

'Do you have *Just Seventeen*?' I asked. The oblong-shaped woman at the counter called to her son who was out in the back, she shouted at him to check if they had any left. The son replied back in English with a heavy Indian accent that made me laugh. He was so obviously one of those chameleon types that spoke like that in front of his parents and then as soon as he was let out, he pounded the streets with another accent. He came out, fighting with the hanging tassels that separated the shop from the stockroom and as I looked up, I saw Suri. I was stunned.

'Hi, Suri,' I said, unfazed.

He looked distressed and handed me the magazine. So this was the infamous Mrs Rama that we never got to see because she and her husband were always 'on call', consultant gynaecologist and obstetrician that they were. At that point, his father came in and asked him to help unload a delivery.

'Pleased to meet you, Mrs Rama, I'm Satchin's sister,' I said, but she looked puzzled and smiled. I paid her and left. I was thinking about Suri as I waited for the bus, had he been taking my brother to see some other parents that he had made up? Had Satchin ever seen them? Did he know? Suddenly, he appeared and put his hand on my shoulder.

'Maya, I have to talk to you, I really do.'

'It's not important, Suri, it doesn't matter. I won't say anything to anyone.'

The bus came along. 'I have to go,' I said. He jumped on and sat next to me.

'Maya, I'm not ashamed of them being shopkeepers, it's easier because . . . well, you wouldn't understand because your father is a businessman.'

'You do know that Ravi is not my father, not my real one?'

He stared at me blankly.

'You do know, don't you?'

He shook his head.

How could he not know? How could Satchin not tell him? Erase Achan from his mind like he never existed. All those years Satchin and I had spent looking after each other meant nothing to him, forgotten with a posh house and a good school. So the memory of our real father meant nothing! I started to mumble incoherently, no wonder he never referred to the past. Suri began to laugh and then I stopped, took a deep breath and told him how we had come to England, how my father had died and as I explained, tears welled in my eyes. It was never talked about. He touched my shoulder and then I described the move to Maggie's house and how Ravi came from nowhere and replaced my father. I talked like time was a sparse commodity. It was an insatiable need to tell someone and to be heard and after I finished, I felt better, much better, as if a weight had been lifted from me. Suri listened, just listened without saying anything. Then he talked.

He told me that he had received a scholarship to go to Satchin's school, that his parents worked all hours in the shop and their only focus was to make sure he had the best education. So he went on all the ski trips and did all the other stuff with the money they saved for him and the money Amma gave him for coming in on Saturdays. There was no six-bedroomed mansion or au pair; they lived in a semi in Wembley. He made it all up so he didn't have to feel different from the other boys.

We shared so much on that bus ride and as we got off, he said he would walk me home. No doubt he wanted to play on Satchin's computer or borrow a book. We got to the drive and he looked at me and said, 'I'll see you very soon, Maya.' Then he turned back, heading for the bus stop. He walked all that way, for me. That evening, before I went to sleep, I began thinking about Suri. His calm smile that I trusted, and the strong hands that gently touched mine as he said goodbye, then I fell asleep and woke up, obsessing about the next time I would see him.

Many times I wanted to go to Maggie, tell her what I felt about Suri and ask her if I should go back to his shop to buy another magazine, but whatever my mother had must have been contagious because Maggie, too, seemed very distant. Something had happened between Tom and her. After he had married without telling any of us, she got very upset and didn't speak to him, just cut him off like that, which I thought was so unlike her, so harsh, without a second thought. Even those you most trusted were capable of doing that. Lots of times I told her to pick up the phone to say that she forgave him, it was a silly thing to remain upset over but she never did, despite missing him so much. Tom also made no effort, he cut us off too. It was strange, there was a period of time when we saw him every day and then he just disappeared. Some people just didn't have enough to give.

Suri came around six days later to collect a textbook and stayed to eat with us. Every time I tried to look him in the eye, he avoided my gaze, and I didn't feel like joking around with him and Satchin like I normally did. It was becoming harder; I couldn't concentrate on anything and in everything I did, he was on my mind.

Upstairs, I started sewing pieces of material together in the hope that this would occupy me and my feelings would pass, that this was what that teenage crush thing was about. A few minutes later, there was a knock at my door. It was him. He quickly handed me a plastic bag and then ran downstairs. I heard him say goodbye to Ravi and Amma and then the front door shut.

My heart beat faster as I opened the bag, finding inside a box, which was awkwardly wrapped in pale orange paper. I ripped it open to find a Dundee cake with a note attached to it. 'For all the times I have wanted to get you something and I never knew quite what. Suri.' My heart jumped and I wanted to go running after him, but I couldn't; Amy Willis always said that you should never, ever show a boy that you liked him, you had to 'make them sweat'. I threw the Dundee cake on the bed and I ran down the stairs, out of the house, chasing after him anyway.

'Suri,' I shouted. 'Suri, stop.' He turned around and when I had reached him, I didn't know what to say. I looked up and smiled at him. He kissed me. Our noses collided and he laughed, then he took both my hands, placed them on his face and kissed my forehead and then my eyes, whispering my name, making it sound so very beautiful.

'Suri,' I said seriously. 'You know that there's only one thing that will ever wreck this?'

'What?' He asked

'Those purple Farahs, they've got to go.'

He laughed again as he took my hand and walked me back to the top of my road, promising that despite his exams he would make time to see me and then after that, we would have the whole summer. I wasn't really listening, this is what it felt like to have all that you have ever really wanted.

It was out of the question to tell Satchin, it would violate the unspoken code of conduct established between us, not to go out with each other's friends. Amma and Maggie were too busy with other things to notice and I didn't want to share this with the girls at school who would want to know all the details, turning it into a kind of sordid competition which was so far from the truth. So I kept it to myself and the relationship became even more special.

He became my best friend and was the only person with whom I could openly talk about my father and talking about him resurrected his memory from the many years that Ravi had taken over. Not that Ravi was a bad father; he always treated us like we were his own, not even differentiating between Ammu and us, but it wasn't the same. Suri also understood where we came from, not sweeping it under the carpet like it was something to be ashamed of.

I loved the ambition that he had, his sense of self and clarity. One day, he said, he would be a doctor and there would come a time when his mother and father would not have to work so hard. He spoke of both of them with such respect, they sounded so lovely (even when he said that his father took pictures of the Queen when she appeared on television!). It made me feel at a loss as to what to say about mine and then he filled in my blanks by depicting my Amma as a determined, caring woman and Ravi as a very generous man.

When it rained, or if I was cold, Suri would give me

197

his coat. Whatever little he had, he shared with me, he went without things so we could go to the cinema or he could take me places. He shared everything; his words, his thoughts, everything. Never afraid to say that he loved me, or write it so it was there on paper in black and white. He handled my insecurities as if they were his own, treading gently and knowing how to calm me when he sensed the onset of a temper, or when he knew that he had touched on something that upset me. When we fought, we fought hard, but it would all be forgotten before the evening was up. 'Maya, I'm not going home until we sort it out, we can't leave things like this.' He would do something or say something stupid: 'Maya have you ever thought about it? We are like beauty and the beast, it's true, isn't it? I bet no one has ever called you the beast before.'

We couldn't really go to each other's houses, not as boyfriend and girlfriend, and when he came to mine, there was never any eye contact or exchange between us. It was so difficult and this probably made the whole thing even more passionate. We would see each other every Sunday afternoon without fail and very briefly on some evenings and then when I left him, I counted the hours until I could be with him again. Over the summer holidays, we spent nearly every day together and after that time, it got to the point where we could finish each other's sentences.

Satchin said that something was going on with Suri and told me that he had found himself a secret woman who was very demanding. 'Did he say that?' I probed.

'No, doesn't say a thing about her except this one is different, but you know what they are all like.'

The irony was, at the time, Satchin wanted to spend more time with me. One day he came into my room saying 'Soda, soda and what will you have, Stanley?'

'Oh, please,' I thought, 'get a grip.' All those years that I had waited for him to talk to me like that again and now I didn't need him, he decided he was ready. Well, I wasn't, it was too late, that time had long gone. He lingered in my room.

'Do you remember, Maya, in the big house when we were sitting on the dining table and laughing hysterically thinking about that fridge game. We couldn't stop laughing and the tea that I was drinking came spurting out of my nose, we were howling and then Achan came out because we had woken him up and told me to stop. "Stop Satchin, because for the amount that you have laughed today, I guarantee you'll be crying for the next three days," he said.'

No, I didn't remember. Achan wouldn't say something like that. 'That was one of the last times we saw him,' he continued.

'Do you think about him?' I asked.

'Not really, I try not to. I've kind of blocked all that off. He's dead now anyway, what's the point? I do remember stuff like a few months after that, though, when I broke your thumb and I put it under cold water so it would get better but you wouldn't stop screaming and then Maggie had to take us to the hospital because your thumb was halfway up your elbow.'

I couldn't have forgotten about that, I was six years old. Satchin had found a tatty black leather swivel chair in the dump nearby and he came back for me to help him carry it into the bedsit. He thought it would be a

199

good birthday present for Amma. We fought over who was going to sit on it first and he gave in when I threatened to tell our mother that he wasn't really taking me to school properly in the mornings as he had promised her. He would walk me halfway and then leave me there, stranded. 'You know your way, Maya,' he would say. 'Just follow the other mums,' as he ran off to find his friends. I followed the other mothers and it was really shameful when they spotted me lurking five paces behind them. They took pity on me and stopped, waited for me to catch up, and held my hand as we crossed the road. Blackmail always worked, so I sat in the chair and asked him to swivel it. He turned it but it was an old thing and the chair fell off its stand and I went flying. My thumb got caught under the iron bed as my body went in completely the opposite direction.

Maggie was irate and started shouting at him, which is why I always thought that he didn't warm to her as I did. It was probably about a month after we moved into the bedsit and so we probably didn't create a very good impression. We made up a story for the hospital and for Amma; that I had accidentally fallen on the pavement on my way home from school, landing on my thumb to break the fall. I couldn't remember that second bit so when the doctor asked me it all came out jumbled and Maggie stepped in and asked the doctor whether it was possible that I could be suffering from concussion.

I laughed thinking about it now. How worried Satchin's little face was and how I played on it, making him give me his whole precious collection of marbles. I lost them the next day to Jatinder who was the worst at the game and who was nicknamed 'blind git' because he never managed to throw them in a straight line. I had to roll the one-ers between my two fingers as my thumb was strapped up and I don't think that Jatinder ever saw as many marbles as he did that day. 'They're all lost,' I said to Satchin, expecting a fight. 'It doesn't matter, Maya,' he replied.

'And do you remember when the bloke from the Special Branch came for me, Maya, and I told him where he could get off?'

It wasn't quite the Special Branch; it was Simon Kingsley's dad who was a retired policeman. I was about eight, it was before we were going to move into 64a, the house across the road, and Amma was over there getting things ready. Satchin had warned me that Simon Kingsley might send his dad around. Satchin had punched Simon in the eye because of something he had said about Amma and Maggie. He came beating on the door. Satchin said he would be right there beside me but in the course of me opening the door, he had gone to hide.

'No, Mr Kingsley, there is no little Indian boy of that name here. If you want to speak to my mother, she is out in the back having a bath.'

He stood in the doorway for a while, looking confused at all the fruit that poured out from the different boxes in the bedsit and then, as I added that she might be some time, he shook his head and left. I heard Maggie tell my mother that someone came around looking for her and Satchin the day after that. Maggie said she thought he was from the Social and so she said she knew of no one of that name and sent him packing.

'Yes, Satchin, you really told him where to go,' I said, as I got up to leave.

I think, deep down, I always wanted to be like Satchin. He never thought about things too much, just took things in his stride, not questioning or being suspicious about people. He also had this amazing ability to have friends constantly buzzing around him and to be loved by everyone and to make others happy, something I felt I failed miserably at. When he hit his teens, there were all these different girls who would call, giggle and hang up. 'Who was it?' Amma would ask Ravi.

'Just another one of Satchin's admirers,' Ravi responded.

He started to see this one girl, Jasminder, who he met at the tennis courts and was really nice, but then Karla arrived on the scene. I didn't really think much of her so kept out of the way.

I also envied the closeness Satchin had with Amma and Ravi, somehow I couldn't get there, not like Satchin could. Before Ammu came along, every sentence was prefixed by Satchin, Satchin sportsman, Satchin brainbox, but now that Suri was in my life, none of this seemed to matter. Suri made me feel important enough just as I was.

'Satchin, I'm seeing Suri.'

'I know,' he replied.

Karla was annoying. Granted, she was very attractive but much less so when she opened her mouth. This hideous laugh escaped like a trapped seal, wailing its way out. It made everyone stop, turn around and stare; all that was missing was the clap and maybe a ball. I couldn't bear it when the four of us went out but something odd had come over Satchin and he insisted on tagging along with us. It wasn't all the time, thank God, because I had nothing to say to the Seal. She was the same age as both Satchin and Suri but it wasn't just the laugh, there was something about her, a plastic type of a feeling, like she was unreal. I don't know how they met, he probably picked her up at an animal sanctuary. After her A levels she was going to study sports therapy or something like that but was waiting for Satchin to make up his mind where he wanted to go so she could follow him.

He had applied to do law at Cardiff but I don't think he told her this because whenever the subject came up, he changed it rapidly, saying he was still undecided. Suri wanted to stay in London and study medicine at King's. I didn't ask him to do this for me but was so relieved when he told me. I couldn't really imagine life without him, despite the fact that we had only been seeing each other for a year, but even so, we had already begun making plans.

It probably all sounds so childish and slushy, imagining our house and deciding on names for our children. Amma would say that it was unlucky to do this; you had to wait until you had things in your hand or else they would find a way of escaping. But I had this deep sense of knowing with him. I'm trying to explain this sense of knowing and it's difficult because I have never felt it since. It's not like walking into a room and thinking 'Wow!' it's more about being comfortable with each other, not having to impress. Everything felt right, there was no uncertainty or uneasiness, even when we argued, and I wasn't trying to convince myself that things would work out. It was effortless. This is how it was with Suri.

He passed his exams and was accepted at King's. Most of that summer, Suri spent working at Ravi's office. Satchin failed his A levels monumentally. Ravi tried to do a postmortem on what was bothering him but couldn't find anything. He needed to look no further than the Seal but that was typical; Ravi couldn't see what was in front of him, even if you placed it there with a big red sign saying 'LOOK HERE'. Satchin had gone to dump the Seal a month before the exams so he could concentrate on them. A week or two before them, she said she was pregnant. Whether she had a phantom pregnancy, I don't know, but she threw him into complete turmoil.

Amma didn't really say very much about him not passing except that once in a while it was normal to fail at things. Failing was all part of being human. Where she picked that philosophical line from, I don't know, because ever since we went to our new schools that Ravi paid for, her whole vocabulary consisted of education, education, education. 'You've got to do your best, makkale, and make the very most of all your opportunities.'

The whole escapade with Karla distressed Satchin, the phantom baby disappeared and my brother seemed deflated and started to search for other things. He suddenly noticed my little sister, who would potter around in his room. She absolutely loved him and sat there for hours with the saucepan lid she carried around and the wooden spoon which she hit against it. This used to drive him crazy but the two of them could sit there and amuse each other. He took her giant panda and made its voice so it would appear like the panda was talking to her. She loved this and Ammu went through a phase where Satchin was all she ever needed and when he went out, she would be in his room, lying on his bed, waiting for him. Amma would carry her and put her in her own bed and the first thing she did in the morning was to look for him.

Suri had been saving up for his first car and for his nineteenth birthday, Mr and Mrs Rama had surprised him with a blue Datsun. It was awful. You could hear it coming up the street, coughing like a bad smoker, and when he pulled up into the drive, the car would suffer a cardiac arrest from which it had to be revived with Ravi's jump leads. We were supposed to be going to a party one evening and Suri and I got into a huge argument because I had had enough of driving around in that thing. I suggested part-exchanging the heap and putting the money he had saved towards getting something better. Tactful as I was, I came out with it directly and inadvertently insulted his parents in the process. Satchin rolled his eyes at my comments and as Suri stormed out of the house, Satchin followed him. The two of them drove off together.

It was because I was embarrassed to be seen driving around in that thing, the safety factor never crossed my mind, not even once. The shiny steel tiffin carrier that my mother packed for Suri knocked against Satchin's feet on the passenger side. Suri was turning back to come and get me, to apologise. The tiffin carrier rolled as they did a U-turn and then it burst open as an oncoming car hit them. The car rolled on its side, food went everywhere, it splattered the windows and the seats and the various tins were sent crashing. Suri managed to crawl out but fell unconscious at the foot of the car door. The emergency services had to cut Satchin free but he never made it to the hospital. He was pronounced dead on arrival.

Putting back a book on the top shelf in my room, I caught a glimpse of the blue flashing siren whose wailing stopped abruptly as the police car parked in our drive. The rain was beating down, lashing against the doors and windows. Had I not seen them walking up the drive, nobody would have known that they were there. The sound of the bell was drowned out in all the noise. I hesitated for a moment, if I didn't go down, maybe they would go away.

'Are your mother and father in?' they enquired. I knew. My heart raced and I began to sweat. No, I wanted to say, go back, it's the wrong house. I took a deep breath so that tears would not rush to my eyes. I tried to call out to the back where my parents were sitting. Nothing came out. The police officers followed me as I tried to make my way into the kitchen. I looked up and saw my Amma's face.

'There's been an accident, Mr and Mrs Thakker.' There was a pause. 'There is no easy way of saying this and I am so sorry to tell you that your son Satchin was killed.'

There were a few seconds of incomprehension. Amma got up and went to hit the policeman, choking. Ravi pulled her off. Ammu suddenly walked in and began screaming. I picked up my little sister and ran out with her up the stairs, putting her into her room. 'Don't cry, don't cry, Bobo, I'm here.' I tried to be strong for her and not cry. I rocked her in my arms whilst she went off to sleep and then I went back to my room and looked out of the window. Amma was crying, sitting outside in the rain, soaking wet, pulling at her hair, and there was absolutely nothing Ravi could do to console her, she wouldn't come in. I sat watching her, and the rain.

I remember the rain now, how it fell on the day that we left Ammamma and how it fell when I was told that my father died, a few drops but it was there, and then a few days later, it fell harder and the aching inside would not go away. I tried to make it, I tried to be strong, playing with my brother and my doll but it wouldn't, it was like the rain was falling inside, trying to build a sea with which to drown me. I tried not to cry so Achan would come back to me but it was too much. Now the rain lashed relentlessly to tell me that my brother had gone.

Maggie came around, coaxing my mother back in. And Suri, was he dead too? I should have asked but I didn't think. The doctor came and gave Amma a sedative. Ravi and Maggie walked into my room. 'I'm so sorry, Maya, darling,' she cried. Ravi was in tears and put his arms around me, but I felt nothing. I felt nothing as Maggie held me and crawled into bed with me, not even controlled emotion. Just a lump in my throat that would not move. 'Maggie, did Suri live?'

'Yes, darling,' she replied.

Every day, I called the hospital to see how he was doing but I couldn't go and see him. One day I got as far as the ward but I headed back home. It felt like I was being stabbed. Everything felt so out of control; fear, anger, resentment, guilt, sadness, all rolled into a big throbbing pain. I had to be strong for Amma. God, I was relieved Suri was all right, that he had survived, but then I felt angry for feeling like this. Angry with myself, guilty, it should have been me in that passenger seat, me. Maybe if I hadn't argued, I would have gone with him and none of this would have happened or if it had happened it would have been me. Why did he turn back? There was no one else to take this out on but Suri. He was alive.

Amma spent days in bed, crying. This woman who I felt was so in control was suddenly like a baby that desperately needed us. Sometimes, as I lay with her, grief went beyond verbal description and it was too much. So I made sure my Ammu was taken care of, knowing that this would somehow console Amma. My little sister would go from room to room, looking for Satchin, even though we had said that he had gone away and would not come back. To see her lying in his empty bed, waiting for him, was heartbreaking. The only thing about him that was still there was the smell on his pillow, which she clung to. Other times, she spoke to her panda, waiting for a response, but it never talked back to her.

Suri sent me letters from hospital but I never read any of them. He made calls to me but I never returned them, he called Maggie but she said I couldn't talk to him just yet. I needed some time.

The train pulled into Atocha, Madrid's central station. Everyone clambered to get out and Casanova was there to assist the ladies. An older woman had knocked her foot against the door and was yelling and causing chaos as everyone rallied around her. I pulled down my case and picked Bogey 2 up. I had half a mind to leave it there as it was awkward to carry and there was no way I was putting it on. Then, I thought of María Carmen's face, her beloved coat left on the train, and the prospect of carrying it suddenly seemed a lot better.

She was nice enough, but very overbearing, like a prima donna who loved the sound of her own voice. The first time I went to their house was about a few weeks after Marcos had asked me to marry him. María Carmen just went on and on, coming up for air only occasionally. Her husband interjected when he thought it was appropriate. He was a stern man and despite the fact that he said very little, his presence was very much felt. He had been the judge in the town where they lived and had only recently retired. You could tell that he was finding it difficult in his new role, the constant chattering of his wife aggravated him and he shot her glances which said that if it was at all possible, he would condemn her to at least ten years of solitary confinement.

María Carmen doted on Marcos and he transformed when he was in her presence, acting as if he could not even wipe his own nose. She had two daughters who were much younger than him, about my age, and were both away, studying at university. They never came up in conversation, not as much as Marcos did anyway. She was desperate to be a grandmother and every other word had '*niño*' as the noun or adjective. Then she got out his baby album and before I opened it, I could imagine how she had him dressed. 'That was when I entered him in the baby competition, not expecting anything and, you know, Maya, he won,' she said, pointing at his crocheted frilly hat.

'When are you planning to get married?' asked his father.

'We haven't decided yet,' I said.

His mother looked over at him.

'Summer is a good time, isn't it, Maya?' Marcos added.

I said nothing.

We had to visit them twice a month, leaving on a Friday night and coming back on Sunday evening. His father made us all go to Mass and I hated this as he never asked, just ordered us into church with no consideration of how I felt. I went without arguing, not for him, but because I could sense María Carmen's apprehension.

'Marcos, you know I don't want our children to be brought up Catholic and I don't want to get married in church, even if your mother says she can arrange it all with the priest. Just a simple register office with our friends and family,' I insisted.

'You've told me already, *cariño*,' he replied. His mother almost fainted when she heard the words register office. She developed a life-threatening illness and gave us her dying wishes, the illness was miraculously cured when we conceded, and he told her that I had changed my mind and we would marry in church if we could.

I managed to bypass the commotion on the train by walking in the opposite direction of all the activity. A doctor, priest, nun and workman had congregated to attend to the señora's foot which anyone would have thought was in the process of being amputated. Bundling the fur coat into a carrier bag which had been left on one of the seats, I went out in search of a taxi. One pulled up almost immediately.

'*El aeropuerto, por favor.*'

'*¿Dónde va? ¿A La India?*' the taxi driver asked.

I told him I was going to England to see my family and he asked me how often I went. I felt almost ashamed to say that it had been almost four years. I had left my little sister learning her two times tables and she was now probably on Pythagoras's theorem. So many times, I had intended to go back for birthdays, Christmas, anniversaries, but I could never get as far as the airport car park without turning back. My family had wanted to come and visit but I always managed to find excuses; the house was being decorated, I had visitors, we were going away, I was busy with work, I had to travel.

I told him I went back often. He smiled.

Barajas was crowded. I called up Ravi before boarding to say what time the plane would be landing and then I tried Marcos. In those years, I had called them and sent postcards as often as I could to Ammu but I allowed time to slip away, it was easier.

'Marcos, it's me.'

'Maya, where are you?'

'I am going to London. Maggie is sick.'

There was a pause and then I realised he wouldn't have known who Maggie was. All of that time, those events, I had erased when I started my life in Spain. I was Maya, Maya with no past, because it was easier, painless.

'Maggie is my . . . my aunt. I have to go but I'll call you tonight.'

'But, Maya . . .' he continued.

'I'll call you later to explain.'

The two seats next to me were empty; I put Bogey 2 and the case in the overhead locker and closed my eyes. So many people came to Satchin's funeral. Suri was still in hospital but his parents were there. We thought Amma wouldn't get through it, but she just clung onto Maggie and I, the way that she clung to Satchin and I when we were children, thinking that we might run off and leave her stranded. I had every intention of seeing Suri after I got through that week, I needed to get through the funeral and then I could talk to him. We were all taking it one day at a time but two days after I went back to school, a tall man, with greying hair and deep-set eyes, stopped me as I was turning into our road and sent me on a different course. He said he was my father, my father, Raul.

Nothing made any sense to me, I looked at him. 'My father is dead,' I said to this man. What was he thinking of?

I looked again. Satchin had the same nose and mouth. 'Mol, Mol, it's me, remember, who's my favourite Maya Mol?' That was right, that was what he said to me, in that voice, that voice in English. My father always spoke to us in English and Amma in Malayalam and then, after he died, we used to sit for hours teaching her words and phrases. Our language became a mishmash of two cultures; the reverence of English, interspersed with playful high intonations and colourful eastern adjectives. Then Ravi came and that went too as he didn't understand Malayalam. When I wanted to annoy him, I spoke in the language that bonded the three of us and both Amma and Satchin would revert to English. But back then, my father was dead.

'Mol, it's Achan.'

I stared blankly at him. I could see where my eyes came from, they were the only things that were different from my Amma's.

'Mol, is there anywhere we can go and talk?'

I stared at him, nodded and pointed towards the park.

'He's dead,' I heard Amma saying years before, dressed in her green sweater. Why? Why would she do that? Put us through that? 'He's dead, he died a hero, you know.' I dropped my bag in the middle of the street and I held him. Grabbing him in case he would go again. Unable to catch my breath, the lump that I carried around in my throat escaped; I began to sob, falling pathetically to the pavement and clutching at his legs. He picked me up off the ground and held me tightly, rocking me. I had to tell Satchin, Satchin, Satchin, look he's here, he's come back. Why now? When Satchin couldn't see. She lied. Why? Why did she lie? I didn't want to let him go so he took my hand and we walked towards the park.

'I'm so sorry, Mol, I came because I heard about Satchin. A friend of mine told me and then I had to see you,' he began.

Which friend? Had he always known where we were? Why hadn't he come sooner?

'A friend? Why didn't you come for us?' I wailed.

'I tried, Mol, believe me I did, but in those early days

213

I didn't know where you had all gone and then when I saw your mother a few years ago, she made me promise.'

Amma had seen him? She knew where he was? What was going on?

'Amma has seen you? She knew where you were? It doesn't make sense. Why?' I choked out.

'I came back to the house after a business trip and it was empty, I thought she had taken you both and gone back to India. I went back to India immediately and I tried to find you there in Mumbai and the village but it was useless.'

None of it made sense. Why did we leave with Tom if we were going to India? Did she mean for us to go there? I couldn't remember them fighting. Why just up and leave? Why go to a bedsit? Did Tom have something to do with it? Was it because of him, because of Tom?

'It doesn't make sense. There was no reason.'

'She was very homesick. We had an argument before I left, Mol. She thought we were all going back and I told her it would be another two years,' he said. 'I said some things that maybe I shouldn't have. I was hard. Too hard. Maybe she thought things would be better without me.'

Better! We had to live in a cold bedsit with rats. Satchin and I looked after each other, he cooked by reheating the food Amma had left us and when I complained, he opened tinned soups. We wore things from the jumble sales that the other children laughed at and we walked on streets where empty petrol cans rusted beside the houses that had been gutted, torched by people's hatred of all things foreign. I had to watch my friend Fatima come to school with various bruises because her father could not cope and there was absolutely nothing I could do because we were told not to trust anyone, to say anything. This was better?

'No,' I cried, 'We stayed here and she said you were dead.'

'Don't blame your mother, it wasn't her fault, Mol.'

Don't blame her? What kind of woman would do that to her children and then marry someone else when she was already married?

'Why didn't you fight for us when you found us? Why didn't you see us?'

'She didn't let me and you seemed so settled and happy, so much time had gone by, and I thought it was for the best. The best for you and Satchin, and you had a little sister.'

'When? When did you come?'

He told me how he had met Ravi Thakker through his friend and colleague, Anil, who was Ravi's brother. Then he had seen Amma. 'Does Ravi know?' I asked.

He shook his head.

'Anil told me last week about Satchin and I had to come and see you, Maya, I couldn't stay away. Even if I saw you for a moment it would be enough. I couldn't go on without seeing you, just once. Was he happy?' he asked.

'Yes,' I cried. 'Satchin was always happy.' I talked to him about Satchin, the way he laughed and fought with me, how he took care of our little sister, the way he was good at everything he did and how my father would have been so proud of him.

My father told me things about when Satchin was little. 'He used to wait for me to come home so he could ride with me on the scooter. Then, as he became older, he grew to hate the sight of a suitcase. The only times he ever cried was when he saw that case being brought down because he knew I was going away.'

He searched for something more to say, but he couldn't. How could he when she had robbed him of that, robbed him of everything? I filled in the missing years and for those few hours we brought him back, he was sitting there on the bench with us.

I wanted to leave the house and go back with him to Chicago but he asked me to wait, saying that I could always come in the future. My place was here at the moment, to look after my mother. How could he forgive her like that? Be so compassionate and still put her first?

'Don't tell her that you've seen me, Mol, promise me. You can come later and stay, when you are a little older, but promise me you won't tell her now, she won't manage with it all.'

We sat for another hour or so, talking, then he said he had to go. I screamed, begged him to stay, to stay with me, but he had to catch a flight that evening. He promised that he would come back soon and see me for longer and, in the meantime, he would stay in touch. If any time I needed to, I could go to Chicago and be with him. He kissed me and left me there on the park bench. 'Don't go, Achan, don't leave me alone, not now,' I cried as he walked off. He didn't hear me.

I sat there for another hour or so and then it was dark. The tears were replaced by a seething anger; how could she have put us through all that? What kind of a heartless person did that? Did Maggie know what kind of a woman she was? What about Ravi Thakker in all of this? She wasn't even really his wife – and my little sister? What would happen to my little sister? It made sense now; Tom disappeared shortly after she met Ravi Thakker, just cut himself off from us, he probably did that because she had left him too, left him for another man. That's what she did, that's what she knew best. I wanted to tell Amma I knew it all; forget what Achan said about her, she didn't deserve compassion. She was a selfish woman who thought of no one but herself. I ran home, opened the front door, dropped my bag in the hall, and ran up the stairs, storming into her room. I found her lying on her bed pathetically, my little sister sitting on a pillow beside her, stroking her face. She looked up at me with red-rimmed eyes and I wanted to shake her and tell her that she deserved everything she got, everything, she deserved to suffer, no one in the world deserved to suffer more, but all I could manage was, 'How are you feeling now, Ma?'

Maggie would have answers, Maggie always found answers. She would be straight with me, she always told me things how they were. I ran over to her house, knocked frantically on her door. 'Maggie, open the door, open the door. Are you in?'

'What is it, Maya, darling? What is it? Is it your mother?' she asked as she opened it.

I shook my head

'What's wrong?'

I couldn't speak.

'You're freezing, you're in shock, darling, come upstairs, the fire is on and it will warm you up.' She led me upstairs.

'Sit down, sweetheart, I'll just go down and make you a cup of tea, whatever it is, we can sort it out.'

She turned her back before I could say no, I don't need tea now, I need answers. I sat there shaking, waiting for her to come back.

'Have a sip of that now, Maya. Take a deep breath and tell me.'

'I've had enough of lies, Maggie, there are things I need to know. I need the truth,' I sobbed.

'What about?' she said, sounding a little jarred.

'About Tom, Tom and . . .' I began, meaning if there had ever been anything between Tom and Amma? I wanted to ask if my mother left my father to go off with Tom.

But she didn't allow me to continue, 'I knew this would happen and you're old enough to hear the truth . . .' She interrupted me, not giving me a chance to finish my question. She began telling me the story of Tom, almost as if Satchin's death provoked an overwhelming need to unburden herself to me. She told me things that I really did not need to know or want to hear about her. Truth is like that, sometimes so ugly. 'So I had no option, darling, I had to work on the streets . . .'

'Stop!' I wanted to shout, that's not what I need to know.

'No, no,' I shouted.

'Darling, I want you to know the truth about me, I want you to hear it all and not bits of information that you've picked up from somewhere.'

She continued and, somewhere in that exchange, our relationship changed. I no longer saw Maggie as she was; the person who could fix things, reassure me or make things better, she wasn't the woman who replaced my own mother. She was a woman with the same failings. After she finished, she wiped her tears and asked me if that answered it, if that had put an end to the gossip I had heard. Was there anything else I needed to know? Any questions that needed answering?

'Nothing,' I replied.

Even when we had nothing, we had each other. I had Maggie to set my boundaries for me, to tell me how things were, yet she too had been dishonest. Never had I felt so lost, alone and confused as I did then. Now there was real emptiness, the people I cared about were not who they pretended to be. Satchin was gone and could not even verify if the memories I had were real. Then there was Suri, Suri who was my everything. He had turned into nothing along with the rest of them. Love was an illusion, nothing was real any more. As I arrived back home, I sat at my desk and wrote a letter. I vented my rage on the wrong person because there was no one else to punish and I wrote some awful things to Suri and ended by asking him never to contact me and to respect my family's wishes by staying away.

I posted the letter almost immediately so there wouldn't be an opportunity to hesitate, to take it all back and think things through with the sobriety of time. I also decided not to say anything to Ravi or Amma; it wasn't right to do that to my little sister, she didn't deserve any of it, neither did Ravi. There was only a year left before I could go to university, so I made it my resolve to bury myself in books and get my exams so I could get as far away from them all as I possibly could.

* * *

'Are you all right, Miss?' the air steward asked as he put the food tray down beside me.

'I'm fine,' I said, wiping my tears. 'Nothing for me, thank you.'

'Are you sure, perhaps I can get you something to drink?'

'No, I'm fine.'

Conversations between myself, Ravi and Amma became monosyllabic and my little sister kept me going in the days I wanted to give up and take a flight to be with my father. He wrote as he promised, not as often as he said he would, but news arrived at Amy Willis's house and she forwarded me the letters as we had agreed. Sometimes I called reverse charges but it was always at an inconvenient time. He was a busy man.

A year later, when I made it to Edinburgh, Ravi and Amma were thrilled. Thrilled is probably not the right word in a house that was suffused by grief but they couldn't have been any happier than I was. Finally to be away from them, to have my own space and room to think. I absolutely hated it there but I have now come to realise that if you are not happy in one place, it doesn't matter how many millions of miles away you are, happiness isn't suddenly going to come and find you. Edinburgh was no better than London. The letters from my father became more infrequent, the emptiness even bigger, and I hated the course. Student life was just one endless round of drinking and small talk. Many times I thought of calling Suri, just to talk openly to someone and to have him listen without judgement. I always got as far as dialling the first five digits and then I would hang up.

In the first two years at Edinburgh, I went home three times, saying that I was overloaded with work and for the first long summer, I got restaurant work and stayed there in town. For Christmas, I went home only because I knew how much my little sister loved it. For those three weeks, she would not leave me alone, hanging on my every word and following me about wherever I went. When I took her to school, she would shout in her loudest voice, 'Bye, Mayo,' and then look proudly at me as she ran off to play with her friends. All as I had done. I hardly spent any time with Maggie, making excuses that I had too much work to do. I didn't cut her off because I stopped loving her, I cut her off because at that time, everyone seemed to belong in the same circle of deceit, none of them could be trusted; they had all hurt me.

Amma and Ravi became mere shadows of their former selves. Amma's long hair, now cut short, was greying. Ravi began working from home so he could help her look after my sister on the days that the lethargy was too much. She and Maggie had shut down the business and Jack was ill so Maggie spent all her time taking care of him. It was sad to see and the only laughter that came into that house was brought by the innocence of my sister, she kept them both going. I couldn't take that away.

I visited them briefly on my way back from the Spanish course. 'There's a change in you, Maya. Have you met someone special?' Maggie asked.

'No,' I said.

As I was packing, getting ready to go back to Scotland, I came across some letters hidden at the back of my wardrobe. A few of them were from my father, hastily scribbled, telling me all was well, along with cheques that I hadn't cashed, and behind them were a bundle of unopened letters. They were from Suri. Opening them up slowly, I hesitated before reading them; they smelt of him. All began by saying how much he loved me and if he could, he would turn back the clock so he was sitting where Satchin sat. 'Sorry' punctuated every sentence. Sorrow and regret filled the page. Every letter ended: 'No matter where you are, Maya, or how much time has passed, I will always, always love you. I hope one day you find space in your heart to forgive me. Suri.'

It had been three years and not a day went by when I didn't think of my brother. Why couldn't his life towards the end have been happier? Why didn't I spend more time with him? Why didn't he get to meet our father? Why did Amma do this to us? So many times I came close to asking her for the truth and all those times, I thought of the effect that it would have on my little sister and on Ravi Thakker. He was essentially a good, decent man, so I kept it inside where it was eating away at me. Suri was the only one who could have helped.

Forgiveness. It was I who needed to be forgiven. That evening, I took the car and drove to his house. I wanted to get out and knock on his door but as I sat there thinking about it, an hour and a half went by. None of it was Suri's fault, my anger was not with him, it had never been with him. I was about to step out of the car when I caught a glimpse of him in my rear view mirror. His arms were around the waist of an Indian girl who was smiling as he went to kiss her. He had obviously moved on and was happy. I started the ignition and drove off.

If you were to ask me when exactly I fell in love with Marcos Gonzalez del Hoyo, I would say it was at that point. I desperately needed someone to hold me and tell me that everything would be fine, that they would be there for me. When Marcos came to visit me in Scotland, I made myself fall deeply for him. He became a way of distracting myself from everything that really hurt, he was safe, I knew where I stood with him. I decided to put the past behind me and start all over again. Spain seemed as good a place as any.

Teachers came and went in quick succession at the school in Madrid. Whether we liked to admit it or not, all of us were running away from different things and hoping to find something better. Just as soon as we got a scent of whatever it was we were looking for, it eluded us and we would distract ourselves, pretending it didn't really matter anyway. Most days after work we went from bar to bar eating tapas and drinking *cañas* and then we forgot about what it was that we were really searching for. It was like socialising with one big family, who all came from the same place, who understood each other. Without having the need to talk seriously about things, we spent our time messing around.

It was with the double act, John and Michael, that this childish behaviour first started. They were two other teachers who began working at the school around the same time as me and who devised this ridiculous game based on a system of points. It was ten points for touching a bald waiter's head, twenty for stealing a stranger's tapas, thirty for drinking someone else's beer and fifty was too outrageous to mention. At the end of the evening, all the points were totalled and the person with the least would have to pay for dinner. I always lost but often I didn't make dinner, as I would suddenly remember Marcos's call and run off.

'He's no good for you, Maya, it's been two years and we still haven't seen him; dump him' Michael would say.

But what did Michael know about anything? Did he understand Marcos as I did? I knew Marcos could be difficult at times: he was set in his ways and possessive but I knew all this, I knew all his faults, that is precisely why I felt safe with him. There was no room for ugly surprises. What did Michael know about anything?

'You shouldn't judge people, Michael, especially if you've never met them.'

'That's precisely what I mean. Don't you think it's a bit strange that none of us have seen him. Can't he be asked to come up for a weekend?'

'He doesn't come because the only time I can get away from you is at the weekends.'

'Well, you know, if you ever dump him, Maya, I'll marry you,' Michael joked.

After a couple of years of teaching English, one of my students, Enrique Sanchez, offered me a job. He was an eccentric fashion designer who owned an exclusive boutique on Calle Serrano, an affluent part of the city. Enrique had joined my conversation class because he had begun to export his collections abroad and wanted to improve his English. The job offer came as a complete surprise because on the occasions I wore my own creations, he laughed at them. Enrique wasn't an intimidating man, just extroverted, waving elaborately when he spoke: 'Maya, *cariño*, those sleeves are hideous and that tuck there, what is that doing for you? No movement, fabric is supposed to flow with you, not walk ten paces behind.'

Once he invited me along to see his autumn/winter collection and there was a certain familiarity with cuffs on sleeves, the cut of a neckline and the 'flow' of fabric. I didn't say anything. It was around that time that I decided to give teaching a break and took a few weeks off to consider other options. One day, he called me up at home and asked me to go for a coffee with him.

We were sitting outside in the Plaza Mayor, the sun wasn't particularly bright but he had these really black narrow sunglasses on and was commenting on the women as they walked by. 'You see Maya, *cariño*, too co-ordinated; nothing original there. Have you thought about whether you are coming back to teach us?' he asked.

'I don't know, Enrique. I've been doing this for two and a half years now, it's time for a change,' I replied.

'Good, how would you like to come and work with me?'

'Yes!' I wanted to shout, but I hesitated and then told him I would think about it.

'What is there to think about, *cariño*? I'll offer you a good salary, plenty of opportunity to travel and you can learn, learn the business,' he said, waving his arms.

'How good is a good salary?'

'You're on what, maybe 150,000 pesetas now? I'll double that,' he said exuberantly.

'Okay, Enrique, I'll try it out and we'll see how it goes.' I was absolutely elated.

Marcos, too, was happy for me. Both of us had settled down into a routine and our relationship was becoming effortless, maybe because I conceded a little more. The BMW was still parked right outside my heart but I knew it would only be a matter of time before he got out of it and would meet me at least halfway. We spent all our weekends together, well, Saturdays, anyway, because Sunday mornings he would spend in the gym and then after lunch he would catch up with his paperwork. I continued going up to his place because he hated the city. He had bought a flat in Palmadoro, in a prime location in the square, and I rented a small duplex in Madrid now that Jen had gone back. She promised that she would write and call as soon as she'd gone back to the States, but I never got to know what happened between her and Steve. The numbers she had given me didn't work and my subsequent letters went un-answered. Spain and the people in it no longer existed for her, she had found whatever it was she came looking for and no longer needed us. That's what happened to some of the people that came to Spain, they returned to their realities and erased everything else, perhaps this was easier.

My flat was small but it was located near the Retiro Park, in an area that resembled a village. Tree-lined streets were dotted with a few obscure shops filled with strange curiosities. The grocer's opposite me was like a little toyshop with fruit beautifully displayed and tins and jars stacked neatly. The most expensive products, like bottles of gin and whiskey, were guarded safely behind the counter, which the owner never left. His wife would help all the old ladies who came in for a chat or give sweets to the little children, pinching their cheeks or cooing at them. Sometimes their two older children would come in and work on the weekends. If they didn't see me for a couple of weeks they would be concerned, though they knew that it was not in my nature to defect to a large supermarket. In many ways, their little shop reminded me of Amma's. I loved going in and it never once frustrated me that it would take half an hour to buy a bunch of grapes because people just stood and chatted. Everybody knew everyone else.

I had named the caretaker of my building, a woman in her fifties, 'Zubi', after a Spanish goalkeeper because she didn't miss a thing. If you asked her my shoe size she probably knew it. On several occasions, I caught her cleaning the landing with her mop, her ear pressed against the front door and it felt like the gasman came every week because this is how often she let herself in.

On my way to work, I'd stop and have coffee at the local bar. The waiters would put out a coffee cup and begin to toast a croissant before I walked in at around nine o' clock. Then I walked to the boutique which was half an hour away, passing the old man who would wish me a good day, as he stopped momentarily from begging on the street, and the lady with perfectly set hair who was always dressed in a suit would just smile as she was walked her two dogs.

In the afternoons there was a three-hour lunch break, so I would go back to the flat, cook and fall asleep watching the customary Latin American soap. All the banging and shouting that came from the open windows stopped at this time as housewives everywhere settled themselves to find out whether Rosa had managed finally to discover the affair her husband was having. Work finished around seven or eight and we'd all go out for drinks afterwards, tapas filling us along the way so that by the time we were ready for dinner, we weren't really hungry.

Working with Enrique was not how I expected, it was better. Every day was different and filled with colour. Some days I did administration, calling and arranging meetings with clients, other days I would talk to suppliers and sometimes I would sit in the workshop and design, working with his team of designers and tailors. Occasionally, I popped into the boutique but it never lasted long as I didn't have the patience to flatter the clients as he did. 'No, *cariño*, you don't look fat in that,' he would say to women popping out of dresses that did them no favours. Six months into the job, he wanted me to go abroad and buy fabrics.

'I'm thinking ethnic, Maya, something Indian, find me a supplier.'

'How do I do that?' I asked, thinking that the only supplier I knew was the shop in Green Street. 'Go there,' he said. 'I have a list of Indian suppliers, take a month and come back with what you think is appropriate.'

'To India?' I asked bewildered.

'Yes, yes, you're from there, aren't you? It shouldn't be a problem.'

I couldn't tell him that I hadn't been back for twenty years, that it wasn't something that I wanted to do, that I was comfortable in Madrid. 'No,' I said, 'it won't be a problem.'

'You can't go, Maya,' Marcos exploded. 'Are you crazy? Tell him no.' That's what I appreciated about Marcos, encouragement and support when I most needed it.

'Marcos, don't be like that,' I replied.

'How long will it be for?' he asked.

'About a month.'

'You know you don't need to work, Maya, tell him you are not going. A month is too long.'

Despite the sulking and the silence, I left on Monday morning for Madrid, saying that I loved him and I would call as soon as I got to India. Then I began to get organised. I made two calls; one was to my father in the States. I thought perhaps he could help me with contacts for when I got there and maybe someone who could accompany me and give me assistance with the language. I also wanted an address for his parents; I didn't have any intention of visiting them but it was always better to have it. He said he would call me back in fifteen minutes. I called up Ravi and asked him the same thing. 'No problem, Maya, I'll have someone waiting for you at Mumbai airport and they will have a list of people that I will arrange for you to meet, also take these numbers just in case you need anything,' he said. I waited for my father to call me back from the States. After two days had passed, it was time to leave. There was no return phone call.

It was intensely humid when I got off the plane in Mumbai. It was as if the heat wanted to wake me from a deep, deep sleep by trying to steam all the dormant feelings out of me. A smell lingered in the air; I couldn't quite make it out but it was like sweat and sadness. You try and push it away by not inhaling properly, but it follows you. At first you cannot see very clearly, everything is blurred with dust and heat. The distant sound of ringing comes at you from everywhere; bicycles and cowbells, scooters and car horns, all keeping you alert so you will not go back into slumber. As I stepped into the airport building, these sounds grew louder as if to compete with the shouting, protesting and bustle inside the terminal building. Sweat-stained khaki uniforms with bushy moustaches and guns fixed me with their gaze as if to say, 'You are one of ours.' I was scared.

The guard took my passport and handed it back to me with a flirtatious glance which I did not respond to. Averting my eyes, I took it, and walked away. Young boys fought over each other to help me carry my suitcase, shouting 'Ma'am, Ma'am, Ma'am', all so desperate that the experience of picking one was impossible. The stench grew stronger as we walked out of the airport, the smell of armpits and urine was everywhere, the noise became louder and suddenly, I was descended upon and then surrounded by countless faces, begging at me, crying out; limbless, blind, old, young, mothers with babies, children shouting 'paisa'. All at once, the stench no longer followed you but was there in front of you; fear and sadness. I handed over whatever small change I had, knowing that it wouldn't make a difference, but at least for that moment, I was unaccountable. They came after me and the only thing I could do was look away. Amongst the chaos, I saw someone holding a big sign with my name written across it. Relief.

Ravi Thakker had called up one of his friends who

had arranged a driver and chaperone to meet me just outside the airport. Krishna, the chaperone, introduced himself and asked me whether this was my first trip to India. I didn't know what to say, this was the country where I was born and then for twenty years, I blocked it off like it wasn't even on the globe.

'I was born here,' I replied.

He smiled, sensing that I was a stranger in my own country.

As we got into the car, he waved the beggars away like irritating flies. Each time we stopped at some lights, they came at us from all directions, putting their arms through the open windows. He continued talking to me as if they didn't exist and when one little girl put her hand through the window, I had just enough time to remove my bracelet and give it to her.

'You shouldn't do that, Maya. Most of it is organised and these children don't get to see any of what you give them. Ignore it.'

How could you ignore what was staring you in the face? But people of better means drove through the poverty as if it were all part of everyday life, they were accustomed to it. Shantytowns built with shacks and cardboard boxes littered the streets, roofed with dirty linen or newspapers that provided no shelter from the rain. Surrounding them were sewage pits and dumps where children played. These towns were set against a backdrop of colourful billboards announcing the latest Bollywood film or advertising domestic appliances, creams and make-up with Indian ladies who looked too fair to be Indian. People drove by on motorbikes, carrying mobile phones, or in fast cars wearing designer clothes, fighting for space on the roads alongside errant cows that wandered freely. Women dressed in saris, alive and vibrant with just a little flesh showing, gift-wrapped by the tucks and folds of their garments, yet the way they would look away shyly, suggested it was wrong to admire them.

As we drove nearer the city, more people wore western clothes and the rhythm changed again, with pop music blasting out of the shops and roadside stalls selling Coca Cola and Fanta in returnable bottles. The smell of roast peanuts and traffic replaced the human stench and *MTV* played in the background, satellite dishes eagerly swallowing up the waves of Whitney Houston's 'I'm Every Woman'.

The driver pulled up to the Taj, a five-star hotel in the middle of the city. The floors were made of white marble and the ceilings were high, beautifully sculptured with intricate designs and painted in fresh, clean white. Hanging from them were ornate crystal chandeliers. The bedroom was immaculate with a pristine bathroom and a double bed scattered with colourful silk cushions. The air conditioning was switched on so you wouldn't have to open the windows because when you did, the opulence of where you were living made you feel guilty. The same contradiction that resided in this place resided in me. The same India, where I was from, gave birth to a mass of antitheses; happiness, sadness, poverty, richness, abundance, hunger, piety, decadence which engulfed its people. All co-existing together.

I called Marcos and said that I was fine. 'Make sure you come home soon, Maya. I am sorry about . . .' The connection went dead. I called up Ravi at the office and thanked him for arranging all my meetings and asked him one more thing: if he could find out from my mother the address where we lived in the town to the north of Mumbai and then fax it to me. He said he would see what he could do. I went to bed.

Krishna came to collect me in the morning to help me find the suppliers that I had arranged to see on Enrique's list. A few sat beefed up behind their desks in their dull, grey offices in tower blocks, hiding behind their moustaches which twitched beneath the blades of a rotating fan. When we asked to see their workshops, they hesitated, politely refused and then waved the most elegant fabrics in front of us to entice us away from the very thought.

Only a few invited us to the workshops; dank and sweaty with no proper ventilation and where children as young as five were working. Nobody looked up to see who we were and got on with weaving, dyeing and embroidering. They seemed unfazed by the hovel that they were working in and just continued; they had other things to think about. From those smelly black pits emerged the most lavish fabrics; pink and red chiffon, gold raw silk, turquoise blue taffeta, delicate white organza intricately woven and embroidered. Beautiful things were born from those pits, like the recess of a troubled mind where occasionally inspirational ideas emerged. The materials came out into the sunshine, without a trace of the suffering or the hungry hands that had toiled on them and the irony was that these fabrics were often shipped abroad to be displayed on a Western model who starved herself to fit into them.

Ravi's list was a little better and whoever put it together either had a conscience or wanted us to see a better side. We collected samples and came to some kind of agreement with a few of the suppliers. With over two weeks left, I kept looking at the fax with the address that Ravi had sent to me and asked Krishna to take me there.

We drove past the sea that vomited a murky brown swell onto a beach and did its best to glisten against the jaundiced sun. Children ran along the beach following a boy who had found a discarded bicycle tyre. An hour north of Mumbai, we found the large colonial-style house protected by enormous gates. Inside the compound, there were many trees. The house looked smaller than my fragmented memories of it and now belonged to a local landowner. Krishna told the man what we were doing there and he invited us in for tea. We sat in the main room behind the veranda. I remembered this room, now dirty white with red-tiled floors. There used to be a sofa in there; Satchin and I would pull the covers off and Ammamma would get annoyed at us. Then I saw a few faded images: a glass cabinet filled with dolls that my father had bought for me; the straw-filled attic which we were asked not to play in because of roaming snakes; Amma sitting on the veranda immaculately dressed, waiting, talking to the postman as he passed with letters; Ammamma's frustration at the dhobi who over-starched our clothes but who she could not bring herself to get rid of; the servants collecting cow dung for its innumerable uses; the house full of neighbours; the puppy. One of the servants interrupted my thoughts as she came out with a tray on which she carried three shiny steel cups. She handed one to me, her eyes narrowed and she looked at me.

'Nalini? Nalini?' she shouted, as she put the tray down and began to talk furiously in Hindi. 'What is she saying?' I asked Krishna.

She says that she had missed you so much after you left and it has never been the same. Then she stopped, looked at her employer, and added, 'Since before Sahib came.'

'Tell her I am Maya, Nalini's daughter.'

He told her. She smiled, then she laughed and those yellow pan-chewing, gapped teeth and that white cotton headpiece transported me back to my young Aya. I held out my arms and she came to hug me. 'Maya, Maya,' she kept repeating, using her hands to show me how small I had been. Her eyes widened and she asked for Satchin. I shook my head and looked down and she came to sit next to me. Her smell of damp linen and wood smoke reminded me of the times when she took me to the kitchen to watch my Amma and Ammamma cook. 'And Ammamma?' I asked. My Aya looked at me and said, 'Collenauta'. She had gone back to Collenauta.

Aya asked after Amma. 'And Raul?' she continued, as she made an awkward face. I shook my head again, thinking how it was possible to explain everything that had gone since. Her face beamed as she made sweeping gestures with her hand. 'What is she saying, Krishna? What is she saying?'

'She says she's glad as he was never good to her. Nalini married a mistake.'

What did she say that for, he loved her. 'Tell her, no,' I said. 'He really loved her.'

235

Aya looked disappointed, moved her headpiece, said something back and fell silent.

'He loved himself,' Krishna translated.

We saw workers planting contradiction in the paddy fields as Krishna and I drove back. He did love her. I know he did. He was a bit slow in communicating, especially bad in letter writing, but that was it.

Riding in a rickshaw to the sea, my Ammamma's voice whispered softly to me as I sat bouncing on her lap, telling me that the labourers were planting their doubts, their worries, hopes and dreams there in the water and the soil, hoping the ground would nourish with its magic and resolve all that needed solutions. Carefully tending to it, waiting patiently until the moon had done the necessary cycles so that the musician could bring the rains. Then finally they gathered whatever answers had been given to them and took them to the mills. Removing all that was unnecessary, the wrapping that comes with every gift, the husk was separated from the grain. It appeared tough at first, resisting the attempts of separation but once it came away, it came easily. They gave thanks.

Patience, she said, is what this first taught them, for this was one of the most important things. Without this, all the rest of the work would be made redundant. They then laid the grain out on the ground so the sun could send its heat to every single one, magnifying life, energy, fertility with which it had been sewn and the wisdom which was so sought after. From the sky, birds saw it sparkle and came flocking around so someone had to stand guard and watch carefully. Brushed and collected, people waited eagerly. Then it was steamed so its goodness that had been fermenting could expand and fill empty stomachs with the magical answers that came from the soil.

Some people didn't want to hear the answers so they ate more, hoping for different solutions, indulging and revelling in the feelings that the food temporarily gave them but when the answers came back the same, these too they discarded. They sought further comfort, sometimes in sweet things like laddoos or jilebies, which quelled human emotion. Others were repulsed by the answers that surfaced and ate just enough to see them through the day. Many went with empty stomachs and these people had no answers, only questions that made them ache with hunger.

We passed the sea again. 'Stop the car,' I shouted to Krishna.

'Here, Maya?'

'Yes, please, stop the car.'

He indicated to the driver. I got out and ran, ran as fast as I could into the sea, the sea that I thought was a murky swell, the predator. I was a part of it, it was a part of me and I let the swell wash over me. Then I sat on the pebbles so my clothes would dry, and breathed, breathed in time with the ripples of the waves. Krishna came rushing over to me with a look of utter disbelief. He rattled off all the diseases I could have caught by that one act. 'What were you thinking of, Maya?'

'I was trying to find the pace.'

He looked completely confused and probably thought it was some bizarre Western notion that I had brought with me.

'Yes, but there is still typhoid, diphtheria, malaria . . .' he began again.

I nodded.

'Let me get you some clean clothes from the car.'

'No, I want to sit here by myself for a while, so that they can dry.'

He went back to the car reluctantly as I sat and listened to the sea and tried to find the pace so I could read the signs. A balloon seller came up to me, children crowded around me and instead of giving them money, I bought the balloon seller's entire collection and handed them out to the children. Colourful balloons ran along the beach. I went back to the car.

'I have to go to Collenauta.'

'But, Maya, it is deep in the South,' Krishna replied.

'I know, but you don't have to come with me.'

'You can't go on your own. I'll arrange the tickets, we'll fly tomorrow,' he said.

Back at the hotel, the waiter came to where I was sitting and said, 'The same as always, Ma'am, omelette and French fries with green salad?'

'Thank you,' I replied and as he was turning away, I said, 'I think I'll try iddlies with sambar.'

'Right away,' he nodded.

It was a typical dish from the South which my grandmother would make for us, smashing up the fermented rice cakes in the liquid sambar. Ever since I can remember, Amma tried to make us eat them. Food was the battleground between her and us, used to establish the balance of power, and Satchin and I stood firm. She was a skilful opponent, packing the iddlies into our lunch boxes or putting tomato ketchup on the side so we would be enticed. We managed to dispose of them quite easily but as Satchin grew older, he started to love them and it became a competition between him and Ravi to see who could eat the most. My little sister liked them too, all mashed up and then she drank the leftovers which my mother put in her pink beaker, but the last time I tasted iddlies and sambar was probably when I was about four, preferring food that had been processed since.

They came steamed and fluffy in a rich brown sauce with long vegetable drumsticks and juicy shallots. I cut softly into them with my knife and fork and rolled my eyes thinking of my Amma's comments: fingers connected you to food in a way no other instrument could. Satchin and I would argue with her about hygiene, insisting that we had to use cutlery. We had learnt this from the other kids who said that Pakis were unclean and ate with their fingers. 'No,' she answered, 'it is important to touch the food.'

Touching food, eating with fingers. I laughed at the thought. Marcos and I were in a bar with some of his colleagues, eating tapas. I picked up a piece of fried chicken with my fingers and he was appalled. He pulled me over to one side. 'Maya, what do you think you are doing? What do you think the cocktail sticks are for?'

The iddlies felt like soft grains of sand which had been stuck together by the tide. Formed into a perfect circle, they were swimming in the sambar. Bits that resembled seaweed floated aimlessly to the surface and a heavy drumstick sank to the bottom like an old oil drum. The shallots bobbed up and down and it would have been difficult to fish them out with a fork so I

239

picked them up and bit into them. They tasted salty. I asked for a spoon so I could drink the sambar, not wanting to slurp it from my plate as Ravi did or drink it delicately from my hands like Amma. The hot peppercorns made me cough and though I didn't want to admit it, it felt soothing, like returning safely home. My grandmother would say that this was the process of self-cleansing, washing out all the impurities that had become stuck throughout the years. Definitely, that is what she would whisper.

My mother posted the letters that we sent Ammamma with our pictures and Amma would read the letters that Ammamma sent back because we couldn't read Malayalam. Every letter ended by telling us to be good, to do our schoolwork and that she loved us. When we moved into Maggie's house, the letters became infrequent and then they stopped. Satchin and I didn't want to upset Amma by asking questions so we presumed Ammamma had gone to join my father. But the reality was probably that she was alive and well and this too had slipped Amma's mind, another lie. I packed my cases that evening, ready to travel South.

Krishna collected me the next day and we flew down to Kerala. A new driver was waiting for us at the airport, dressed in a checked shirt and loongi which he lifted up and doubled after he met us so it showed his legs, matchsticks, thinner than my own. His smile seemed to electrify his face which was really dark. 'I am your diver,' he said proudly, shaking his head from side to side. He said it in Malayalam, except the word 'diver', which someone had taught him incorrectly and he showed us to the car. Krishna had booked a hotel near the airport so we stayed there the first night. The driver ate outside in his car and I asked Krishna to call him in so he could eat with us but he refused. After dinner, I went outside and spoke to him in my broken Malayalam, asking him to come inside, that we would pay for a room, but he insisted that he wanted to sleep in his vehicle.

The next morning, we set off after breakfast. Vijay, the driver, said it would take three to four hours. The city roads were good, then he had to drive along dirt tracks, avoiding ditches and animals, using his horn at every conceivable opportunity, competing for space with colourful buses and bicycles. He waved back at people whenever he could and laughed, and because his laugh was infectious, I started doing it too. The roads became quieter but he still used his horn. The noise would startle women carrying huge bronze water urns, who turned to look whilst their children began running after us. Everywhere you turned there were palm trees, banana plantations and lush vegetation, and those who could afford umbrellas walked under huge black ones to shelter themselves from the sun. The heat was not as intense as in Mumbai; it was hot but very different, the air seemed a lot fresher too and not infused with the intensity of pollution. We stopped briefly at the roadside to buy some coconuts.

The seller looked relieved as if we were the only customers he had had that day and began choosing three coconuts. Vijay shook his head and said only two but between the sales pitch from the seller and I, he conceded. Sharpening his rusty axe, the seller took great pleasure in knocking off the coconut heads and handed them to us with the straws he had made out of reeds. I pulled a few rupees from my pocket and his eyes nearly popped out. Vijay said it was too much and there was slight apprehension as the seller stood with his hand held out and I said to Vijay that it didn't matter. The seller looked thrilled and as we made our way into the car, he began to pack up his goods. He had made enough money for the day and was making his way home.

Stringing a badly phrased sentence together, I asked Vijay if he had family. A smile beamed from his mirror and he lowered the sun guard to show me a picture of his daughter and wife.

'I got her married last year,' he said proudly.

She couldn't have been more than sixteen. 'To a man with lots of land,' he added.

'Are you married?' he asked shyly.

I shook my head. The look that he gave me was that of a parent who is disappointed in their child. 'I will pray for you,' he said. 'Pray that a good man comes and takes you.'

Krishna noticed that the seats were beginning to get sweaty and suggested we stop in the nearest large town before Collenauta and find somewhere to wash. There were lots of signs in Chotagam for hotels. At every hotel, Krishna would stop, get out of the car to inspect their rooms, and come back disappointed. 'It doesn't matter as long as it is clean,' I said, trying to widen the choice.

The best thing he could find was called the Laxmi. There were mosquitoes everywhere and the bed had a net surrounding it but it was covered with holes. The bathroom had no bath or shower, only a simple yellow bucket and matching mug with a makeshift drainage system. The toilet was a hole on a step between two concrete slabs; basically you had to hoist yourself up and employ a squatting position to be able to use it effectively. 'It's perfect,' I said to Krishna, who looked at me, unconvinced.

We washed and had lunch, which consisted of sad-looking grains of rice, stuck together as if they really didn't want to be there in a mangled spinach sauce served on a banana leaf. I played with mine, thinking there was no popadom which I could hide it under so there was no option but to eat it. Dessert was a deflated gulabjambo, which I had to leave because it was full of syrup in which a battalion of red ants had lost their lives. We paid the waiter and continued on the journey. 'How far now?' I asked Vijay.

'One hour.'

The trees swept onto the roads as if to claim it all back, brushing against the car and depositing a confetti of curious-looking insects on the car windows. When the foliage cleared, all you could see for miles were green paddy fields soaking up the sun, surrounded by tall reeds and sugar cane plantations, against a background of moody purple mountains. People were dotted around the fields and as they looked up, they waved. An hour and a half and several winding inroads later, we finally arrived at what appeared to be Colleanauta.

The noise the car made brought people who were praying in the temple, drinking in the toddi shop, bathing or washing clothes in the lake and working on the land to congregate where we had stopped. It was in the centre of the village square which had a temple and a rice mill next to it. Vijay beeped at them so they would move out of the way. Some of the children jumped back, startled, thinking that God had sent us, others stood there and watched, laughing. They stood with baited breath. In my fragmented Malayalam, I asked for Ammu Menon. They began to whisper to each other.

'Nalini.' Someone shouted and then someone else began to shout, 'Nalini, it's me, Luxmiammayi.' Why was it they thought people never aged? Someone from the crowd stepped forward, squeezed his way towards me and invited me into his home.

The man was very tall with greying hair and a beard, which he had tried to dye dark brown but had turned out a henna orange. He also had a constellation of spots on his right cheek. Something was very familiar about him. Krishna said maybe it was better if I went on my own. I made my way with him through the crowd. Some of them followed and others stayed by the car and a few carried on with their business, speculating and gossiping. The man showed me into his home which was behind the temple. We took our shoes off and entered a type of courtyard which had a broken water fountain. Sitting on the bench was an old woman. An elegantly-dressed lady came out and looked at me suspiciously. 'I'm Maya, Ammu's grandchild,' I said awkwardly, looking over at the old woman just to make doubly sure this wasn't her.

'I know,' he replied.

I looked again at her; was it? She didn't smile or give me any indication.

'You look exactly like your mother,' he said. 'I am Gobi, Gobi Kathi.'

Stunned, I had to sit down.

I didn't even think of finding them. The old lady, she was my other grandmother and he, he was my uncle. I didn't know I had an uncle.

'Uncle?' I asked.

'Uncle,' I said again, excited.

He nodded dismissively. 'How is Raul?'

I didn't know where to begin, what could I say? 'He's . . . he's well.' I stammered.

'We haven't seen him for nearly thirty years.'

That couldn't be right, didn't he come and see them when he came looking for us?

'I thought he came here some time back.'

His brother laughed coldly. 'Not since he ran off with your mother.'

Ran off with her? He never ran off with her. They were introduced, his family had arranged it, and they moved to Mumbai.

He told the old lady who I was and she glared at me. No long-lost embrace, smile, receptive welcome or nod, just a glacial expression as if I had no right to sit there in her house.

'Your mother was a taker, nothing but a taker, she took the gift I bought her and lured him.'

I had no idea what he was talking about. What gift?

'Both of them, your mother and grandmother, they worked their magic on him and took him, finally got what they had always wanted, his money.'

Gobi told me that Achan was about to marry someone else when suddenly he left with Amma, leaving his fiancée stranded. 'It was shameless, he told her he loved her,' he shouted. His father could not cope with the embarrassment and shortly after, suffered a heart attack

245

so Gobi came back to look after things at home and married the fiancée so the family would not lose face and standing. The elegant lady who stood there looking at me disdainfully was to have been my father's wife.

'And Ammu?'

He huffed. 'She had gone to live with your mother and father in the north and years later she came back but nobody spoke to her and she died. Died in her shack just across the lakes.' He waved his hand in the direction of the temple. 'Died' was said with bitterness as if he was glad that she got what she deserved.

All this way and she was dead. Dead and he was happy she was dead.

'Where was her home?' I asked.

He repeated the way I said home and laughed, giving me a few directions. He made no offer to take me there, no glass of water or hug goodbye. I went over to my other grandmother to say something, to hold her hand but she turned her face. This is what Amma had done to them. I put on my sandals and walked across the sandy ground to find her home. A few people that were waiting outside the Kathis' house trailed behind me. I said nothing, and made my way to the house that he had described.

Just behind the lake on a hill stood a solitary shack amongst some trees. Nobody wanted to live there because they said it was cursed. Cursed with her magic. The people that were following me stopped short of the hill and I climbed up alone and above it were a row of mango trees and a broken fence. You couldn't really see the shack, as it was covered with vegetation, but I spotted something wooden and, sensing that it might be the

246

front door, I kicked it open. As I did so, something screeched and flapped around.

The room was filled with cobwebs and smelt of rot. A basic shack is where she spent the rest of her life. I took a stick from the ground and poked at the webs so I could see a little more clearly. A mat lay on the floor surrounded by some cast iron pots and I spotted some pictures beneath a battered wooden crate by the mat. On the crate was a statue, pale blue, covered with cobwebs. I went in, grabbed the pictures, looked just for a fleeting moment at the statue and considered running out again. Instead, I crouched next to the pots, gently brushing the cobwebs away. Tears ran down my cheeks but I didn't really know why I felt so sad. The Goddess was looking at me. 'Tell me what really happened?' I asked her. I picked her up and went running as fast as I could to the other side of the lake where it was quiet.

A gentle stream ran behind the hill and I sat near some rocks. The pictures were of Satchin and I as babies with Amma, some were of my Ammamma holding us, a smile that stretched from ear to ear with her teeth that she had put in especially for the pictures. Dressed in her cream cotton kasava mundu, she didn't work magic, she worked love, I thought. It's wrong what Gobi said about her. I put my head between my knees and cried. Exhausted. Someone put an arm around me and I looked up, feeling defeated.

'Little Maya, she spoke so much about you.'

Saffron-stained chest, carrying a simple black bag and wearing only a loincloth, an old man smiled at me. He said he was the astrologer.

'How did she die?' I cried.

247

'It's not important how she died, what's important is how she lived and she touched at least a thousand lives using her gifts, something many never get to do in one lifetime. When you do what you love, Little Maya, you experience the greatest sorrow and the greatest joy and this is how it has always been. Sorrow because this is the only way life can teach. It gives you the opportunity to confront your fears. She knew when she came back that she would have to face the wrath of the people because they fear all that they do not understand; they fear what is different. She faced their ignorance with the greatest courage and when none of the villagers ate what she cooked, she fed those who knocked on her door, touching them and guiding them along their paths in ways that you cannot even begin to imagine. Not once did she think of stopping or moving away so life would be easier. She knew you would come, we didn't even bother to work out when because she was certain. She gave me this for you.'

He pulled out a small note from his bag but I couldn't read it. I gave it back to him and asked him to read it. He searched again in the bag and pulled out an old pair of spectacles.

Maya Mol,
When you are ready, the truth will come and find you. I know you are brave enough, for invisible things too are passed through the genes. Your journey, you know, begins here in the place where you are from. When you find truth in all his various forms, face him, take him by the neck, forgive and let go.
From letting go comes a peace and a love that is

impossible to buy or have anyone else give to you. It is an absolute freedom from all that we seek to prove. And when you do this, all that you have within you will be enough.

Do what you love, find the pace: listen for the magical conversation that is always taking place through the food that you savour, the words that are spoken to you, the music that you hear, the people that you meet, and you will never feel alone. This, Maya Mol, is abundance.

Know that I will love you no matter where you are or what you do and that I am always, always with you, even on the days of doubting, when you think that it is all just an illusion.

Ammamma

He folded it up and gave it back to me. Putting the spectacles back in his bag, he pulled out another note. 'This is for your mother, give it to her,' he instructed.

'Read it to me.'

He shook his head. 'It is for when you are ready to meet her,' he replied.

'Did your father leave, like your Ammamma said he would?' the astrologer enquired.

'I don't know, I don't think so,' I said, and I thought for a long time in silence.

'Did she go peacefully?' I asked.

'She couldn't have gone any other way.'

He said a prayer, the same one my mother always said but the one I never allowed her to complete, and then he told me the story of King Mahabali, the story Amma began and the one I never let her finish. He told me about sacrifice, the King's sacrifice, Ammamma's sacrifice to let us go. He ended by saying that this was only possible because she truly believed that the spirit always lives on.

I took the letters and went back to find the car.

Krishna and the driver were busy signing autographs for the school children who had hijacked the car. It was very late and their mothers came out of the houses, dragging them back home. Some asked if we wanted to stay and have dinner and then a fight broke out as to whose house we would eat in. We thanked them all and said it would be better to leave. Before we knew it, various savouries tied in cotton were thrust through the car windows and the villagers waved us off. None of my father's family came to say goodbye but then I didn't really expect them to.

'Did you find her?' Krishna asked.

'Yes, I found her.'

The journey was silent, each of us lost in our own thoughts, playing against the orchestra of crickets and frogs. We arrived back at the hotel and went to sleep.

The next day, Vijay left us at the airport. He cried as we left. I don't know if this was because of the size of the tip we gave him or because he would miss us but he said that he would say a prayer for me every week so that God would send me a good husband with a large plot of land, even a plantation. Krishna and I took a flight back to Mumbai the next day. It would have been possible to go back to Spain that very day, but I wanted to stay, not in the Taj, but in a home. I asked Krishna if he could arrange it. He said he lived outside of Mumbai with his parents and if I wanted to stay, I would be more than welcome, but it was basic. So I packed up my things and he came to collect me.

Krishna worked for Ravi Thakker in one of his offices in Mumbai. He had been there ten years, since leaving college. He wasn't married and said that you didn't have to look for these things, if they were meant to happen they would, when the time was right. His mother thought differently and left pictures of various girls in the dining area with a short résumé of their lives, hoping that one might catch his eye.

The house was sparse but they had everything they needed and it was, most importantly, filled with warmth. Krishna had bought it for them a few years ago and they were very proud of him. The latest purchase he had made for his family was a colour television, which they kept safely locked up in a metal cabinet and only brought out for special events. His parents were very welcoming, his mother probably thought I had ulterior motives for staying and tried hard to communicate with me. Not understanding a word of what she was saying, I smiled and probably unwittingly said yes to a host of wedding plans.

I spent days on end sitting in the kitchen area with his mother and their servant girl. I watched spices being ground with stone, leaves being soaked and dried in the sun, fruit being preserved into pickles, dishes prepared from scratch with love and attention. Each person was working through their own thoughts and kneading dough or grinding lentils was a temporary respite. The end results were amazing: brightly coloured and full of freshness, not packaged for convenience and thrown together in disposable haste; answers so clear that it was impossible not to see them.

Packing the soft fabrics suffused with aroma and colour as passionate as the people who had made them, I said goodbye to Krishna's family. His mother wept. Krishna took me to the airport and as I was saying goodbye, I handed him an envelope. As I sat on the plane, I took my Ammamma's letters and placed them at the very bottom of my handbag and there, I saw Krishna's returned envelope with a note scribbled, 'Maya, you have given me enough, find what you are looking for and come back.' I knew there would come a time when I would revisit all my letters but for now, other things were pending. I wanted to savour everything that India had given me; a sense of peace and stability like I had never felt before. I sat there on the aircraft thinking about it all, when my thoughts were interrupted by a gushing sound. The airline was spraying disinfectant on the plane hoping that whatever we brought back was not contagious.

Perhaps sensing that he was losing me, Marcos came to meet me at the airport. I didn't tell him exactly which flight I was taking so he must have waited there for hours. He came with a bunch of white lilies. I never thought he heard me when I said they were my favourite, overriding the conversation we were having with friends by talking about the make of a particular vase they had in their dining room. It was the first time I had ever received flowers from him, simple scented lilies, just as I loved. 'Maya, I've been doing a lot of thinking whilst you have been away and you cannot possibly imagine how much I have missed you. How was it?'

What could I possibly say so that he would understand? That India had revived a part of me that was lying dormant? That colours, aromas, contradictions, emotions from the place that we are from are born with us, and at some point we are asked to rediscover them? That I had caught a glimpse of the pace?

'It was good,' I replied.

As we got into the car, he looked at me and said, 'Maya, I have come to realise how much I love you. I am ready to move out of Palmadoro, I know I've made mistakes in the past, but I'm ready. Here, I have something for you.'

Isn't it a funny thing when the things that you most want come and they don't seem as important any more. He produced a single solitaire diamond ring. 'Will you, Maya? Will you marry me? *Te quiero, Maya, cariño. ¿lo sabes no?*'

Sometimes we are not ready to face whatever it is we have to or maybe things are sent along to distract us from all that we resolve to do. Would she have been disappointed? I thought. No, she would have understood.

'Yes,' I said. 'Mr Gonzalez del Hoyo, I will be your wife.'

Enrique was delighted with the samples. '*Cariño*, just what I was thinking of. You got the colours right as well. This purple will work so well for the autumn collection. What do you think, Maya?' I smiled as he showed me the designs for the fabric.

'Maya, there has been something I have been meaning to ask you. How would you like to set up an office for me in London? We need a base there and you've lived in London, haven't you?'

London. It took me by shock. London. I couldn't go there. I thought momentarily of Amma and all the questions I had for her and then of Marcos, this man I was tied to. Yes, there was Marcos, I couldn't leave him; he needed me, I loved him, he had his faults but I loved him. London was out of the question.

'I'm getting married, Enrique. I can't just go to London, not now.'

He mumbled something about Marcos, but I didn't hear exactly what he said and I chose not to ask him to repeat it.

Work continued amongst a host of wedding plans which I left with María Carmen who was only too delighted to accept responsibility. I absolutely loved my work and took every opportunity that Enrique gave me. I never noticed the hours as they flew by; it wasn't like I was trying to distract myself from all the things that I had in my mind, I was just waiting, waiting for the right moment. Then four months later, an opportunity came to visit a few clients in the States like I knew it would. It only took a week to visit them all in New York and then I caught a flight to Chicago.

Ravi's parents lived there and I thought momentarily of paying Fingers a visit but this idea soon evaporated at the thought of her insisting that I stay with her. I checked into a hotel and then called a cab. The cab driver took me to the address that I had taken from one of Raul's letterheads. Excuses, always excuses. Sometimes the truth is staring you in the face but you don't want to see it. 'Maya, I tried calling several times but there was no connection.' 'I left you a message, didn't you get it?' 'Maya, I won't be able to make it now in the summer, are you around in the fall?' 'Maya, I can't talk right now, I'll call you back or better still, I'll write.' Then the fragmented shorthand would come to me with a note saying how much he loved me, along with a cheque.

I rang the apartment intercom and a voice asked me who I was. 'I'm looking for Raul,' I said.

'Sure, come on up,' said the young man's voice.

I walked two flights of stairs and the apartment door was left open.

Not very big for an oil tycoon, I thought.

A very handsome man emerged from behind the door and I was taken aback. 'I'm sorry to disturb you but does Raul live here?'

'Yeah, he does, but he's not in at the moment. Come on in and take a seat, he shouldn't be long,' he replied, showing me to a hideous red leather sofa.

'I'm Maya. His . . .' My voice trailed off.

'A friend from England?'

'Yes,' I replied, wondering who he could be.

'Dad's always talking about his time in England.'

Dad? This was his son? He couldn't be, he was around the same age as me. 'Dad?' I repeated, looking around at the pictures of strangers on the side table, holding my composure.

'Can't you tell? Everyone says we look so alike. I'm Ralf,' he said in his plastic voice.

'Raul doesn't look old enough,' I said, trying to figure out his age.

'He does, I'm only twenty-two,' he laughed.

He was three years younger than me, my father was still married to Amma, we were selling up things to move to England, Ammamma was left at the gate in the rain.

'And your mother?' I blurted.

He looked confused. 'She is back in Ohio with my little sister, they're not together any more. Do you have brothers and sisters?'

What? I thought, I wanted to choke. Did I have brothers and sisters? 'I have . . . had two,' I said, choking.

'Can I get you something to drink, coffee, something cold?' he asked.

Something to drink? Something to drink? What was he talking about?

He got me a glass of water.

'And your sister? How old is she?' I managed.

'Jemma's eighteen,' he replied, puzzled.

Eighteen. That made me seven when he had her and Satchin nine. He left us living in a hovel so he could play house with another family. I looked up and saw a vain solitary picture of him placed proudly on an awful mahogany sideboard. I wanted to get up and spit on it.

'Is that your sister?' I asked, walking over to the sideboard, looking at a picture of the three of them. She was sitting on his back, oh yes that pathetic piggyback ride that Satchin and I fought to have.

'Yeah, but that was taken a long time ago, she doesn't look anything like that now.'

Next to it was another picture of the two of them with a Labrador. 'Tikko,' I stammered.

'Yeah, how did you know that?'

I wanted to scream. 'I don't know,' I whispered.

Aya's words rang in my ears. 'He loved himself.' I moved towards the door.

'He shouldn't be too long. He'll be really disappointed that he missed you,' he said, looking over at the door.

'Somehow I don't think so,' I replied, opening it.

Ralf looked confused.

'I'm sure he won't be long,' he insisted. 'Shall I tell him that you'll come again or give me a number where you are staying and I'll get him to call you.'

'No,' I replied, as I tried not to run in my haste to get out. 'No, don't do that.'

'She married a mistake, she married a mistake,' the words screamed again and again in my head as I ran down the stairs. I got out of that building as fast as I could and was immediately sick on the pavement. He was not my father; he had never been a father and was better dead.

The fear of rejection is bigger than the actual state but he had made it easier by·slowly chipping away, not handing it to me in one big block. Unlike me who rejected all those who really mattered. Thoughts of Amma came to me as I got myself together. Almost four years of silence, I had rejected her, made her suffer. After first meeting Raul, every subsequent word I spoke to her was full of hatred and it got to a point where I couldn't bring myself to speak to her at all. All those years I made Ravi Thakker feel useless, yet he was the only thing that was ever solid in our lives. Satchin didn't meet Raul again; years that I had filled with remorse that Satchin didn't get to see him were replaced by gratitude. How is it possible to get things so wrong? I wanted to take a plane home, hold Amma and say that I was sorry, so sorry for everything I had put her through but guilt overwhelmed me and I didn't know where to start. It was better without me; maybe they were better as they were, getting on with things. I caught the plane back to Spain. Throughout the journey, I just kept thinking, 'When you are ready, the truth will come and find you.'

Peroxide blonde hair in the bathtub that he said belonged to the black-haired cleaning lady, Lucía. Reliable Lucía, mother of two, had suddenly decided to go blonde? A woman with the same hair colour came up to him for a slow dance at a friend's wedding. 'Go on, it's okay, dance with the lady,' I said to Marcos, not even thinking. Marcos Gonzalez del Hoyo was probably a lot like Raul Kartha or Kathi or whatever he called himself. Magnetic, yet showing vulnerability when he sensed he was losing, not deep vulnerability but just enough so you became hooked on the pattern of making things better because you thought the fault resided in you. Trying harder, giving more, until most of yourself had gone and before you knew it, there was really nothing left. Control. It had a lot to do with control and power. How could he have left her with two small children and not even care?

Instead of going to Palmadoro on the weekend that I landed, I took a week off work so I could piece things together in my head. As I went for a walk that first morning, I saw the lady with her two dogs, her head was lowered and she didn't glance up. '*Hola,*' I said again and when she looked sideways, I saw her eye was black and bruised. She stayed in my mind that entire day and the day after that. I wanted to run after her and tell her she deserved better, that she was worth more, deserved much more. I sat and thought about how much of myself I had compromised to be acceptable to another, how much I refused to see things to make myself feel secure and all along everything was as secure as I believed it to be. Marcos kept calling. It was finally time to do something. I took a train to Palmadoro later that evening. Marcos said that he would come and collect me from the station. 'I'm fine,' I said. 'I'll make my own way.'

When I walked in the door, white lilies were waiting on the table. It was very late and he had not arrived back from work. I fell asleep, exhausted. He did not wake me when he came home as he normally did. The next morning, I said we needed to talk but he was rushing off and said that he would make sure he came home early and we would go out for dinner. María Carmen called to say that she would be coming over to show me some wedding invitations. I wanted to tell her no, stop, but it was already too late. She had put the receiver down and was on her way. Maybe it was too late. This was the day my father Ravi called to say Maggie was ill.

The plane landed at Heathrow airport; it was raining and grey. There was a knot in my stomach: anxiety, relief, happiness, apprehension, sorrow, weariness, all rolled up in a tight ball, waiting. Before we got off the plane, I asked the air hostess if she would be flying back to Spain. 'Yes,' she smiled. I handed over the coat with some money for postage and an address where she could send it. I attached a note to María Carmen saying that I was very sorry and that I would call to explain.

My father and my sister were waiting at the airport. I left my trolley and ran over to them. Shorty had grown so tall. I hugged them both, squeezing out all the years I had been without them. 'Amma?' I cried.

'She's back home, cooking for you.'

'And Maggie?'

'Maggie is very ill, Maya, I don't think she has very long.' He tried to prepare me.

I was so desperate to see Amma but half an hour would not make any difference to the time that had already gone. Maggie needed me. I needed to see her.

'Can we drive by and see Maggie first?'

Ammu looked at me shyly. She didn't say very much and throughout the car journey, there was none of her parrot chatter. I asked her questions and she said very little.

Ravi dropped me off in front of Maggie's house and said he would go home, tell Amma where I was and come and collect me in an hour. He and Ammu drove off. I stood outside her door and waited. I don't know what I was waiting for but as I wiped my tears, I rang the doorbell. An African lady opened it.

'You must be Maya,' she said. 'Your mother left an hour ago and she said you would be coming.' She smiled as she showed me in.

There was no odour that lingered of warm lamb stew, electric heating or wax from candles. It smelt of sterile bleach. The green carpet on the staircase was worn and dirty. The pictures still hung on her landing: one of a sheep dog, another of Tom; Satchin and me holding

Ammu and one of Maggie and Jack. Jack had died a few months ago; I hadn't made it to the funeral. The African lady, Joyce, was talking to me but I wasn't listening, I was thinking about the times I came running down these stairs. 'Not so fast, Maya, you'll ruin the carpet,' Maggie would say. It now looked like sundried moss. The last time I ran down them I was filled with disgust and contempt for what she had told me and didn't want to believe it. It hardly mattered. Joyce opened Maggie's bedroom door and said, 'Maggie, I have someone to see you.' There was no reply, no Maggie laugh. I walked in and there she was, lying in bed, almost unrecognisable.

Soft, pallid, white skin hanging from her face, she looked half her weight, with a red scarf tied around her head, her blue eyes set deep into her face as if they were preparing to say goodbye. She looked at me and tried to smile. 'Maya, darling,' she managed. I went over to her, put my arms around her frail body and kissed her forehead. 'At last,' she whispered.

'Don't say anything, Maggie.'

She took a deep breath and said, 'Did you find it in Spain?'

'Yes and no,' I cried. 'Why didn't you call me earlier, Maggie?'

She closed her eyes. Joyce came and moved her head slightly so she would be more comfortable.

Joyce told me that the two people she kept calling for over and over again in her sleep were Tom and myself. They could not find Tom. Ravi had looked but had had no luck. 'She's holding on,' said Joyce, 'She's a fighter.'

Nobody had called me earlier to say how ill she was, that was probably her doing. She was as stubborn as any person I have ever met. Sitting in a little pair of high-fashion tan corduroy trousers that she made me when I was eight, we were arguing at her dinner table. 'You are not leaving the table, Maya, until you eat all those vegetables up. There are people going hungry for that.'

'Well, let them eat it,' I shouted back at her.

'I'll just sit here until you finish,' she said adamantly. Hours went by and she was still there.

'I hate you!' I screamed at her.

'Well, I suppose someone's got to,' she laughed.

'And I hate your doll. She's horrible and I call her Creepy,' I added.

Hours went by and it was nearly dinner time and I conceded. But Maggie never made you feel like you had lost. She got up, left the table and said, 'You want to come and watch some television with me?'

I sat there on her bed, watching her sleep. Most of her had already gone and the part that was clinging to life was a mere flicker of the person she once was. 'It's not important how you die, it's who you touch,' the astrologer had said. Without her, I could not even begin to think what would have happened to us. Squeezing her hand, I could not control my breathing and began to sob. 'Don't go, Maggie, please don't go, I haven't told you how sorry I am for what I did, for leaving you the way I did. For judging you and not giving you a chance. It wasn't you, there was so much going on at the time. You can't leave without knowing how much I love you, you can't, Maggie, you have to know how sorry I am and that I love you.'

A tiny squeeze came back and then I heard the doorbell, and Joyce's footsteps running downstairs. 'She is upstairs,' Joyce replied. My heart beat faster, was she here? Had she come to meet me? Was it her? My hands became sweaty and tears streamed down my face.

NALINI

Soothing coconut milk poured into the potato and onion stew as it boiled doubts away. It was the only thing Maya really liked to eat. Served on a bed of pancakes made with pulses, throbbing black gram and angry red split lentils. Hardened seed surrounded by layers to survive external conditions, taking hours, like the years of absence, to soak and soften into a gentle centre, all that I knew she was. Grinding resentment in a blender, surrendering the liquid into a harmless batter, poured into a solid cast iron pan. Finally coated with ghee, soft and golden, which melts into kindness. My daughter was coming home. Sprinkling just a little turmeric, so she would hardly notice it was there, I placed the mixture in the fridge and went upstairs to change.

Wounds are sealed with turmeric and from the thousands of fronds from the crocus flower, which make saffron. Bright yellow and reddy-orange like the warmth of the sun, sent to heal any place of hurt or injustice. It is a funny thing but we are unable to administer our own medicine, healing others to cure our own insatiable grief. I often wondered why my mother did this, but now I know. I fed the mourners chicken with a marinade of turmeric and saffron as they came to offer their condolences after Satchin's funeral. When they had gone, I came down in the middle of the night, took a pair of scissors, and cut the heads of every single flower they had left as a mark of their respect, black night absorbing the colours that nobody could see. The morning sun shone in the lounge and brightened the stains, which covered the sadness on the carpets and the walls with sporadic yellows and reds, like a child's finger-painting.

Nobody explained this kind of pain to me, not even my mother; the split second when you see big, dirty trainers lying in the hallway and you smile with relief, thinking it was all a cruel joke. Then you remember, and your heart breaks. You breathe in his scent as you enter his tidy room but there is no loud, irritating music and your heart breaks again. An extra plate that is unwittingly set, a phone call from someone who is unaware that he is gone and the heart splits open. Grief is all engulfing.

Nothing pulls you out of it, not even seeing another suffer in the same way; the sobs that I heard from the other side of the wall were Maya's, who stored her tears for night time. We grieve alone. Months went by and it didn't get easier. Getting out of bed and facing reality was like a punishment. I wondered whether telling someone about the lies would ease the pain, make it all go away. Because, maybe, the loss feels so great that losing everything would feel exactly the same and it wouldn't really matter anyway.

'Ravi, I have something to tell you,' I cried, as he came to console me.

'No, Nalu, I know,' he responded calmly.

'No, you don't know, you don't understand. Maybe Satchin was taken because I lied.'

There was a pause and to silence my fit of distress, he assured me that he knew, that it was not important. What was important was that he was there for me and would always be.

Three years passed before that conversation was resumed. Punctuated with delusion and question marks. By then, the very things I worked to protect had gone. My greatest fear was losing Satchin and Maya, most of my actions were determined by this, ever since they were babies. I was meant to look after and protect them as I had promised, but then I lost them both, in ways I had never imagined possible. Maya left for Spain and I sensed it would be a while before she returned, if she ever did.

Grief brings you to a place where you realise that nothing really belongs to you, it is all borrowed and what you are faced with is the cold, blank reality that truth stays, it is the only thing that accompanies you, standing all tests of time. My mother was right when she said it just came in just two shades; black or white, ingrained in the soil with the hands with which it is planted. Truth grows constant, bearing its fruit, follow-ing your every move. Ravi needed to be told.

'Nalu, whatever it is, I know and it doesn't matter.'

We were sitting at the kitchen table, he was trying to

clear some plates but I made him sit down and listen. I told him that I wasn't the woman he thought I was, I was already married, my husband had left us but in my heart, he was dead. Dead because that was what he deserved but he came back again and I paid him to leave so he would never make contact with the children. I lied to them. Satchin would never know but there was Maya, she needed to be told. Ravi did not flinch.

Raul had informed Ravi's brother that I was his wife the very night they came for dinner and Anil notified his mother who hurried downstairs the very next morning to enlighten her son. Ravi told her that he was aware and asked her to leave. All that he was certain of was that he loved me, and knowing me like he did, he said I must have had my reasons and when the time was right, they would emerge. After Satchin died, the reasons became irrelevant.

'Why didn't you say anything?'

'We all make many mistakes but the intention is all that matters, Nalu.' he said.

'And when I sold the shop?' I cried.

'You did what you thought was best at the time. It is past, Nalu. What's important is what we have now and you have suffered enough.'

'You should have said something; why didn't you?'

Ravi put his arms around me and I decided to face what I had neglected for so long.

Maya, Maya needed to know. I wanted to call her back from Spain, sit down with her face to face and explain, and then if she wanted to find him, that was her decision. We had barely spoken in the last few years, each consumed with our own grief, and as time went

267

by, she seemed to get further away from us, building her own life in another place. She seemed very happy. Many times I asked her to come home. 'Soon,' she kept saying, but she didn't return. Then one day as I was in the garden planting some coriander seeds, I decided it was time to let her go. Never once did I stop loving her and it was then that I understood what my mother did for me and what she meant by letting go. I went back into the kitchen.

Volcanic dried red chillies and mustard seeds bubble in boiling hot oil and burst, releasing their insides. The pungent smell fills the room with a black choking smoke, clinging to all that surrounds it, years of stagnation, guilt and sorrow that I had not been a good daughter, wife or mother, failing miserably in every role. I opened the kitchen door and windows, and the suffocating fog is enticed away. Courage revisits and blows a gentle, hopeful breeze telling me there is now space so I am able to start again, building brick by brick on new foundations. It happens when you are ready and not a day before.

Taking a loan from the bank, I leased a new shop, not as big as the previous one, but a little shop which would give big things. I painted the walls myself in a deep red. The carpenters came to fit the kitchen, make the counters and to lay the wooden flooring. Ravi had bought me a brass fan, imported from India, and that was the last thing to be fitted. Maggie said she didn't want to come and join me. After Raul had left with the money raised by selling the first shop, we were consumed with our respective fears; I was afraid that he would come back and she thought there would come a time when Jack would find out about her past and also leave her. So we didn't really work or concentrate but wallowed. Three days a week at home, we pickled bottles of fear that came back to us returned until there was no business left. When Satchin died, it came to a definitive end and then Jack became ill and so Maggie absorbed herself by taking care of him. She would never return.

Ana, my old cleaning lady, and Anita came to help me. Everything in the shop would have the fundamental ingredients of dried red chillies and black mustard seeds. The wind chimes rang and the priest walked in the morning before we opened. The old man smiled, his teeth had fallen out but he looked at me, beaming. Not saying a word, he smashed a saffron-stained coconut, took out his tin and left a blessing which he decorated on my forehead. The shop was adorned with fresh fruit and flowers, and little Annapurna was given her place, surrounded by scented incense. We were ready to open.

People somehow manage to find what they need. Most of our customers brought their doubts, regrets, guilt and worries to the shop. As they sighed, the room filled with all that was bothering them; a broken marriage; the death of a loved one; a lie so big it was unable to be contained; an unresolved argument. It all stuck to the walls and counters. Out in the back, I would explode the chillies and mustard seeds in boiling sesame oil. The thick fog would leave no hostages, wafting into every corner of the shop, attaching itself to the walls and suffocating all the sadness that was already there. Customers would wheeze an irritable cough and their chests became heavy. The windows and doors were opened and the fan extractor would suck everything away: bitterness; regret, animosity, all swallowed up. A gentle breeze would circulate with the rotating motion of the brass fan, calming, soothing. The mixture of fried condiments were added to whatever felt appropriate on that day; sometimes it would be in the marinade for dry savouries and other days it went into the pickles. People came in and they went out lighter, letting go of what they needed to.

Ammu came into the shop on Saturdays, not because I asked her to but because she loved being there. She would spend hours propping herself up against the counter talking to the customers, or in the kitchen with me. The packages and bottles were filled with her whistling or singing. At ten, she was a little version of Ravi, putting other people before herself. Ammu was constant. When Satchin and Maya both left, it really upset her and when she saw me lost somewhere in my grief, she would sit with me as if to reassure me that she wasn't going anywhere.

Watching her learn and ask me questions about the spices brings me full circle.

'Why does cinnamon take away bitterness, Amma? Will this combination take sadness away?' 'Why do you have to serve it in that order?' The questions I asked my own mother, who sat and explained as she let me practise. Sitting on the floor beside her, with the fresh spices that we had collected in our baskets, my mother and I crushed the spices with a heavy stone so they would lose their coarseness and left them out in the sun in preparation for the vegetable man, who came every week.

Normally, nobody would let him in but my mother always invited him for tea and savouries. Lifting the basket of vegetables off his head, he would leave them on the floor with his worries, enraptured with spreading the village gossip a little further whilst devouring all that my mother placed before him. Then just before leaving, he would pick out all the rotten brinjals, aubergines and drumsticks that were strategically placed on the top and delve to find the freshest produce and hand it over to my mother. He would pinch my cheeks with his soiled hands, say 'Aye chanthakari' (beautiful girl) and leave.

I worked four days a week at the shop and would be back home by four o' clock, giving me ample time to prepare a good meal so that the three of us could sit and eat together. Leaving space for Ravi also healed the marriage. It wasn't broken, I just hadn't participated in the years following Satchin's death – and probably even before then. Meeting Raul again had set me back in time with the need of constant reassurance that Ravi would not leave me or the children. Desperation does strange things. The space between us was occupied once again by new plans, conversation, understanding and love and that is how life became for the three of us and for the first time, I was not afraid.

The shop was always busy but not so that people could not move. Only occasionally did I go out in the front to serve, when I sensed that Ana could not take time to speak to the customers individually. One Thursday afternoon, Ana had to leave early so I was serving. The shop was empty when the chimes went and a handsome, young man with black ruffled hair, dressed in a white T-shirt and blue denim jeans walked in. I looked down and then I looked up again, it was Suri. Startled, he stopped abruptly in the middle of the shop beneath the brass fan and stared at me.

'Auntie,' he managed to whisper.

I didn't know what to do so I came from behind the counter to where he was standing and I held out my arms. He took hold of me and began crying like a little boy. I stroked his hair, like I had done with my own son; when Satchin had fallen from the scooter; when he failed his exams and felt he had let us down. Tears trickled to the floor.

'I'm so sorry, Auntie,' was all he kept saying. It was as if it was yesterday but six years had passed since that terrible day. It looked as if he carried those years with him. Sadness poured out of him as if he had never been allowed to display it. 'So many times, I wanted to come and see you and tell you that I am so sorry,' he sobbed.

'It was an accident, Monu,' I cried, as I squeezed him tightly. 'It was an accident.'

Softly, I spoke to him until he calmed down. I walked over to the door, put the 'Closed' sign up, went to the kitchen, made some tea and put some savouries on a plate. I told Anita she could go home if she wanted. Suri took a stool and sat behind the counter facing me, his eyes bloodshot and heavy.

'It has got better, Monu,' I whispered, as he coughed and caught his breath.

'How are you, Auntie? Are you okay?'

'Everything is fine now. Eat, Monu, and drink your tea.'

'And uncle and Ammu and . . . ?'

Maya, I wanted to finish. His Maya.

Maya who he liked from the moment he came to work in the shop. She was twelve, always dressed in clothes she had made herself, except on the days the boys came and then she wore tracksuits so they wouldn't laugh at her. But Suri was never laughing at her. Maya did not even notice the way he adjusted his hair before seeing her, how he went out of his way to help her or asked Satchin to invite her along to whatever they were doing. Satchin refused, so he would sneak away a few moments to go and speak to her on his own, inventing silly excuses. Maya, not understanding, would be frustrated with his lack of common sense. 'How many times do I have to tell you, Suri? The boxes are kept in the cupboard in the storeroom,' she would shout.

Suri spent many evenings at our home, having dinner with us and then suddenly this stopped. I asked Satchin if they had fought but he said no. Then the days when he did come, he could barely look at Maya. Something changed between them. It was Suri who began to change her, softening the jagged edges, he opened a soft centre and she showed she cared. One day, Ravi and I were driving back from the supermarket and we saw them together, holding hands as they walked slowly to the top of the road, then he left her there. A few days after that, Ravi spoke to Suri and said wouldn't it be better if he took her to the front door and then he could come in. He smiled with that warm, embarrassed smile that could only belong to Suri.

He was too injured to come to the funeral but he sent us some white lilies which the florist mixed up so a neighbour brought them later that evening, after all the guests had left. That was what triggered the decapitation of the rest of the flowers. Not that I ever wanted it to have been him that was killed, nor did I hate him. I'm still not quite sure what it was, maybe anger or desperation. Maya could not deal with it, she couldn't deal with any of it and also cut Suri off like she did the rest of us, Maggie included, retreating to her room and her books, and just as I was getting myself together, she went.

'Maya is fine,' I filled in.

His face brightened. 'What is she doing?' he asked avidly.

'She has a job with a fashion designer.'

Suri managed to laugh as if to say he might have guessed.

'Is she here in London?' His voice strengthened with excitement.

'She's in Spain, Maya has been there for the last four years.'

'Spain,' he repeated. 'Is she . . . is she married?'

I didn't really want to mention that she was engaged. Engaged to a man that we had never met or knew very little about. 'Tell me, Maya, what is he like? Send me pictures,' I asked eagerly when we spoke. She said they would come to London to see us to discuss wedding plans, but they never did. 'Go and talk to her,' I wanted to say to Suri. 'Call her.'

'She's engaged,' I mumbled, not wanting him to hear the sentence.

Suri looked disappointed. For a few minutes, it felt like he was back there with her, walking her home. Then he changed the subject, telling me that he was on his way to see his parents. His mother had called to ask him to stop by and get some savouries for some visitors that were coming around. He didn't know where to begin but as he drove by, he caught sight of the shop.

'It's a shop that finds you. She'll like this one,' I said, handing him some lightly-coated fried banana chips. 'And take some pickles for her as well, these are good,' I added, giving him a case of six, hoping Suri would take some for himself.

He told me that he was almost a doctor; he had passed his exams and was training. Then, before leaving, Suri took a piece of paper, wrote his number and gave it to me. 'If you ever need anything, Auntie, all you have to do is call,' he said as he kissed me goodbye.

Just as he was going out of the door, he started to say something. 'Tell her, tell her . . .' He didn't finish.

You tell her, I wanted to say as I ran to hug him again, but all I managed was, 'Suri, I'm proud of you. Very, very proud of you.'

He kissed me again and left.

I wanted to call up Maya that evening and tell her that I had seen him but she was on holiday and when I eventually spoke to her and she told us she was marrying Marcos in Spain and not in England, it seemed better not to even mention it. Maya was happy, she had moved on. Again, she promised she would visit soon and then a week later, when Jack died, she said she was coming home but, once more, it didn't happen.

Jack had suffered his second heart attack. The first one had left him paralysed on his left side and with a speech impediment. Maggie was engrossed, taking care of his needs, absolving herself from everything she needed to tell him but didn't. When he died, she fell apart, lying in bed for days on end, not eating. I would take Ammu to see her but there was nothing we could do or say, she didn't care if we were there or not. Her house was filled with clutter and boxes of his clothes and possessions she had packed but could not bring herself to give away. Weeks went by and most evenings, I sat with her, telling her stories about the customers, hoping she would come out of it but she didn't speak. The doctor said it was delayed shock but I knew something else was going on.

Guilt and regret, instead of clinging to the walls, clung to the cells of her right breast and rapidly began spreading. She had probably known that it had been there for some time but let it fester, almost as if there was nothing worth fighting for, as if it was some kind of punishment that she was ready to accept. Tom had left, Maya had gone and now Jack. By the time she saw the doctor again, it was inoperable. It had spread too far. Refusing treatment, she stayed in bed.

'Fight, Maggie, fight! There's Maya, Tom. We can find him, you can get well,' I begged. 'Maya will come right now if you let me tell her,' I pleaded.

'No, I don't want to see her. I don't want her to ever remember me like this. I'm not going to tell you again, Nalini, I don't want Maya to see me.'

I took Maggie bowls of fiery peppered rasam, infused with red chillies and mustard seeds, which she didn't finish. I don't know why it didn't work; maybe because for some of us, it is only in death that we are ready to let go, to forgive ourselves. Whatever it was, the rasam had absolutely no effect and, if anything, she seemed to get worse.

'I've done some awful things, Nalini,' she cried.

'What is important is that you are a good person. You know that, don't you?'

'I left the little one behind; Mary was only six and she needed me, she couldn't sleep unless I tucked her in. But I had to leave, Nalini, I just had to. I knew Noreen would take care of them all and I thought coming to England would be better; I'd be able to give Tom a better life. You never saw me as a whore, you almost made me believe I wasn't, and then Jack came and none of that seemed to matter. I thought I did it all for Tom but I don't think I did. If only he understood, Nalini, but he hates me. Maybe I have grandchildren and they don't even know I exist. 'A grandma slut' pretending to be someone else. Jack deserved better, didn't he? And little Maya, you should have seen the look of disgust on Maya's face when I told her – absolute shock and disgust. I wish I hadn't said anything then maybe she would've stayed and not been so distant. I don't want her to come back because she is sorry for me. I want her to remember how much I loved her, how she was like my little Mary, and remind her how it used to be between the two of us. Promise me you won't tell her how I am now, you'll only tell her how much I loved her after I'm gone?'

'I promise, Maggie,' I said, calming her.

We watched her deteriorate. The bouncing red curls in her hair were the first to give up, falling limp and lifeless onto her pillow. Even my attempts to tie it up in a red chiffon scarf could not hide what was happening to her. I fed her liquid with a little teaspoon because she could not eat and it dribbled from the side of her mouth. Pain, as she breathed in, and sadness consumed her eyes. The emotional anguish seemed worse than the physical suffering and there was nothing we could do to make it better, she didn't want us to make it better. The doctor had given her a few weeks at most. She drifted in and out of consciousness and one day in her sleep, she called out for Maya.

'I love you, Tom, I love you Maya, darling,' she murmured, and the nurse told us that was all she ever said in her waking moments. Ravi called Maya home.

We hadn't touched Maya's room since the day she left. The lilac wallpaper that she chose after insisting that she could not sleep with polka dots was still there, with a matching duvet that looked so worn, but I could not bear to throw it away. Everything was as she left it; the stuffed toys that sat messily on her bed; her books, stacked high on her desk; pictures on the wall she had painted; bright fabrics sprawled across the furniture and photos were everywhere. There was one of Satchin, Maya and me squeezed together in a photo booth, taken the day I stopped work at the factory. We went out to Wimpy to celebrate and on the way back, Maya insisted on going into the booth. There was a school photo of Satchin and Maya and many pictures of Maya holding Ammu as a baby. I wished that she was coming home because she wanted to, not because she had to. Not to see her Maggie die. They would be arriving soon. Ammu hadn't slept all night because she couldn't wait to see her. My hands began to shake as I saw the blue car pull into the drive and I ran down the stairs as fast as I could. I opened the door but she wasn't there.

'She's gone to Maggie's house,' Ammu informed me.

My heart would have burst if I had had to wait any longer, so I asked Ravi to take me.

MAYA

The door opened and she stood there. Hair, now long again, with streaks of white, chappels showing feet painted with dusty pink nail varnish. I could not see her eyes clearly as they were brimming with tears. I got up, walked towards her, and her face just sunk into the side of my neck. Soft, moist tears ran down my back. I clung to my mother as I have never clung to her before. For all the times I have wanted to hold her: day one at the factory when she came back with swollen hands; the morning she married Ravi; the day Satchin died and she sat alone in the rain; when I was sick on the sidewalk in Chicago after seeing Raul's son. We stood there holding each other as if we were the only two people left in the world.

Lightly scented jasmine, that is what my mother's hair smelt of, not a trace of spices from cooking.

'You're home now, Mol,' she said, taking a deep breath.

Dressed in a chiffon green sari, with her hair unbraided, she looked beautiful.

'There are so many things I want to tell you, Ma.'

'We have time,' she whispered.

Maggie opened her eyes and just momentarily, I thought she would muster enough fire and emit her Maggie laugh but she said nothing. And closed her eyes again. Both my mother and I looked at each other. In dying there is unity, forgiveness and understanding. We sat on either side of the bed.

'It has been too long. I'm so sorry, Ma.'

'Mol, I understand, I wasn't a good mother to you, was I, not being there for you when Satchin died?'

'It wasn't that, Ma,' I managed.

There was a movement in Maggie's hand and I wanted to believe it was to tell me that she could hear, that she was asking me to continue and resolve all that needed to be resolved.

'I saw him a few days after the funeral, smartly dressed, he touched my face, wiped my tears, told me he was my father and that he wanted to be there for me.'

Amma shuddered and looked horrified and was about to say something when I continued, 'He told me how you had left him and he spent years looking for us and then when he finally found us, you had married and he could not bring himself to disrupt our lives.'

'No, Mol, it wasn't like that. He was . . .'

'Wait, Ma, I need to tell you how it was. I thought you had left him for Tom and that you had abandoned Tom and married Ravi for his money. I felt disgusted but, because of Satchin, I couldn't talk to you about it

281

and promised myself that I would never come back. You didn't need me.'

'No, no, no,' she cried.

'When I was in Spain, I was trying to forget you. It didn't seem to hurt as much there and then I went to India and nothing seemed right. I met Raul's family and they treated me like dirt and then I found where Ammamma lived. It was horrible, Ma.'

Amma looked intensely at me, with tears streaming down her face.

'She died happy, with all of us beside her in black and white pictures. And after India, something came alive in me, it was a sense of belonging, the smells and colours of that country were all running inside of me, so potent that I felt unable to handle it. I went back to Spain, almost like I didn't want to believe it, any of it. I wanted to feel that Raul loved me, that Marcos loved me, because it was easier, but I also wanted to know the truth. I went looking for him. He has a son, you know, and a daughter. Three years younger than I am. How could he do that, Ma? How could he have more children after doing what he did to us?

'I'm so sorry, sorry for being so wrong about every-thing, for not having faith in you,' I cried.

She came over and held me.

'Mol, the day I had to tell you and Satchin that your father died was one of the hardest things I have ever had to do. He didn't deserve you two, you know, that is why I did it, because I knew your lives would be better without him. He left no note, nothing, only debts, and I cannot even start to think what would have happened without Tom or Maggie. Two children and a lady who

282

spoke very little English. I worked for you both to give you everything you deserved. Almost allowing myself to forget, I married a man who loved you both as if you were his own. I would have done anything to keep Raul away, but I never thought he would come back. What for? So the day he returned, Maggie and I sold everything to pay him to keep away from you. Then I became fearful that he would try to come back at any moment and when Satchin died, I thought it was my punishment for trying to keep what is not yours. Then you left and I knew it was.

'But I have learnt that life does not punish, it teaches you to let go, let go of all you fear or that fear becomes you.'

We sat rocking each other for some time.

Maggie died in the middle of the night; I think it was when Amma and I had dozed off for a few moments. They say that, sometimes, the dying hold on for you and the moment you turn your back, they feel it is the most appropriate time to let go.

It was the afternoon of 7th February and, unusually, the sun came pouring in. Ammu came to wake me. For a second I forgot where I was and that Maggie had died and when I remembered, I felt strangely peaceful.

'Maya, are you ready to eat?'

'Yes, Shorty. Come sit with me for a moment.'

She came over and sat by the bed and I pulled her in and gave her a big hug and kissed her.

'You know I've missed you, don't you, Shorty?'

She looked embarrassed and then after a little while that parrot chatter that I remembered came back. She talked non-stop, playing with my hair and telling me about her friends at school and all of them who wanted to meet me. How could I have spent so much time away from her?

We both got up. I had a shower and changed and went downstairs to eat. The table was beautifully laid and Amma and Ravi were waiting for us. 'Sit here, Mol,' said Amma.

'Ravi, I'm so sorry,' I said.

'Maya, it's finished.' He stretched his hand across the table.

'No, let me finish. I'm sorry that I was a nuisance as a child, that I never gave you a chance, and I want you to know you're the best dad anyone could have had; Amma couldn't have chosen better.'

Amma smiled and lifted the lids off the dishes; deep-filled masala dosas with hot potato stew. I was home.

Amma organised the funeral and the food afterwards. Fish baked in a tamarind sauce, coated with fried mustard seeds and red chillies. After all the guests had left and everyone else had gone to bed, I sat in the kitchen with her and talked, then I remembered the letter that the astrologer had given me for her. 'Wait, Amma, I have something for you,' I said as I went in search of my bag. 'It's from Ammamma to you,' I said as I handed her the note. She took it eagerly, unfolding it.

'What does it say?' I asked enthusiastically.

Nalini Mol,
Not a day has gone by that I haven't missed you and
I know that when my time here comes to an end, I will

*be able to return to you. Sacrifice is like that, Mol, I
know that spirit lives on.*

*Don't ever think that I wanted to leave you and the
children; if I had stopped you from going you would
not have turned into the woman I knew you could be.*

*If you can pass on one thing to our Maya, teach her
the most important thing that I have taught you.*

*I love you always,
Amma*

'What does she mean, Ma?'

'Forgiveness. I need to show you what the spices can
do. Come to the shop with me and learn.'

'I have to go to Spain to speak to Enrique and Marcos.'

'Does Marcos deserve a visit, Mol? You can call him.
And Enrique, ask him for some more time off, he will
understand. Just stay for a week, I can teach you the
very basics.'

At around midnight, I called Marcos.

'Maya, where are you? You didn't call, what am I
supposed to think, it's been days now? My mother is
becoming hysterical with the preparations, she needs
you here, I need you here. When are you coming home?'

'Maggie died four days ago, Marcos, there were other
things to do,' I replied.

There was no sorry, nothing, only, 'but it doesn't take
a week to pick up the phone, does it?'

'It does if you are not really thinking of coming back.'

There was silence and then laughter. 'Don't be silly,
Maya, the wedding is five months away, I have been to
see some houses for us.'

'I said I'm not coming back.'

'You have to, I love you. What about the prep-arations? My mother, the guests?'

'I'm sure Carmen can step in,' I said, thinking of the peroxide blonde.

There was silence. 'Maya, listen, there is nothing going on with Carmen, there never has been, we work together. I don't know where you got such an idea. Just come home and we'll talk about it,' he pleaded.

He sounded pathetic.

'There's nothing more to say, Marcos, I'm not coming back, I *am* at home.'

'But, Maya . . .'

I hung up.

No sadness, nothing, I just felt alive again. I went to bed. On my ceiling there were some luminous stars that Satchin had bought me for my twelfth birthday. Maggie was with him now; both of them were watching us. I fell asleep.

The next morning, I went to the shop with Amma. She had given Ana and Anita the week off and had the closed sign up so the two of us could spend time in the kitchen. 'It's forgiveness, Mol. I know there is no more resentment inside of you but forgiveness also includes oneself.'

We chopped the onions as she told me how she knew she was carrying a baby girl when she was pregnant with me. I kicked a lot less than my brother and it felt so different from the first time. We chopped our way through so many bags of onions that it made us cry. Sizzling in a cauldron of oil, everything that was bitter and raw turned sweet. The astrologer said it would be a girl and he was never wrong. An almond-skinned child with a soft centre who would grow into big things if she allowed life to teach her. We made a marinade of bitter cumin seeds, rough ginger and garlic, peeling them with the patience with which they had grown and smashing them up so they shrunk significantly in quantity, almost making the hours of peeling redundant.

Things that appear small often have a huge effect; smiles, gestures and words that appear insignificant to the eye. 'Give thanks,' Amma said, 'for the root of the ginger appears ugly, the cumin seed bitter and the smell of garlic can repulse, but in these things too there is beauty and beauty comes in unexpected small quantities, these are things that are constant.' Mustard seeds seem so tiny and insignificant that their healing qualities go unnoticed; if a grain rolled to the floor you would not notice, not like its slender red counterpart, the chilli. Together, they make an explosive combination, permeating the body through the breath and the pores of the skin like no other scent is able to do, cleansing, purifying and taking away self-doubt.

Fried in a cauldron of smoke with the magic of dreams and possibilities floating in the air just as fragrant as fresh lilies to those who understand, eliminating regret and sorrow into absolute nothingness. Mangoes signify fertility, tender and succulent orange flesh slithers gently off the knife. Then, in the centre, there is an unexpected stone, solid and furry as if to remind us that all that is sweet comes initially from something hard. Deceptive, yellow lemons whose sourness betrays them, like the sunny disposition of a bitter person. Steamed together, hot vapour and warm rain like the monsoon that brings up all that is ugly from the ground.

Cinnamon sticks, coarsely sweetened, float to the top like driftwood, escaping rough seas to perfume with experience that which surrounds it. 'That is how I drifted when I first married,' whispers my mother, as she stirs with her heavy metal ladle. 'No anchor and then Satchin was born and I was so scared of the responsibility. Could I manage? Could I protect him? Would I be a good mother? When you came, I really understood what it was to be a mother; things fell into place and made sense. Everything I had ever asked for was given to me in two wrinkled bundles and I promised you many things.'

I smelt my childhood as it went into the cauldron; sticky monsoon days; damp walls; cherry blossom; spicy pickles; the urine-stained mattress; the Trebor factory; lamb stew with dumplings and bar fires. As the cauldron cooled, the odours vaporised in the air so that none of it seemed to matter. We bottled a sense of understanding and I was grateful for the place that I had come to.

'I have to go out for the afternoon, Maya, to get a few things for Ammu's play. You'll be okay in the shop pouring the mixture into bottles, won't you? There won't be any customers, I'll keep the closed sign up and lock the door.'

'Do you want me to go instead or come with you?' I asked.

'No, no, you stay here,' Amma replied.

She picked up her coat, kissed me and left.

So I stayed, pouring ladles of pickles from the cauldrons, filling empty jars, putting the lids on top and covering them with elaborate pieces of sari material cut into small circles from red silks, blue chiffon, cream cotton. I took the fabric glue and elastic bands to attach them to the lids. Looking at my mother's bronze Goddess sitting comfortably on her own handmade shelf, I was thinking how familiar she looked and remembered my Ammamma. Smiling, I began counting how many bottles I had filled and forgot where I was at, when the bell went. I thought Amma had locked the door and put up the closed sign.

'Hello,' a voice came. 'Auntie? Auntie, are you there?'

A familiar, gentle voice. I went out to the front to see who it was.

'Suri,' I screamed. I ran over to him.

He looked at me with disbelief. 'Maya,' he whispered. 'Maya!' He spoke my name like nobody could.

I held him.

'Maya, what are you doing here?'

Fighting a barrage of tears that ran down his shirt, I replied, 'I came to see my family to tell them I'm sorry. I am so sorry, Suri.'

'No Maya, you don't have to say sorry to me, ever,' he held me tightly.

We were whisked back for that moment into simple innocence and love. He wiped my tears and touched my lips with his fingers.

'Shhhh,' he whispered.

Solid as ever, he had grown into the man he had looked certain to become.

'I wrote some awful things, I didn't mean it, not any of it.'

I didn't want to be pulled apart from him or for him to move away. 'Maggie died, you know?'

'I know,' he said, slowly releasing me. I wanted to

grab his hands and pull them back. 'Your mother called to tell me. I'm really sorry, you know, about everything.'

'It wasn't you, Suri, I wasn't angry with you, there were just so many things happening at the time. I want to explain.'

'It's all in the past, your mother tells me you're happy now, living in Spain and about to get married.'

No, Suri, I wanted to shout as I searched for a ring on his finger. But I didn't say anything and I don't know why. Perhaps it was fear or maybe because things don't stay with you if you don't feel you truly deserve them.

'Did you become a doctor?'

'Almost there.' He stared at me. 'Does he make you laugh?'

No, I thought, and it doesn't matter because he's not around.

'Yes,' I said. 'He makes me laugh.'

'Good, because that's important.'

'Does she make you laugh?' I enquired.

'No,' he replied.

There was silence and in those seconds he waited for me to say something but I didn't.

'Listen, Maya, I have to go, it's been . . . it's been just the best seeing you. And I wish that . . . I wish you every happiness.'

'Take care,' he said as he let go of my hand. He turned his back to leave. I wanted to stop him, to tell him that I wasn't getting married and the only person who I had ever really loved was him. But I couldn't.

I called Enrique later that week to tell him that I wasn't coming back to Spain. He began by telling me that

Marcos was calling three or four times a day, asking for a telephone number or an address. 'I told him where to go, Maya, I'm glad you came to your senses finally,' he said. 'Now listen, what about this London office of mine? Who can I get to run it for me? More than an office, I think, I need a boutique,' he continued in his flamboyant manner. 'The pay is very good because that is all these designers think of. You know what their first question is? Not what does the job entail, who are your clients, but . . .'

'How much?' I interrupted.

'You're on what, three hundred and fifty thousand pesetas? I'll double it,' he joked.

The process of acceptance and forgiveness for me took many, many months. I came to accept the past and all those I had hurt unintentionally and learnt to forgive those who knew no better and had hurt me. Sometimes there is no point in trying to figure out why; it is better to accept and to move on. Amma and Ravi helped me set up the boutique in Bond Street and I ordered the most beautiful fabrics from India with the money Maggie had left me. She would have loved it, all of it. I spent hours and hours designing, cutting patterns and making outfits. Whilst I was cutting and sewing I learnt to find the pace and my own sense of contentment. Four months passed and the shop was ready to open. Amma had organised the priest to come in and bless it.

He came early that morning and blessed it, imparting no wisdom, just smiling, breaking a coconut and saying a prayer. I was ready to open.

Ammu was the first to arrive with Amma and Ravi.

She had made me a good luck card and asked me to design a pink taffeta outfit that she had drawn.

'But, Shorty, what about something else, like . . .'

'No,' she exclaimed. 'Just like this one, with the sleeves puffing out like this.'

'Okay, okay,' I said. 'Let me measure you up.'

'There's no point because I want it at least two sizes bigger so you can take it down when I need it.'

'That's not how I work, Ammu.'

'Mayo, aren't you supposed to do what your clients tell you? I'm your client, don't you want my custom?'

I sighed.

'And can I have a receipt?' she asked.

'But you haven't paid for anything.'

'Dad, will you give me some money to give Mayo a deposit?

'There,' she said. 'I'll see you back at home but I'll come back to be fitted in four weeks, that's how it works, isn't it?'

I laughed and they left.

The bell went again, 'What is it now, Shorty? I suppose you want a discount,' I asked from beneath the counter where I was searching for a box of invoices.

'Ehmm, just wondering if you sold any purple Farah trousers?' said the voice.

'Suri, Suri,' I shouted, bumping my head as I got up.

'Ahh, you need a doctor to take a look at that. Come here.'

A warm hand touched my forehead, the other rested on my waist.

'How did you know, today of all days?' I asked.

'I got an anonymous tip-off from a squeaky little

292

voice, who told me pretty much everything and then ended the conversation by saying, "bye Suri, I'll see you soon."'

'Maya, why didn't you tell me? Why didn't you tell me when I saw you back then that you weren't getting married?'

'Because, because I had to let go and trust.'

He touched my face, holding it in his hands, and began kissing my eyes, my cheeks and then my lips. It felt like the first time, like I had finally, finally come home.

Suri and I were married the following year, in the month of Shravan. I know my brother and Maggie were there, not because that is what I wanted to believe but I saw luminous stars on the ceiling and a little Indian girl carrying a rag doll very like the one Maggie had made for me.

Amma and Ravi stood proudly next to us as did Suri's parents and my sister Ammu who was a kind of bridesmaid, kind of because in Keralan weddings you don't really have them, just a simple exchange of garlands and rings. She stood there with us, in a pink taffeta meringue that I made for her, with flowers and ribbons bouncing everywhere. I knew that in years to come she would look at the photographs with distress. It didn't matter.

Suri and I held hands and walked around the fire that the priest lit for us. He said a prayer, took out his tin of sandalwood and left his blessing on our foreheads.

Amma made the wedding feast and she served Suri and I. 'From left to right,' she said serving on the banana leaves and as she was doing this I heard a grandmother and a granddaughter running along the beach, laughing, and someone, somewhere whispered to me:

'I will always, always be there for you, even on the days of doubting.'